THE
AFTERMATH

A hundred years ago, The Sisters came, a
string of asteroid strikes that destroyed
human civilisation and brought on a
decades-long winter.

Now, communities are starting to rebuild,
and trying to piece together the knowledge
that was lost. The old tools are broken,
superstition is rife, and the land is hard and
unforgiving.

And some, inevitably, have dreams of
conquest.

The Aftermath tells the stories of a future on
the edge of survival.

DEC - - 2018

First published 2018 by Solaris
an imprint of Rebellion Publishing Ltd,
Riverside House, Osney Mead,
Oxford, OX2 0ES, UK

www.solarisbooks.com

ISBN: 978 1 78108 504 2

10 9 8 7 6 5 4 3 2 1

A CIP catalogue record for this book is available
from the British Library.

Designed & typeset by Rebellion Publishing

Printed in Denmark by Nørhaven

SHELTER

SOLARIS

IT TURNED OUT that over a century of blockbuster films and catastrophe novels did nothing to prepare humanity for the disaster when it came.

The Spacewatch programme, perennially short of funds and resources, failed to spot The Sisters; they were just too small and moving too fast, the shrapnel of a comet shattered by some collision on the edge of the asteroid belt. The crew of the International Space Station saw it, though, a quick series of blinding, soundless detonations scattered across the face of the world.

Later, the Commander of the ISS, a woman of a poetic frame of mind, said they were like rapid camera-flashes as God took a snapshot of the final moments of human civilisation.

By the time she said that, there was no one left on Earth who could hear her.

Thanet

CHAPTER ONE

THE WEATHER THAT summer was dreadful, even by Berkshire's mediocre standards. Storms swept down from the north carrying hail the size of peas and left the Vale carpeted in dirty white. Fields were waterlogged, ponds flooded, rivers broke their banks. One morning, out for a walk to check the damage, Max looked out into the murky distance towards Oxford and it was like looking out across an inland sea dotted with trees and hedges and little hillocks.

Late at night, in the fortified smallholdings of the Parish, aged gaffers sat by their fires and muttered darkly about the summer of '22, which up until this year had been the worst summer anyone could remember and during which hundreds of people had died of varying causes, from drowning to starvation to being struck by lightning.

Max was too young to remember that time; all he'd known was year after year of miserable summers, monsoon autumns and yellow-grey winters of dirty snow. Times had been hard, but none of these things had, during his lifetime, actually killed anyone directly.

"Summer of '22," Rose said one night, as they sat in the parlour listening to hail hammering down to the roof.

"Don't you start," Max said. "I'm sick of hearing about the summer of bloody '22." He got up from his armchair, went over to the window, lifted back the curtain, and peered out into a vertical sheet of driving hail. He sighed.

The next morning, the yard was still paved with white. Some of the younger kids waded ankle-deep through it, kicking up slushy clods of ice and getting in everyone's way. John Race, Max's foreman, wandered over, coat collar turned up and pipe clamped between his teeth, and nodded hello.

"If you so much as mention the summer of '22, I'm going to give you such a slap, John," Max warned amiably.

John took his pipe from his mouth and examined the bowl. He sniffed. "We're going to be in trouble if this goes on, Max," he said.

"Well, *that'll* be a novelty, us being in trouble."

"There's going to be a lot of folk around here in trouble."

"Yeah." Max scratched his beard. "Well, we'll cross that bridge," he said.

John sucked his teeth. The Taylor farm had crossed a lot of bridges, these past few years, but he didn't say anything. Max knew it as well as he did.

Max clapped him on the shoulder. "The weather'll pick up, John. You wait and see." And he strode off across the compound to check how the repairs were going on one of the outbuildings.

AND, THOUGH IT seemed unlikely when Max said it, the weather actually did start to improve. The wind dropped, the hail went away, the temperature rose. The sun shone weakly and apologetically through high cloud. The landowners made repairs, assessed the damage to crops and livestock, traded for supplies and manpower. Peace descended on the area.

It did not descend everywhere, though. On one of his walks, Max stopped on the brow of the hill and was presented with a vista of flooded fields that went on as far as he could see. The people on the Ridge didn't mix very much with the people of the Vale, even though there were some towns – Didcot, Abingdon – that were almost intact. Max's teenage years had been a bit wild, and he had spent some time in Abingdon as part of a vaguely-expressed interest in going to Oxford to find work. After a couple of months, he'd turned round and come home.

Abingdon, as it turned out, was about as far as he'd ever got from home. The country seemed finally to be emerging from the Long Autumn, the almost century-long period of driving rain and cooling which had followed the arrival of The Sisters, but travel was still hard and people still tended to stay put, in general. Max liked his comforts, his armchair by the fire in the parlour, his breakfast bacon sandwich, his nice warm bed. Camping out in the countryside didn't appeal.

Sitting here, now, he could see Didcot, and the dirty grey smear beyond that was Abingdon, but everything else was lost in floodwater. Off to the north, in the direction of Letchlade, a column of smoke was rising into the sky. Through his binoculars, a cluster of buildings was just visible, sitting on a low hill rising out of the shallow water. One, maybe more, of the buildings, was on fire. Slow movement nearby resolved itself into a line of four or five boats making their way along a flooded lane away from the fire.

Max sat and watched this little scene for quite a while. The boats were too far away to make out individual people – they were almost too far away to make them out as boats. Impossible to know, of course, what the story behind all this was. The people in the boats could be rescuing people from the houses. He laid the binoculars down beside him and hugged his knees.

Back at the farm, he didn't say anything about what he'd seen. Rose was getting dinner ready, the smaller kids were running around causing havoc as usual; Nell was trying to get them to wash their hands before they ate. He hung up his coat and took off his boots.

"Everything okay, love?" Rose asked, and he smiled and said it was, although later that night he found he couldn't sleep and he lay thinking about those boats moving slowly along the lane far away.

AROUND THE END of August, they had things squared away around the farm enough for Max to feel able to head over to the Coghlans with a case of homebrew and a flitch of bacon. So one morning he harnessed March and April, their two most equably-minded horses, to the wagon and kissed Rose goodbye.

"Give Betty and Andrew my love," she told him. "And you take care."

"I'm only going to Blandings, Rosemary," he protested.

"You should take Patrick," she said.

He glanced up at the wall surrounding the compound. His eldest son was standing on the parapet, crossbow slung across his back, looking out across the countryside. Sixteen years old and protector of everything he surveyed.

"Patrick's busy," he told her.

She thumped him on the chest hard enough to hurt. "Don't you take the piss out of him."

"I wasn't," he said innocently.

"You were and you know it. I remember you at that age; you were just like him."

"At that age I was on my way to Oxford," he told her. "Remember that?"

Rose waved it away. "You came back."

"Yeah," he said, looking around the compound. "Yeah, I always come back."

"Go," she said. "Go, you daft man, if you're going to go."

"Look after your mum!" Max called up to Patrick, who just shrugged and kept scanning the area beyond the wall. Rose punched him again.

THE BRIDGE ACROSS the Thames at Streatley had washed away long before Max was born; years of floods had swollen the river and simply eaten it away, along with most of the other bridges both upstream and downstream. At some point, an enterprising group of people had come along and set up a ferry. They had cleared the main road through the Gap where the river cut through the Chiltern hills. And then they set up shop taxing travellers.

Those had been wild days; Max's grandfather had told him of bands of armed and desperate people besieging the village, of firefights between the people operating the toll and travellers who thought they could go any-damn-where they wanted and didn't see why they should pay for the privilege.

These days, things were quieter. Max arrived near dusk and joined a line of wagons and riders waiting to board the ferry. He could hear, on the other side of the river, the bells of St. Thomas's calling the faithful to evening prayer.

A group of men armed with shotguns and crossbows guarded the slipway down to the big flat-bottomed boat that winched itself from bank to bank. When Max reached the head of the line, one of them came up and nodded hello. "Howdo, Max," he said amiably.

"Terry."

"Off on your travels?"

"Going to Blandings." Max reached behind the seat and brought out a bottle of homebrew. He handed it down.

"Give the old woman my regards," said Terry, taking the bottle.

Max drove on into Goring, where stallholders were just packing up after market day. There was a pub on the other side of the village – no one knew what it had originally been called, everybody just called it The Goring – and here Max pulled off the road, drove round the back of the main buildings to the stables, left the wagon in the hands of one of the ostlers, and went inside.

The bar was full of farmers and traders, most of them wearily drunk after market day. Max ordered a beer, nodded hello to the few faces he knew. A young woman brought his pint, and he beamed. "Hallo, Evie," he said. "Room for a little one?"

Evie was small and slim and blonde, her hair tied back. She looked tired. "Should do," she said. "Most of these old lads will be going home in a bit." She looked out into the bar. "I hope. How's the family?"

Max had been coming here for... oh, longer than he wanted to remember. Evie's parents had both died within weeks of each other during a particularly bad flu season which had swept through the area a few years before, leaving her alone to run the pub.

"They're fine, thanks. Been busy?"

She grunted. "Market day. We've got some stew on; that do you?"

He grinned. "That'd be smashing, thanks, Evie. I'm starving."

"Yeah," she said, looking him up and down. "Like Rose would ever let that happen."

Max took his pint over to a table at the other side of the bar, where he joined a couple of gaffers he knew vaguely.

"Been talking about things up north," said one, a ruddy-faced man called Bob, when pleasantries had been exchanged. "You heard anything?"

Max shook his head. "I saw something the other day, over to Letchlade. Houses burning, people on the move."

"Bandits," grunted the other gaffer, one of the Robinsons from up towards High Wycombe.

"I don't know about that," said Max, trying his beer. The Goring ran its own microbrewery, and produced the best beer in the Hills. That was what Evie said, anyway.

"Our Rita's husband has people up Oxford way," Bob said. "He's not heard from them in months."

"*That's* hardly conclusive proof," said Robinson.

Evie came over with a steaming bowl of mutton stew and a chunk of bread and put them in front of Max. "They had boats," he said, dipping his spoon into the stew. "The people I saw."

"Every bugger down there's got a boat," Robinson said. "One day it's going to flood for good."

"He's been saying that since we were boys," Bob told Max.

Max chewed a mouthful of stew, washed it down with a sip of beer. "Any idea *what* exactly's going on up north?"

Bob shrugged. "Something in the Cotswolds. Don't know what."

"Cotswolds," Max mused. "Bit of a distance, that."

"If they're messing around in Letchlade, that's not such a distance," Bob pointed out. "If they decide to come south, they're going to have to come through here."

"Mm," said Max, tucking into his stew.

THE GORING'S ROOMS were small and cramped, but they were clean and dry and the kitchen provided plenty of hot water for washing and a big bacon and egg breakfast the next morning. Some of the slates on the roof had been loosened during a storm the week before, and Max spent a few hours up a ladder repairing them to pay for his board before setting out again.

The old roads were nearly unusable. Almost a century of rain and frost had patiently cracked and lifted the tarmac or washed it away altogether. Main roads were still choked with the rusting wrecks of ancient cars and lorries, almost hidden by weeds and overgrowth.

The preferred option for getting about was horseback, or failing that on foot, but in some places – the Chilterns was one shining example – two generations of settlers and farmers had worked to keep at least some of the roads clear and open for wagon traffic. So it only took Max half the day to travel the well-used road between Goring and Wallingford.

Just outside the town, he turned off down a side road, and a few minutes later, he reached a pair of tall iron gates set into a high brick wall. There was a nest of sandbags atop each of the pillars on either side of the gateway, and attached to the wall beside the gates was a sign which read, BLANDINGS. FUCK OFF. He drew the wagon to a stop and waited, and a couple of minutes later, a figure poked its head over the wall.

"It just occurred to me that there's nobody round here who can read this sign, you know," Max mused out loud.

"For the illiterate," said a voice from one of the sandbag nests, "we have Mr Browning." And there was the sound of a heavy machine gun being cocked.

"Afternoon, Betty," said Max. "Andrew."

The figure on the wall waved and dropped down out of sight. Another figure rose from behind the sandbags. "Mr Taylor," said Betty. "And what can we do for you?"

"Brought you some bacon."

Betty grinned. "I knew there was a reason I liked you. Come on in. Andrew?"

Andrew, a tall, slim young man in jeans and a black pullover, with an L85A2 assault rifle slung over his shoulder, unlocked the gates and cranked them open.

"Follow Andrew," Betty called. "I'll be with you in a bit."

The estate was much too large to be easily defensible; its perimeter wall was more than four miles long, so they relied on what the Coghlans described with a wry smile as 'passive defence'. Down the years, local brigands had learned to steer clear of Blandings, but every now and again someone drifted down from Bedfordshire, or up from the Plain, and in their ignorance decided to try their luck. Betty quite welcomed moments like that; she said they served as a reminder that she was serious about that sign by the front gate.

Max followed Andrew down one of the safe paths to the house, then round the back to the stable block. They unhitched the horses and Andrew went to feed and water them, while Max carried the flitch of bacon into the kitchen.

"This is nice, Max," Betty said, coming into the kitchen and taking off her duffel coat. "Many thanks."

They hugged. "Brought you some homebrew too," Max told her. "It's in the wagon."

Betty grinned. "Much appreciated. How's the family?"

"Not too bad, thanks. Rose sends her regards."

"I haven't seen her in... two years? Three?"

"Nearly four. Patrick's birthday party."

She shook her head. "I need to get over to see you more often, Max."

"You've been busy, probably."

"Nah. I forget there's still a world on the other side of that wall, and that's not good. I should get out more." She clapped him on the shoulder. "You'll stay, yes?"

"I didn't come all this way to turn round and go back again."

Betty looked at his face and cocked her head to one side. "Is everything all right?"

He thought about it, wondering whether, at the last moment, to cross this particular bridge after all. "I do have a favour to ask, as it happens. Advice, as much as anything."

"Well, advice is always free. We'll talk after dinner. Go and clean up; there's plenty of hot water."

NIGHT FELL OVER the Chilterns, cold and windy but dry at least. At Blandings, lights began to come on, here and there, in some of the rooms. Electric light was one of the reasons Max liked to come here. That and the seemingly inexhaustible supplies of hot water.

He had a long bath. Afterwards, he caught sight of himself in the mirror, a short, stout middle-aged man with curly black hair and an unruly beard. It seemed he had more lines around his eyes than he remembered, but that must have been the electric light.

Years and years ago, before Max was born, a particularly stubborn and stupid group of bandits had chanced upon Blandings and decided they wanted what was inside. The estate was very heavily defended back then, and the initial assault had been beaten back, but the bandits, like bandits everywhere, were too dim to take the hint and go away. They laid siege to the place, which was hardly a problem because Blandings could have existed independent of the outside world for almost a year if need be. But it had been a severe irritation, so Betty's father – Mr Richard, everyone called him – got word out and a number of farmers had got their people together and marched up here and helped to sort things out. Max's father had been among them, and when Max was little, he delighted in telling the story of The Battle of Blandings, much to Max's mother's annoyance.

The other farmers had drifted off down the years, preoccupied with their own troubles, but the Taylors and the Coghlans had remained close, had done each other favour after favour until no one really remembered who owed whom what and it didn't really matter anyway.

Rose, for some reason, didn't like them. She put up with Max's periodic trips to Blandings, was perfectly polite about the Coghlans, but she'd grown so annoyed by Max's insistence that the children call Betty 'Auntie Betty' that they'd had sharp words about it, and in the end, as he usually did, Max backed down in favour of a quiet life and being able to get on with stuff without being argued at.

Dinner, cooked by Andrew, was pork chops and potatoes and salad. On the other side of the estate were six big greenhouses, patiently constructed, pane by pane, from windows taken from neighbouring towns and villages. The Coghlans always ate well.

Afterwards, Andrew brought in coffee and brandy – both worth their weight in gold, if gold had actually been worth anything any more. He sat down and looked at Max and said, "So, mother says you have a problem."

"I'm not sure if it's a problem or not," Max said, and he told them what he had seen. The burning buildings, the boats, the strange distant serenity of it all. "Don't know what it was," he finished. "Could have been anything."

"But you don't think so," said Andrew.

Max shook his head.

"Could you make out what *kind* of boats they were?" Betty asked.

"Sorry?"

"Were they canoes? Rowing boats?"

Max thought about it. "They were almost as wide as the lane they were going down, sort of rectangular. I couldn't see how many people were on them; quite a few, and quite a lot of gear."

Betty and Andrew exchanged glances. "Things are starting to change," she said. "I've been hearing some strange things about Oxford."

Max nodded. "I've heard that too."

Betty shook her head. "There's been a takeover, some people from the Cotswolds."

Max raised an eyebrow.

"Yes, I know," she said. "I don't have a clear idea what's going on yet, but I wonder if whatever you saw in the Vale isn't something to do with it."

Max sipped his brandy.

"The days when people lived in tiny little communities are coming to an end," said Betty. "It made sense back in the early days when times were hard and things were scarce, but people are more secure now, they're banding together. There's a big bunch of people down in the West Country, a couple of other large communities, here and there, that we've heard about."

"Isn't that a good thing?"

"Depends," Andrew said. "For people like you, the other farmsteads, maybe not."

Max thought of the faraway burning buildings. The boats moving along the flooded lane. He took a breath and said, "We need better weapons, Bets."

"You can't fight them, Max," she said kindly.

"I will if they try to take what's mine."

"There's too many of them," she told him.

"Suppose they come here," he said. "Suppose they take over the ferry and the toll and they hear about all your stuff and they want it."

Betty got up and started to collect the dinner plates.

"Well then," he said.

"They could *try*," Andrew suggested.

"I'm not going to give you guns," she said. "Not yet, anyway. Not until we know what's happening in Oxford. That could just be rumours. What you saw could just have been bandits."

"But you think it's something else."

"We don't know," Andrew said. "The boats sound purpose-built, shallow-draught for moving over flooded country. Not *hard* to build, but why would you, unless you had a use in mind for them?"

"It's not as if there hasn't been flooding down there before," Betty said. "You and I both know people with boats."

"We should be organising now," said Max. "Us, the Lyalls, the Carters, everyone else. We should be ready."

"You should be *forewarned*," she said briskly, stacking the plates in the middle of the table. "Nothing wrong with that. If the time comes, I'll help you, but I'm not going to hand guns out like sweeties, Max. That only causes trouble."

"I can always go somewhere else."

She picked up the plates, stood there looking at him. "Oh, Max," she said sadly. "Sure, there's old Robert Mason over to Wycombe. He's got lots of guns and he'll sell them to you without a moment's thought. Perry Allen in Sonning – I'll write you a list, if you like. Lots of people have got guns and they don't care who buys them. That's how wars start."

He stood and followed her into the kitchen. "From what you say, a war's coming anyway."

"We don't know that," she said, putting the plates in the sink. "From what I hear about the people down West, that's working all right." She turned and looked at him. "Let me ask around, Max, okay? I know some folk in Witney and Chipping Norton. I haven't spoken to them in a while, but they'll know what's going on. If they say things are getting bad, we can have this conversation again. Okay?"

Max didn't say anything.

"Meanwhile," she went on, "you do us a day's work tomorrow to pay for your keep, and you go home, and you talk to the locals. Let them know that maybe something's coming, maybe it isn't."

He thought about it. "When will you know?"

"Well, that is what my father used to call an *imponderable*." She rinsed her hands under the tap, dried them with a threadbare tea towel. "I'll send Andrew when I have some news for you. Okay? In the meantime, don't panic, and do *not* buy guns from old man Mason because they'll probably blow up in your face."

He grunted.

She stepped forward and hugged him. "Cheer up, Max," she said. "We live in interesting times. That's always fun."

"You've got an odd idea of fun, Betty."

She laughed and clapped him on the shoulders. "Go to bed, Max. You've got a hard day's work ahead of you tomorrow."

LATER, BETTY WENT back to the study and sat for a while reading, but her heart wasn't in it and she laid her book aside and looked into the fire. The wind had got up outside and it was booming in the chimneys the way it had when she'd been little. Back then, it had frightened her and her father had had to sit with her at night until she fell asleep. These days, there were other scary things, and now there was no one to sit with her.

There was a knock on the door and Andrew looked into the study. "Okay?" he asked.

She smiled at him, still amazed after all these years by how much he looked like his father. "Interesting times."

"What are we going to do?"

"Well, we're not going to panic, that's the first thing we're going to do." She thought about it. "We need some help." She saw the look on his face as he realised what she meant. "Don't be like that."

"I don't like dealing with them," he told her. "Every time we do, we wind up owing them a favour."

"That's the way the world works," she said amiably. "We owe them a favour, they owe us a favour. It all averages out, in the end."

"What are they going to do, anyway? Send us a battleship?"

"They may not want to help at all; they have their own stuff to worry about. I'll get in touch tomorrow and see what they say, and then we can make plans. Or not."

"You're just going to send Max back to the Parish and tell everyone to sit tight and not do anything?"

Betty thought about some of the things she'd been hearing about the situation further north, things even she had trouble believing. She was glad she hadn't mentioned them to Max; it wouldn't have made matters any better.

"The weather's going to break in a month or so," she said. "The monsoons will be here, then it'll be winter. Nobody's going to try anything until the spring. What Max saw is just reconnaissance, people looking for a foothold. There will be time to prepare."

"I hope you're right. I really do." Andrew had heard the same rumours she had.

"When have I ever been wrong?" She saw the look on his face and smiled. "All right. In the meantime, let Max have that spare water purifier and any odds and ends of farm tools he takes his fancy to. And don't work him too hard tomorrow. He looks tired."

CHAPTER TWO

OFF IN THE distance, a pair of waterspouts twirled up from the surface of the Sound and touched the low clouds. Chrissie leaned on the railing and watched them skein about each other, their tips lost in boiling spray.

"Not funny," Adam said.

She sighed. "No, it isn't," she said. "But there's no one else."

He put his hands in his pockets and hunched his shoulders deeper into his parka. He'd only got back from Wales the day before, but there was no point making a big thing about it.

She said, "What do you know about Thanet?"

He shrugged. "It's in Kent. I think."

Chrissie pushed away from the railing, turned, and began to walk along the seafront. Adam walked beside her. A respectful distance ahead and behind, her minders walked along too. It had been a long time since Guz had seen a political assassination, but you could never be too sure.

"We've heard some unpleasant stories about what's going on out there, but that's about it," she said. "So we decided to have a proper look."

He thought about that. "Who did you send?"

"Eleanor Christie; you don't know her, but she's good, very capable."

"And she hasn't been in touch."

"She's missed all her contacts for the past month. She could have had an accident, but we need to know." She glanced at him, a stout, red-haired woman in her early thirties. "I wouldn't ask unless I had to."

Adam nodded. "Yeah, I know."

"We'll run you up the coast to Worthing, but you'll have to walk the rest of the way. I don't want to risk dropping you on the beach at Margate. Try to find out what's happened, and if you can, either retrieve her gear or destroy it."

He nodded again.

They walked for a while in silence, turned away from the seafront and headed through Hoe Park. "How was Wales, by the way?" she asked.

It was easy, on the neat rainswept streets of Guz, to forget that the rest of the country was not like this. A Sister – one of the small ones, but even the small ones had erased towns – had touched down at the mouth of the Bristol Channel, sent an accelerating wall of water upstream, according to the stories. Cardiff and Newport were inundated; Weston-super-Mare had simply been erased. By the time the wave reached Gloucester, it had been almost sixty feet high and moving at around a hundred miles an hour. The whole South Wales coast was deserted now; everyone had fled north, forming scattered communities in the Brecon Beacons.

"They want to talk," he said. "Some of them do, anyway; the rest just want to be left alone."

"I haven't had a chance to look at your report."

"Good; I haven't had a chance to write it."

She grunted. "Well, we'll get you debriefed before you leave again."

They reached the place where they had chained their bicycles to a set of railings, unlocked them, and pedalled off through the town. The weather was easing off, and people were coming out onto the streets. They looked, for the most part, content and well-fed and prosperous. Adam thought of the people he'd seen in Wales, just one bad day away from starvation.

Plymouth had come through the disaster almost unscathed, and in those early days when order was breaking down across the country, the garrison at HMS Drake had managed to keep a lid on things. Later, people had started to drift into the town from all over the West, looking for security, and for quite a long time they had buttoned themselves up against the world and the chaos in it. Times changed, though. The weather was improving, finally, and in the past few years the people who ran Guz had looked farther afield, wondering what was going on, sending out representatives to have a look, check things out, make assessments. It was still early days, they were still formulating a position, but Adam had a sense that the country was beginning to wake up from a long and terrible nightmare.

At the gates of the naval base, they showed their identification and were waved through. Reaching the Bureau, the minders peeled off in the direction of the canteen, while Adam and Chrissie went on up to her office.

"I really wouldn't send you if there was someone else," she said, taking off her coat and hanging it on the back of the door.

"It's okay," he said.

"No, it isn't." She sat down at the desk and started unlocking drawers. "It isn't okay. You must be shattered."

In all honesty, Wales had not been terribly taxing. Just a lot of walking and talking to people, sleeping indoors when he got the chance, living rough when he had to. He said, "What do you want me to do if Eleanor's being held?"

"Use your initiative." She opened a drawer and took out a

cardboard folder. "But it might be best if you don't start a war with these people just yet."

"Not authorised to start wars," he said. "Got it."

She glanced at him, decided to let it go. She held out a sheet of paper. "Here's a chit; when you're ready, get yourself down to the stores and kit yourself out. *Anna Mendonça*'s leaving the day after tomorrow; you can go with Ricky."

"I can go now," he suggested. He'd only been home to check on the cat, which was being looked after by old Mrs Spicer downstairs, but the cat appeared to have forgotten who he was.

She shook her head. "Try to get a little rest, at least. Twenty-four hours, and then back into it. You'll get a nice long leave when you get back."

"You said that when you sent me to Wales," he reminded her.

She thought about it. "I don't remember that."

"I should have got you to write it down."

Chrissie looked at him again. Then she took out a clean sheet of paper, scribbled some words on it, and signed it. She held it up. "Happy now?"

He shrugged.

"Go home," she said. "Rest."

HOME WAS A flat in a three-floor conversion in Beaumont. Going up the front steps, he saw the cat waiting at the top. He held out his hand and made kissing noises, but the cat, a stray ginger tom he'd named Happy because it seemed permanently pissed-off, just looked at him for a few moments and then wandered away.

Upstairs, everything was as he'd left it a month ago when he left for Wales. Although to be fair there wasn't very much; he hadn't spent enough time here, over the past couple of years, for it to feel much like home. It was just the place he came to when he wasn't away. Maybe the cat had been a mistake, now he thought about it.

He spent twenty minutes with sticks and wadded-up paper and coal, lighting the fire, then he took off his boots and stretched out on the sofa. Closed his eyes and listened to a hail shower rattling on the skylights and thought about the hills of the Brecon Beacons, where only a handful of people spoke English and everyone was too busy simply trying to survive to distrust him. It was hard country, scattered farms, no real organisation to speak of. The death toll in Wales, during the Long Autumn, had been ferocious. It had been hard enough in Guz, but out there in the wilds, well. He'd liked the Welsh; they were tough, capable, direct people and to have survived out there at all was quite a feat, but they were tired. Some of them had heard about Guz and wanted to cross the Channel into the West Country. They thought it was a land of milk and honey, which it was not, but at least there was a semblance of order here, almost cut off from the rest of the country by the shallow inland sea which had once been Wiltshire.

During the Long Autumn, everyone had hunkered down, no one travelled very much. Entire communities died of starvation or disease unremarked by their neighbours just a few miles away. He'd been up in Northamptonshire the previous year and found it almost completely deserted, stripped of its population by what sounded, if the stories were accurate, like a flu epidemic which could have wiped out the whole country had people moved about more. The North was still pretty much a mystery to the people in the West, and Scotland might as well have been a place of legends.

As for the rest of the world, it was anyone's guess. Guz had maintained contact with the elements of the Devonport Flotilla which had been at sea when The Sisters came, but one by one they had fallen silent. From time to time, there were sporadic, garbled radio transmissions from the East Coast of America. The US had taken a big fragment of the comet in the face, and things sounded as if they were still very bad there. France was a charnel house, the Low Countries were mostly underwater. Adam imagined little communities everywhere, like Guz, or probably more like the fortified farms he'd seen in the Beacons, getting by with only the most basic technology and medical care, eternally dreading a crop failure or a livestock disease or a burst appendix, on the edge of failure for so long that they couldn't remember anything else. Exploration, finding out what had happened to the rest of the country, let alone the rest of the world, was a luxury no one could afford.

Which put Guz in something of a position, because it was a luxury it *could* afford.

Adam got up and lifted one of the skylights, leaned on the frame and looked out on a vista of rooftops and houses. The hail squall had passed over, hung like a curtain to the west, lit by a sliver of moon veiled by broken cloud. Some of the rooftops had windmills, and below them there was light in the windows. Most, though, were dark. Guz might have been the largest population centre in the West – maybe in the entire country – but there were still not enough people to fill it. Movement down in the street made him crane his neck; a patrol of constables, making their rounds.

He ducked his head back into the flat and looked around, wondering if he would ever be here long enough to redecorate.

"So," SAID MR ROSS. "Do they represent any threat to us?"

"God, no," said Adam. "They're barely coping."

Mr Ross had a cast in one eye, and an arm lost above the elbow to some long-ago accident. He habitually tucked the empty sleeve of his jacket into his pocket. He made a note on the pad in front of him and sat back and looked at Adam across the table. "The decision hasn't been announced officially yet, but we're going to be trading with them."

"They haven't got anything to trade," Adam said. "A few scabby sheep, and they can't even spare those."

"As you will be aware," Mr Ross told him, "threat is not

always to be measured in terms of force of arms or numerical superiority. We have to be careful who we take in."

Adam nodded at the notepad. He had been sitting in this airless little room for hours now, going over his trip to Wales, going over it again, answering questions, going over it again. Debriefing was always the same. Nitpicking and dispiriting.

"If you go back a few pages, you'll find a line somewhere to the effect that they're on the verge of starvation," he said. "They're not going to come in here and start a takeover."

Mr Ross sighed. "You know," he said, "these debriefings don't only serve for you to report what you have seen and done in the field. They allow us to make an assessment of how you're performing."

Adam blinked slowly at him.

"Your superiors – myself among them, let's not forget – have noticed a certain tendency for you to over-identify with the communities you visit."

"I'm supposed to tell you what I think."

"You're supposed to tell me what you see and make a dispassionate assessment."

Adam blinked at him again.

"A degree of empathy is valuable," Mr Ross went on. "It helps you do your job more effectively. Your job is to make contact with groups outside Guz and report back on what you find."

"Thank you for that."

Mr Ross inclined his head in assent, as if the sarcasm had bounced straight off him. Which it had not. "A distance is also valuable," he said. "Your job is to gather intelligence. What happens to that intelligence, at a policy level, is out of your hands." He closed the notebook and laid his pen on top of it.

"To be more concise, you can shout and scream and stamp your feet all you want, but we are not, for the moment, letting the Welsh in here. Understood?"

"They didn't even know what happened," Adam told him.

"About The Sisters. They've been living up there all this time thinking there was a nuclear war. They thought the world had come to an end and they were the only people left."

"Hm. Well, absent a miracle it almost did and they almost were." Mr Ross took his briefcase from under the table, opened it one-handed, and put his notebook and pen inside. "The Committee will be setting up a working group to determine the best way forward in terms of trading with the Brecon Beacons," he said. "They will be needing a briefing paper from you."

"I just..."

"No, this was your debriefing, which does not leave the Bureau. As you very well know."

"I'm going out on deployment," Adam said. "Tomorrow. Again."

"You'd best get the briefing paper done before you go, then," said Mr Ross, standing and picking up his briefcase. "Good to see you again. Good luck on your deployment."

"I CAN'T GIVE them this," Chrissie said. "Come on."

"It'll have to wait till I get back, then," he said.

They were in her office, a bottle of whisky, two glasses, and a sheet of paper on the desk between them.

"You said yourself they need help; the working group won't do anything until you give them a steer, and those people up there are going to starve."

He poured more whisky into his glass, sat back, and put his feet up on the desk. Outside, night and rain brushed the windows. On the sheet of paper, he had written, *Send boats across the Bristol Channel. Bring them all here*. "They wanted a briefing paper," he said.

Chrissie picked up her glass and slumped back in her chair, cradling it in her hands. "Just between us, please tell me you didn't say they could come here."

He drank some whisky.

She sighed. "You don't *do* that. How many more times do I have to tell you?"

He drank some more whisky.

"We're not a bloody guest house, Adam. We can't take in every raggedy Bob and tattered Brenda."

"They're good farmers," he said. "They've had to be, to scratch any kind of a life for themselves up there. Bring them over here, put them on some of the old farms inland, they'd work like demons."

"That's not how it works," she said. "You know that."

"It's how it used to."

"Yes, and remember how much trouble it caused?"

Some years before he was born, Guz had contacted a small community living on the marshy fringes of Wiltshire. Like the people of the Beacons, they had been starving, barely getting by. A decision had been made to take them in, welcome them with open arms, and for a few months all had been well. Then their leader, a young man who styled himself Father John, had begun quietly spreading sedition, turning people against Guz's military authorities, recruiting followers. There had been a brief season of assassinations, then an attempted coup, which the Commodore of the time had put down with an iron fist. When it was over, more than a hundred people were dead and Father John was nowhere to be found.

"There is also," she said, "a policy of not depopulating an area. The land needs to be worked, communities need to establish themselves and grow. Nothing's going to get done if we just abandon the countryside and come and live here."

"Even if it means leaving people to die?"

"We're not going to leave them to die. We're going to trade with them. Food, medical supplies, logistical support, animal husbandry."

"They've got nothing to trade with," he said. "How many

more times? You're not telling me we've become a charity now, are you?"

She shook her head. "No, we have not. But we'll trade on account. Eventually they'll have something we can make use of. In the meantime, we'll send them some Marines."

He sighed. "You want a stronghold. That's it, isn't it?"

"Well, I certainly don't; I've got more than enough work to be getting on with here. What's going on in the Committee's mind, I couldn't tell you."

He drained his glass. "They've managed to survive for almost a hundred years in some of the hardest country I've ever seen. They're not going to take kindly to being turned into a colony."

"It won't be a colony," she said. "We'll be helping them out. From what you say, they need it."

"We could always move them to Northamptonshire," he said.

"No, Adam. No." She sat up and held the bottle out to him. "Go home. Take this with you and go home."

"There are times," he said, "when I wonder what the point of this job is." But he took the bottle anyway.

CHAPTER THREE

THERE WAS AN apocalyptic light in the sky when Max finally turned the wagon onto the home stretch. The horses were tired – *he* was tired – but they all sensed the familiarity of the landscape that spoke of home.

He sat up in the seat and looked to the West. He thought the sunsets were getting a little less spectacular, these past few years, which was a hopeful sign. In his grandfather's day, the sun had barely fought its way through the driving clouds. Turning, he glanced back at the wagon, checking automatically that the tarps were still tightly lashed down.

When he turned back, three figures were standing in the middle of the road.

He sighed, let the horses walk on a few more steps before reining them in. Then he sat where he was and looked at the three figures. They were all dressed in combats, scarves wrapped around the lower parts of their faces, hoods pulled up. They were all holding crossbows. *Not three miles from home.*

"Lads," said Max amiably.

"What are you hauling?" asked the tallest of the three. His

voice sounded high and confident; he couldn't be more than fifteen, which made him a problem because kids that age thought they could do anything and not get hurt.

"Oh, this and that," Max said. He watched one of the figures move around and take April's bridle. The horse whinnied and shied a little, but the figure stroked his forehead and hushed him in a whisper, and that was a problem too because the three of them were no longer all in one group and Max couldn't watch them all at once. "You lads from round here?"

The tall one and the third one looked at each other. The one stroking April's head looked up at Max.

"This is stupid, you know," Max told them amiably. "I've got some sickle blades, a little water purification plant, some odds and ends of tools. What are you going to do with all that?"

"Get down," the tall one said. "Nobody needs to get hurt."

"I agree," said Max, sitting where he was. "Don't scare the horses now," he said to the second one. "They're tired, but they're easily spooked."

"Get down," the tall one said again.

Max looked at them, one after the other, and he sighed. "All right," he said. He shuffled along to the end of the seat and started to climb down.

"Keep your hands where we can see them," the tall one cautioned.

"All right," Max said again, and he held his hands over his head as he felt with his toe for the step.

"Mind you don't slip," said the third one, and they all laughed, and in one motion Max stepped down onto the road, pulled the shotgun from its clips behind the footboard, lifted it, and fired.

The blast caught the tall boy on the right side, shredding his combats, but he didn't go down. Max had time to see the crossbow drop from nerveless fingers and blood start to well through his ruined clothing, then he was pumping the shotgun and half-turning for the second one. He had a better aim this time, centre of mass, almost point-blank. The boy folded convulsively as if punched in the stomach, staggered, sat heavily in the road, and toppled over.

Max was already moving, back along the side of the wagon, keeping low so the loadbed was between him and the third hijacker, hoping the kid would see sense and leg it. He pumped the shotgun and the breech jammed; another poorly-handloaded shell. Violence never goes quite the way you plan it. He cursed shoddy workmanship under his breath and tried to clear the slide, and there was a sudden thump and searing pain in his side. He looked down and saw the point of a crossbow bolt protruding from his jumper, and then it *really* started to hurt. He looked over his shoulder and saw the tall hijacker on his knees in the road, hopelessly trying to reload his crossbow left-handed.

"You little twat," Max muttered. A scrape of heels on the road announced the third hijacker coming around the corner of the wagon. Max hit him in the face with the barrel of the shotgun, then stepped forward, reversed the weapon, and hit him again with the butt. The hijacker stumbled back. Max took the barrel of the gun in both hands, and swung it with all his strength at the side of his attacker's neck. The man dropped bonelessly and lay still.

And then all was silence, save for the song of a solitary bird in a nearby tree. Max bent down painfully, picked up the crossbow where it had fallen, and turned and limped back to the tall hijacker, who had slumped over on his side, his face pressed into an expanding pool of his own blood.

"You had a chance to stop that," Max told him.

The hijacker lay where he was, panting, unable to speak. All Max could see of him were his eyes, scrunched up in pain. He stood there watching, and presently the boy stopped panting. Max stayed beside him a few moments longer, then he sighed and sank to his knees in the middle of the road. After a few moments, he bent over and rested his forehead on the ancient cracked tarmac.

DUSK WAS ROLLING up out of the Vale. In the main house, Rose went from room to room, lighting lamps. Upstairs, she could hear laughter and a stampede of footsteps as the younger kids did their best to avoid getting ready for bed.

In the living room, Nell looked up from patching a pair of jeans and said, "He's overdue."

Rose went over to the other side of the room and unhooked one of the oil lamps. "He's been overdue before," she said, lighting the lamp. "And he still turns up." She adjusted the flame and hung it up again, moved on to the next. "You shouldn't sew in this light; you'll ruin your eyes."

Nell pulled a face. "I'll be all right."

"I keep telling you."

Nell laid her work aside. "He's never been this late before, Ma."

Poking the taper into the glass chimney of another lamp, Rose paused for a moment. The flame caught, its strengthening light flickering on her face. She remembered her father bringing these lamps home with him from Oxford, must have been thirty years ago now. They'd once had three, but one had got broken when the girls were little and instead of replacing the glass, Max, with his usual lack of sentimentality, had gone out and got a new one, and then looked crestfallen when she wasn't delighted with it. Max didn't put a lot of stock in mementoes. A thing was a thing; either it was useful for something or it wasn't.

Rose lifted the lamp onto its hook and turned to look around the living room, its comfortable worn furniture, the fire burning in the grate. For a moment, she imagined that it was her mother sitting there in the armchair by the fire, not her daughter. She walked over to the window. The compound was filling up with shadows, the outbuildings sinking back into darkness. Above the wall, the rushing clouds were losing their sunset colours. There had been a time, even when she was young, when everyone locked their doors and pulled down the shutters and huddled inside come sundown. Even now, only the brave or unwise travelled after dark, and Max, bless him, was neither. He could, of course, just have been a bit late leaving Blandings. There might have been a problem with the wagon, or a tree fallen across the road. Any number of things. If he'd decided to stay an extra night to drink with Betty Coghlan, she thought she'd kill him herself, or at least make him wish she had.

Patrick was walking across the compound towards the house, shotgun slung over his shoulder, lantern hanging from his hand. He saw her standing at the window and raised his other hand. She waved back, and he walked out of view around the corner. Doing his rounds.

"He'll be back soon," she said, half to herself.

THE TAYLOR COMPOUND sat atop a low rise like a ragged, blocky crown. Its wall – a ring of old shipping containers dragged here from a nearby railway siding back in the days when there was still petrol for tractors and filled, down the years, with earth and rubbish – enclosed the main house and several outhouses, storage silos and sheds. Back when Rose's mother was a girl, there had been enough space in the yard to accommodate all the livestock in an emergency, but those days were long gone. Scattered in the fields surrounding the compound were byres and pens and sties, patrolled day and night by armed guards. Beyond the livestock were fields and woods and wild overgrown country, and beyond that, lost in uncertain distances, was the Vale of the White Horse, an almost primeval wilderness.

Over the years, the people of the smallholdings of the Parish had done their best to maintain the old roads, but it had become necessary to cut new paths and tracks. It was down one of these, winding and narrow, that a cart drawn by two horses came in the early morning. The cart moved slowly, the horses plodding along and pausing often before starting off again. They seemed in no great hurry, but they knew their way. The track wound between trees and bushes and along the edges of fields, and finally came to the gate of the Taylor compound, and here the horses stopped.

There was silence for a short time, then a commotion on top of the wall, and slowly the gate slid aside and a number of figures carrying weapons and lanterns came running out.

One of the figures vaulted up onto the wagon's loadbed and looked down at what lay there. He held his lantern up by his head, revealing strong features, curly hair, the quick shine of an earring.

One of the figures in the loadbed stirred and opened its eyes. "Hallo, son," Max said dreamily. Then he closed his eyes again.

HARRY ARRIVED AT first light the next morning, in a wagon with his two eldest sons. He pulled the horses to a halt at the gate and called out, "Taylors!"

Patrick, looking down on him from the wall, called back, "We don't want any trouble, Harry."

"Patrick!" Rose shouted up from the compound. "Don't you *dare* speak to Mr Lyall like that. Let him in."

Patrick glanced down at her, and for a moment it seemed as though he might disobey, but he nodded to the men down in the yard, and they began turning the big crank handle that winched the gate aside. When the gap was wide enough, Harry urged the horses through.

In the compound, a group of Taylor farmhands surrounded the wagon. Harry looked down at them and his heart broke.

For a moment, driving up the track to the farm, he had briefly entertained a fantasy that this was like the other times he had visited the Taylors. The band of armed men around the wagon dispelled that fantasy. He felt his eldest son, James, stir uneasily on the seat beside him and reach for the crossbow.

He said, loudly enough for everyone in the compound to hear him, "We don't want any trouble."

"Tell your lad to put his bow down, then," Patrick called from the top of the wall.

"You can tell him yourself," Harry said, more angrily than he had intended. He nudged James and said quietly, "Don't be a twat, son," and after a moment James put the bow down again.

Rose walked across the compound, through the group of people standing around the wagon, and stood looking up at them. Harry thought she looked exhausted. "Rosemary," he said. When she didn't answer, he said, "Where's Max?"

"Inside." Rose gestured at the house. "Dying."

Harry sighed. "All right, Rose," he said. "I'm going to get down now and you can tell me what happened."

"They stay where they are," Patrick called, nodding at James and his brother.

Harry looked up at the boy, then at Rose again. "All right," he said. And he got up and climbed down from the wagon and walked over to Rose. She stared at him wordlessly, then turned and led the way to one of the outhouses across the yard.

Inside, three tarpaulin-draped shapes lay on the floor. Rose silently pulled the tarps back, revealing two young men Harry did not know, and one he did. He stared at the lifeless face, nicked here and there by stray shotgun pellets, and found himself remembering, quite at random, a Christmas years and years ago, before Alice died. He reached out and gently covered his son's face again.

"Who are the other two?" Rose asked.

"Never saw them before," he replied.

"We don't know for sure what happened, because Max was unconscious when he got here," she said. "They were in the wagon." She nodded at the bodies. "They were dead, Max was dying. Anyone else would have left them where they were, but Max loaded them onto the wagon while he was bleeding to death because that's what Max is like."

Harry said, "They could have been attacked by someone." A bunch of bandits from somewhere in Bedfordshire had arrived in the area a couple of years before, stealing livestock and attacking lone travellers. Harry and Max and some of their men had gone out and dealt with them.

Rose went over to a corner of the shed, came back holding a shotgun, its stock broken. "This is Max's," she said. "There's a round jammed in the breech. Two of the boys were shot, one's got head injuries and a broken neck, Max had a crossbow bolt in his gut. Shall I draw you a picture, Harry?"

Harry scowled. He knew men in the area who would start a fight at the least provocation, but Max Taylor wasn't one of them. Max would go a long way out of his way to avoid trouble.

"I want to talk to Max," he said.

Rose shook her head. "No, Harry," she said angrily. "No. Even if he was conscious, I wouldn't let you near him. He's going to die and your son's responsible." She gestured at the bodies with the ruined shotgun, then turned and threw it across the shed. Harry winced at the noise it made as it hit the wall and crashed to the floor among a nest of empty jars.

"You don't know that," he said.

"Oh, I do." She turned away. "Take them away," she told him. "And then I never want to see your face around here again. Yours or your family's."

"I don't know what happened," he said. "And neither do you."

"Fuck off, Harry!" she screamed. She walked to the door,

took a long, shaky breath and said more quietly, "Just fuck off. Take your boy and go home. Please."

After she'd gone, Harry stood looking down at the bodies, a great sad weight growing in his chest. He'd lost children before, to illness and accidents, but this was different and he didn't know how to feel about it. It seemed that the sense of loss he felt was balanced precisely against his anger – anger at Rob, anger at Max, anger at the Taylors in general, anger at the two other boys whose names he didn't even know.

"Dad?" James said from the doorway.

Harry sighed. "Come and help me take your brother home," he said.

CHAPTER FOUR

"HEY," SAID RICKY. "Going on holiday, are we?"

"Good morning, Erika," said Adam.

She trotted down the gangplank onto the quay. "I thought you only just got back."

"Yes, I did."

She looked at him. "You look awful. Are you ill?"

"I have a hangover."

"Don't think that's going to get you off working on *my* boat, sunshine."

"I thought perhaps I could sleep it off for an hour or so," he said. He loved boats but had never worked out why they always involved early mornings.

Ricky picked up his rucksack. "Come aboard, you daft sod. We have coffee."

"Coffee would be nice," he admitted, following her. "And then some sleep."

One advantage Guz had had over practically every other place in Britain on the day The Sisters came was an unusual concentration of skills. HMS Drake was home to engineers, chefs, weapons experts, logisticians, psychiatrists, doctors, musicians, helicopter pilots, meteorologists, divers, boatbuilders, and more Marines than anyone knew what to do with. These were people who knew how to do things and how to get things done, and the first thing they did, in the early panicked days and months and years after the disaster, was impose Order. It had been a sturdy, no-nonsense sort of Order, but by and large that was what people needed.

What Guz chiefly had, of course, was sailors – Plymouth had been a Navy town as far back as the Armada – and people who knew how to build boats. Almost by default, it had become a maritime superpower.

Anna Mendonça was an old-style square-rigged ketch with .40 calibre heavy machine guns mounted fore and aft. She spent most of her time going back and forth along the South Coast, trading in small high-value items with some of the coastal communities beyond Southampton, and if sometimes the items turned out to be people, landed at dead of night on Sussex beaches, that was just part of the job.

They were out of the Sound and making their way up the Channel before Adam felt competent enough to come up on deck.

"Better?" Ricky asked.

"Loads, thank you," he said, looking around. It was a drizzly afternoon. To port the Devon coast loomed up through the dimness; everywhere else was a vague misty distance. "Is that the Spanish?"

She looked at the three boats – two trawlers and what seemed to be an ancient cabin cruiser – riding at anchor side by side a mile or so away. "Yup. Gives me the willies."

The Spanish – it was assumed they were Spanish, from the names painted on their boats – had started to appear a year or so ago. There were never more than four of them at a time, and they never did anything. They just sat offshore. No one ever saw them arrive or leave; they moved under cover of darkness.

There had been much debate about what to do about them. They didn't respond to radio or hails or signal lamps or flags, just rode at anchor for a day or so and then left again. In the end, it had been decided to leave them respectfully alone; if they ever chose to make formal contact it was obviously going to be in their own time.

"Never seen them before," Adam said, accepting the proffered pair of binoculars and focusing on one of the trawlers. "It's quite spooky, isn't it."

"You know nobody's ever seen a crew?" Ricky said. "Not once. This is the way stupid stories get started."

It was as if the sea were haunted. "Yeah." He handed back the binoculars. "I know what you mean."

"Commodore's talking about paying them a visit, maybe next year."

"Really? I hadn't heard that."

"That's because you're always somewhere else."

This would be true. "We're going to Spain?"

Ricky shrugged. "I hear the idea's to repay the compliment. Do a recce of the coast to see if we can find a port, anchor offshore for a bit, then come home."

He thought about it. "Seems a rum way of going about things."

"The Commodore knows what she's doing."

Adam, who tried to limit his contact with Guz's military authorities as much as possible, shrugged. He wondered whether a Spanish phrasebook would be waiting for him when he got back from Thanet.

IF THE SEA was haunted, the land was even worse. Sodden by continual rain and drizzle, it was an impassable nightmare of overgrowth and fields gone wild and sudden bogs under lowering clouds. It was a slog just to get inland from Worthing.

At the end of the first day, he pitched his tent beside an old road, its surface turned to crumbs by decades of frost and rain and the patient lifting of weeds and vegetation. He heated up some soup, and when he'd finished eating, he took a little metal box from his rucksack. There was a handle set into the side of the box; he gently pulled it out, turned it a few times, then pressed the button on the side and said, "Hello."

A minute or so later, a voice from the box said, "Hello."

He pressed the button again. "Well, I'm on my way."

"Understood," said the voice. "Check in at your next contact point."

"Will do." He pushed the handle back into the side of the radio and put it back in his rucksack and sighed.

HIS NEXT CONTACT point was Brighton, where it was market day, farmers from the Downs bringing their produce into town for trade. The place looked tidy and well-organised, if a little shabby around the edges – there were only a few hundred people living here, not enough to keep everything maintained and painted. Today the population must have been almost a thousand, though, and the streets and lanes were crammed with carts and wagons and hawkers and livestock.

He'd brought trade goods with him – some magnetic compasses, odds and ends of medical gear – and for the price of a couple of surgical scalpels still in their original packaging and an old watch he managed to get a room in a boarding house for the night. The owner, a taciturn man named Mr Brown, allowed after some questioning that he might know someone who would be prepared – for a small price – to give Adam a lift further east along the coast.

The someone turned out to be Nigel, who had a cart drawn by a single mule and piled up with what looked like bales of military surplus clothing looted from an old warehouse.

Unlike Mr Brown, Nigel was not remotely taciturn, and as they plodded through the drizzle along the rutted and crumbling A27, he gave Adam chapter and verse on any subject that came into his head, and that was how Adam first heard Frank's name.

"Pendennis, he's called," Nigel said. "Frank Pendennis. Lives like a king, so they say."

"Have you ever been up there?" Adam asked. "Thanet?"

Nigel shook his head. "No need to; I've got all I need here. Besides, I hear Frank doesn't take kindly to strangers just wandering in." He took his pipe from his mouth and spat into the road. "I see them here sometimes, though. His people."

"Bit far from home."

"Just every now and again." Nigel clamped the stem of his pipe between his teeth and spoke round it. "Trading. Big ugly fuckers with guns, walking round like they own the place."

To be fair, that could really describe a lot of people wandering around England these days. Particularly the guns. Adam was carrying a service automatic and some spare ammunition, but that was really only for defence against the packs of feral dogs roaming the countryside. He'd always thought the best way not to get into trouble was to avoid it entirely.

"What do they trade?" he asked.

Nigel shrugged. "Vegetables, mostly. Tomatoes. Have you ever seen a tomato?"

Adam shook his head.

"Fucking horrible things," Nigel said. "Wouldn't give you the last drop of piss off the end of my cock for one."

Adam filed this information away in the part of his brain where he put the stuff he didn't want to think about. "What do they trade for? With their vegetables?"

Nigel thought about it. "Nothing much, now you mention it," he said. "Medical supplies, mostly. What they really do is try to talk people into going back with them."

"Why?"

Nigel shrugged. "No idea, old son. Maybe they're cannibals, eh? Looking for a good meal." He laughed and clicked his teeth together.

In this way, with much jolly banter, they made their way to Pevensey, and a couple of days later Adam was on the Kent Downs just north of Folkestone. Because he was there anyway and he might as well, he swung east and took a discreet look at Dover. There seemed to be some activity around the harbour, but the rest of the town appeared deserted, and he turned north again.

As he drew closer to the Thanet coast, he started to see more and more people. Some were on horseback, others in wagons; mostly, they were on foot, in little groups, carrying a motley array of tools and equipment. A lot of them were clearing roads, cutting the rusted carcases of cars out of the encroaching vegetation and dragging them into the fields on either side. He watched them from a distance through his binoculars and they did not look particularly happy or enthusiastic, but they were getting it done. There were farmsteads; none of them fortified, which was interesting. Did these people have no enemies, no one who wanted their resources? Or did they just not care?

After a day or so, he decided it was the latter. There were guns everywhere, mainly shotguns and mostly in the hands of people who seemed to be acting as overseers. He pondered that for a while before moving on.

He was working from Ordnance Survey maps, over a century old, the theory being that by and large towns and cities and most of the main roads would still be in much the same place as they were before the disaster, even if they were inaccessible. The maps were good enough for navigation, but beyond that they might as well have been blank. His briefing before he left Guz had been based on not much more than an entry in an old encyclopaedia and some unconfirmed word-of-mouth that had drifted down the coast with fishermen and traders. Eleanor had reported seeing what he was seeing now – an apparently organised but impoverished community with some kind of well-armed ruling group – and then fallen silent.

The countryside was huge and wet and empty and wild. It was easy for him to pass through it unseen, particularly as the work-crews and patrols weren't making any great effort to hide. Navigating with map and compass, he gave Margate a wide berth, staying away from roads and trudging along the edge of overgrown fields.

He laid up for a few days in an abandoned village near the coast, cautiously scouting the area, trying to get a feel for the place – in truth working himself up to take the next step; it was never easy. Searching the cottages and little houses, he found a rucksack and odds and ends of camping equipment and assembled a disguise for himself; a traveller looking for safety and shelter. He certainly, he thought, *looked* the part.

One morning, unable to put it off any longer, he stashed the gear he'd brought with him from Guz, made one last brief radio contact, then shouldered his pilfered rucksack and set out again.

It took him a week to work his way back to Brighton, coming in from the north a few days before market day. Asking around, he found a builder named George who needed a labourer for work on a row of houses inland from the seafront, and he spent the rest of the week replacing smashed windows.

As the next market day approached and the town's population began to swell again, he took to wandering the local pubs in his off hours, spending an evening nursing the same pint and keeping an ear open for local gossip. This led to him, on the afternoon of market day, wandering down a little street off the seafront and finding himself looking at a group of men all wearing long waxed coats with hoods and with shotguns and rifles slung over their shoulders. They were big and beefy and many of them were shaven-headed and they were clustered around a cart full of produce.

"Hey," one of them said as he walked by. "Hey, old son. Fancy a tomato?"

He took a few more steps, stopped, turned. "What?"

The shaven-headed man held out a small red fruit. "Tomato. Only the best. Give it a try."

Adam looked at the fruit, thought about it, then shook his head. "Nah. I haven't anything to give you for it."

"Listen," the shaven-headed man said, lowering his voice until it was a conspiratorial rumble. "Between you and me, these things are just going to rot, nobody wants to pay our prices. You can have this one for free."

Adam shrugged. "You should drop your price, then." But he took the tomato and turned it over in his hand. It felt squishy and overripe, and there were spots of black mould on its skin.

"Look, it took a lot of work to grow these. Give it a try."

Adam bit into the tomato and was rewarded with an unexpected and unwelcome spurt of juice and seeds. Nigel had been right; it tasted awful. But he chewed and swallowed anyway.

"I'm Albie," said the shaven-headed man. "Albie Dodd."

"Adam Hardy," he said, running his tongue over his teeth to dislodge errant seeds.

"You from round here?"

"Horsham."

"In town for the market?"

"Working. Fixing up houses."

Albie nodded. "What's your line then, Adam? Brickie? Roofer?"

Adam shrugged. "I can fix windows."

Albie looked thoughtful. "You know, we could use people who can fix windows."

"Who's 'we'?"

"Thanet."

"What's that?"

Albie grinned. "It's not a what, it's a where. Margate. In Kent."

"Never heard of it."

"We've got a good place there. Well-organised, a lot of people. You could do worse than think about coming back with us."

Adam snorted. "Right. And the moment we're out of town you shoot me and take my stuff. No thanks."

Albie looked hurt. "We don't need to rob the likes of you."

"Not that you'd get very much."

"Look," said Albie. "We're leaving tomorrow morning. There's a bunch of people coming with us. Come along with us, have a look at Thanet. If it doesn't suit, you can always leave."

Adam made a show of thinking about it, shook his head uncertainly. "Nah," he said. "I don't know."

Albie shrugged and grinned. "It's a free country, right? Nobody can make you do anything you don't want."

It was certainly a free country; nobody was ever going to argue with that. There were, in fact those, and he worked for some of them, who felt that this was the whole problem. "Sorry."

"Don't worry. It was great to meet you, Adam."

They shook hands, and Adam walked off down the street.

It was raining the next morning as he walked into town, rucksack over his shoulder. George had been a little annoyed at the news that he was leaving, but that was life, wasn't it?

The Thanet people – Thaneters? – were gathered around a couple of wagons outside a rooming house. There were perhaps twenty people in the wagons, all of them locals, by the look of it. The big bulky men were all on horseback. There was a jolly air about the scene, like a family going off on holiday, and as he approached, Adam felt a thrill of apprehension. Last chance to turn away…

But of course that option was never there in the first place. His initial reconnaissance of Thanet had confirmed what he'd thought – he couldn't walk into Margate, poke about a bit, and walk out again. *Frank doesn't take kindly to strangers just wandering in.*

Albie saw him approaching and broke into a huge grin. "Change our mind, did we?"

"Yes," he said. "Yes, something like that."

CHAPTER FIVE

THE FIRST MORTY heard of it, he was coming back from market day in Goring, having failed to sell the four sheep he'd taken with him. He'd given one to Evie Holt as payment for a night's bed and board at The Goring, and on account for several more, but he was bringing the other three back and wondering what Karen would say when he got home.

What Karen would say was uppermost in Morty's mind most of the time these days. She was never angry with him, never used a harsh word, but the weary tone of disappointment in her voice when he let her down yet again was starting to grind him down in ways he only dimly recognised.

He was thinking about this – and not urging the horse along, particularly – as he reached the Parish and saw a rider coming towards him along the Ridge Way.

As the rider came closer, Morty saw it was one of the Andersons – Jim or maybe Tim. He didn't know the family well – they were over on the other side of the Parish, but then he didn't really know anyone here very well, apart from old Kath Mercer and her nest of twats.

He drew the horse to a halt as the rider approached. "Hi," he said, noncommittally.

"Hi," said the rider. Tim, Morty thought. "You from round here?"

This was the sort of question which was guaranteed to buff up Morty's resentment for the Parish in general and the Mercers in particular, but he swallowed his temper. "Morty Roberts," he said, putting on an air of amiability which he did not feel. "The Roberts farm."

Tim looked momentarily nonplussed. "Oh. Right. Sorry. Didn't recognise you for a second there, Monty."

Story of my fucking life... "Morty."

"Yes, of course. Just back from market?" He nodded at the sheep penned up in the back of the wagon, and Morty knew he was wondering what would possess anyone to buy such scrawny scabby creatures.

"Yes," he said. "That's right."

"You heard about Max Taylor?"

Morty sighed inwardly. The Taylors were one of the two big landowning families in the Parish. Been here for generations, big farm, lots of animals, doing really well for themselves, blah blah, yadda yadda. They might as well have been Roman emperors for all he cared about them.

"No," he said, feigning interest. "What's happened?"

"He's been shot. Came home with the bodies of Harry Lyall's eldest and two other lads."

The Lyalls were the other big family, although even now Morty wouldn't have been able to describe any of them; they were just names, distant rumours. He thought it was like the days when there were kings; you knew they were there, but you never saw them.

"Oh?" he said.

"He's really sick. Nobody knows what happened."

Morty put on the appearance of giving a fuck, and shook his

head. "The things that happen when I go away, eh?"

Tim gave him a strange look. "You okay, Monty?"

"Sure," he said. "Never better. Got to get on, though. Things to do, yeah?"

"Sure," said Tim. "See you later."

"Yeah," Morty said under his breath, shaking the reins and urging the horse to start plodding along again. "See you later."

IT WAS, THE aged gaffers of the area said – the ones who could be bothered to talk to him, anyway – just one of those things. Some farms were doomed to fail, nobody knew why. You could work your heart out all your life and you would still fail. Some trick of the landscape, a quirk of microclimate. Perhaps they were even cursed. No one knew.

Which was all fucking well and good for the gaffers, with their thriving farms and their big families and their dozens of workers. They didn't have to drag themselves out of the door every morning, bone tired because they'd been working from dawn to dusk the previous day trying and failing to make their farm work. They were doing just fine, the patronising cunts, with their ramshackle folk wisdom and their pipes clenched between their teeth. Patting Morty on the head, *Eh well, you'll never make a go of it, son, but we can't be arsed to give you a hand but here's a little story about what this bloke did once seventy years ago.* Fuckers.

The Roberts farm – and that name had long since become a bitter joke in Morty's mind – was the smallest and meanest of all the farms in the area. It sat on the southern edge of the Parish, where the Downs swept away towards Lambourn and Newbury and distant Hampshire. Nothing much would grow there, for no particular reason anyone could see. Sheep grazed on the land refused to thrive. The old farmstead had been occupied and then abandoned more times than anyone could remember. And then Morty had turned up with his runaway bride and become the laughing stock of the whole of Berkshire.

A few hundred yards from the farm, but out of view of the house, Morty stopped and put down the tailgate of the wagon and let the sheep jump down. They looked at him accusingly for a few moments, then wandered off in different directions, and Morty carried on towards what he satirically called 'home'.

The place was so utterly rubbish that it didn't even have a compound. It didn't need one; there was nothing there that anyone would want to steal. Even wild animals turned their noses up at it and went looking for better pickings. There was just the house – once the home of some mucky-muck executive or other – and surrounding it was an inexpertly-maintained fence with an almost-dead privet hedge running along it. Inside, there were hen houses – all but two of them empty – and a small, dead, kitchen garden. The rest was weeds and bushes and overgrown shrubs which Morty could not cut back fast enough.

There had been a time when Karen would have been waiting for him in the open doorway of their home – although when he thought back to that time, it seemed to Morty that it had been brief. These days, though, there was no sign of her. He drove the wagon around to the ramshackle stable block behind the house – once a two-car garage – and unhitched and fed the horse.

No sign of Karen in the house, either, and that was more and more usual these days. He mooched around the kitchen, looking for something to eat, but the best he could come up with was a slice of stale bread and a chunk of cheese which, when he'd cut the mould off it, was about two inches square. He'd had a big bowl of mutton stew at The Goring last night, and it already seemed to him like a thing from a fairy story.

She turned up an hour or so later, dressed in jeans and a thick pullover and an old parka she'd found abandoned in one of the cupboards in the house. She was humming to herself as she put the key in the lock, but stopped when she realised it was already unlocked.

"You're back, then," she said, coming into the kitchen and seeing him sitting at the table.

"Yup," he said. "Where've you been?"

"Any luck at market?" She took off her coat and hung it from the hook on the back of the door.

"Sold the lot," he said. There was no chance of her checking the livestock; most days it was all she could manage to go and feed the chickens.

"What did you get?"

"Couple of bags of chicken feed and a side of bacon and some veg." He could go over to one of the neighbouring farms tomorrow, the Wrens maybe, or the Prestons, and offer to muck out their stables in return for some food. He'd done it before, so often that none of them was embarrassed about it any more.

She looked round the kitchen. "So where's this bacon and veg then?"

"On account. They'll bring it over tomorrow."

"They? Who's they?"

"Old gaffer from up Risborough way. He's coming through to see the Lyalls. He'll drop it off on the way."

Karen sighed, and Morty felt himself shrink inside. "You bloody fool," she said with that tired tone of voice. "How many times have I got to tell you? Maybe your memory's going. You don't sell stuff on account. We can't afford to do that."

"He's good for it," he told her. "You'll see."

"Yeah, right, sure."

"Where were you, anyway?"

"I'm tired," she said, heading for the hallway. "I'm going to have a lie down."

He watched her go upstairs, heard the bedroom door open

and then close, and then he was alone with his piece of bread and his tiny chunk of cheese.

He'd known her since they were kids, on the outskirts of Southampton. Her father, the widowed and perpetually-fierce Terry, had had four daughters, all of them older than Karen and all married off. Terry didn't want to let Karen go because she was the only one left at home to look after him. That was, at least, what she had told Morty, in those long-ago days when they were courting. What passed for courting, anyway.

He fell in love, of course, promised her all manner of things. She was noncommittal, worried about what Terry would say if he knew she was seeing him. "Dad's got a temper on him," she said, and that was true enough. Terry was legendary for it.

In the end, he talked her into eloping. It was difficult, at first, but then all of a sudden she was enthusiastic about it, making plans about where they would go and what they would do when they got there. They talked about the children they would have, the house they'd live in. He said he'd get her a kitten, and he did, eventually. It grew into a cat which adored her and despised him. The one time he'd tried to pick it up, it had laid his cheek open with a single swipe of its paw.

But that was still in the future when he sneaked out of the house early one morning, hitched their most rickety wagon to their sickliest horse – he couldn't find it in his heart to take anything useful from his family – and drove to the crossroads where Karen had promised to meet him.

She wasn't there. He called her name and there was no answer, got down from the cart and looked around in case she was hiding. Got back onto the cart and sat there in terror, unable to work out what to do.

Karen arrived an hour later, full of apologies. Terry had gone to bed late, she'd had to wait for him to fall asleep. Morty was frantic, torn between waiting longer for her and sneaking back home. Another couple of hours and his family would be up;

they'd find the horse and cart gone, and him gone, and then he didn't know what would happen. He was so relieved to see her that he didn't notice until later that she had only brought a big bag of clothes and assorted personal junk with her – none of the food and barter goods she'd promised to provide for the journey.

He'd only brought with him a couple of changes of clothes and what little food he could scrounge – his family couldn't spare much – so they wound up stopping at farms on the way. They'd pitch their tent in any compound which would let them in, and he'd do a few days' work in return for their keep, but nobody wanted them to stay. Everyone seemed suspicious and impoverished and only grudgingly willing to help the two young strangers. More than once, Morty had to endure some gaffer or his wife spelling out just how stupid it was to travel round the country with nothing more than a rusty old twelve-bore for protection. Karen didn't voice her disappointment, but at night with the drizzle hissing down onto the tent and water dribbling through holes in the ancient fabric, she sighed and turned away from him.

They wound up drifting, just two more souls on the road among the tinkers and traders and homeless who washed back and forth across the South. He tried to be upbeat, but Karen took to sighing heavily whenever he pointed out that at least they were together and they were in love. It was, at least, a mild summer, and less rainy than most. There were whole days when the drizzle dried up completely and the sun could be made out through the overcast. In dark moments, he knew he had let her down.

They stopped for a while in Newbury – Berkshire was, for the two of them, a faraway land of legend, and it was something of a let-down to discover that the people living there were not that much different to those in Southampton – and one day, while he was going from farm to farm looking for work, he heard of a community on the very edge of the Chilterns, where they overlooked the Vale of the White Horse. Good people, he was told. Welcoming to strangers. Plenty of land available for a young couple who were in love and were prepared to work hard to make their new lives become a reality.

Karen was not so keen. She was rather taken with Newbury; there couldn't have been more than a thousand people in the town, but they had the place running well. There was a sense of purpose and organisation which had been quite absent in Southampton, where people mostly kept themselves to themselves and looked after their own business.

"We can go up there and have a look," he suggested. "It's not that far. If we don't like it, we can always come back, but I hear we could have our own farm. Imagine that."

Karen looked at him with that long-suffering, pitying expression he had grown so familiar with during the weeks of their elopement. Finally, she sighed and said the words which sealed everyone's fate. "All right," she said. "But just a look, mind."

CHAPTER SIX

ROSE WOKE BEFORE dawn and went to check on Max. Nell, who had sat up with him during the night, was reading a book by the light of a lamp. When her mother came into the bedroom, she just looked up, said nothing. She looked worn out.

Max was asleep – or something like sleep, anyway. His forehead was hot and there was a smell of sickness in the air. Rose dipped a cloth in a bowl of water by the bed and laid it on his forehead, went to wash and dress, then went downstairs.

Patrick was already up, cooking bacon and eggs for the younger children. Rose felt her footsteps falter as she walked into the kitchen and saw them all sitting around the table, but she kept going, mentally put her shoulders back and her chin up.

"He's doing okay," she told them. Laura, her youngest, got up from the table and ran over and hugged her legs. Rose tousled her hair. "He'll be fine." She and Patrick looked at each other, and she shook her head fractionally to forestall anything he might be thinking of saying.

"Can we see him, Ma?" asked Christopher, just a couple of years older than Laura and already a solemn boy.

"Not today. He needs his rest. Maybe tomorrow." She looked at her children and wondered how much longer she could remain strong for them. It seemed to her that she had been doing it all her life.

Old John Race came in just as they were finishing breakfast and a couple of the younger children were clearing the table. He shook rain from his coat and hung it on the peg behind the front door, made a business of taking off his boots. "Morning, Taylors," he said to everyone. "Morning, miz."

He'd never, in all the time Rose had known him, called her by name. It was always 'miz'. The kids loved him; he kept a couple of old coins in his pocket and delighted them by performing simple little sleights of hand, making the coins disappear and reappear. Not this morning, though.

Rose clapped her hands. "All right, everyone," she said. "Washed and dressed, please."

Normally, there would have been complaints and grumbling and Laura would have found something to do in the kitchen so she didn't have to go upstairs. But this morning the kids filed out, leaving her and John sitting at the table. Patrick checked that no one was listening outside the kitchen, then closed the door and joined them. Rose felt her shoulders slump.

"We should find Doc Ogden," John told her. He'd removed the crossbow bolt and stitched up the wound, but like almost everyone else his medical knowledge was basic at best. "Max lost a lot of blood, there's almost certainly an infection."

"No one leaves the compound today." She said it to both of them, but she was looking at Patrick.

"You need to think about that, miz," said John. "The longer we wait, the harder it's going to be to treat him."

Rose shook her head. "Today the family stays together." She didn't just mean her family; she meant the other families who worked for the Taylors and depended upon them for food and protection, the people who had been her family ever since she was a little girl. "Make sure everyone knows that, John."

He thought about it, then nodded.

Patrick said, "Ma..."

She shook her head again. "No, Patrick. We stay home and we take care of our business. Anyone comes to visit, we're not entertaining today. Understood?"

It was obvious it wasn't; he was still too angry. But he said, "Yes, Ma."

"Tell them thanks for their concern and your father's hanging on, but we don't want to see anyone."

"Yes, Ma."

"Now go and make sure the children are getting ready." She saw the look on his face and added, "Nell's sitting with your father; they'll just be up there throwing water at each other. Go on."

He got up unwillingly and left. He left the door ajar, though. Rose went and closed it, came back to the table and rubbed her eyes. "So," she said. "What's everyone saying?"

John shrugged. "Just a lot of rumour. Nobody really knows anything."

"Lyalls?"

"Sitting in their compound. Just like us."

"Good. That's good. I don't want any accidents, John. No harsh words, no punch-ups. I don't want this to get any worse."

"No, miz."

She looked round the kitchen. Yesterday morning, it had seemed like the happiest place in her life, the place her family came together and ate and laughed. Now it seemed embattled, under siege. "If Max doesn't improve, I want you to go and talk to Doc Ogden tomorrow. Just you. Nobody else. Don't make a fuss about it."

He nodded. "I was thinking maybe we should let Blandings know, too."

"No. I don't need Betty bloody Coghlan's help."

"With respect, we need all the help we can get."

"No." She'd never really understood the web of favours which bound the Taylors and the Coghlans. For most of her marriage they'd seemed a distant irritation; now they were a looming threat, an alien influence on her husband. "We'll do this ourselves or not at all."

John sighed. "It's market day in Goring next week..."

"*No*, John."

He sat back and looked at the tabletop.

"I'm sorry, John," she said wearily. She reached out and put her hand over his. "I need you to be strong. I need *all* of us to be strong. And I need everyone to do as I say. All right?"

"Yes, miz."

"I need you to make sure no one does anything silly."

"Yes, miz."

"Anyone who does anything silly can go and find somewhere else to live. You tell them I said that."

He looked at her. "What are we going to do if the Lyalls do something silly?"

All through the sleepless night she had lain in her bed in the spare room, staring up at the ceiling, thinking about that. "We'll cross that bridge," she said.

HARRY STUMBLED ON autopilot through a hangover so intense that it felt as if his teeth were about to explode. He ignored the looks on the faces of his family and went and stood in the drizzle for a while. Even the raindrops falling on his face hurt. He did a circuit of the yard, another, realised he was avoiding the shed where they had put the bodies of Rob and the two strangers.

Alice had always said the farm was haunted. Like most of the other holdings in the area, it had begun life as a big family house, one of the expensive executive homes of the Chilterns commuter belt, handy for the station and the motorway to Reading and London. After The Sisters, in the first freezing rain-lashed days of the Long Autumn when everything was breaking down and no one knew whether the world was ending or not, Alice's great-great-grandfather had come here and found the house empty, abandoned by its owners, a message scrawled in lipstick on a mirror in the hallway, *GONE TO ALEX'S*. Who Alex was, and who the message was intended for, he never found out.

They hadn't been gone long; there was still fresh food in the fridge, although there was no electricity to run it. There was still one car in the three-car garage. There was a bedraggled and starving cat which had obviously decided, in the way of cats, to go off and hide while its owners tried to find it. *If* they'd tried. Back then the first instinct of everyone had been to flee, whether they had an idea of where to flee to or not.

Alice's great-great-grandfather had fled from London, part of a great shockwave of people who had some dim, ancient sense that they were safer out in the countryside than in the city. They had been wrong – nowhere was safe, particularly – but no one was thinking straight, there was no power, no communication, no order, no idea of what had happened to the world.

The house was secluded, set behind a high wall in a few acres of grounds. It was easy to miss – Alice's great-great-grandfather had almost walked past the lane leading to it in the driving sleet. He went through the abandoned rooms, opening cupboards and wardrobes. He stood in the garage and looked at the car, weighed up how far he would get on one tank of petrol in the chaos outside. He found some cat food in one of the kitchen cupboards and put it in a saucer, and in time the cat came to eat.

Others found the house. There was a family called Richards whose car had been hijacked by an armed mob as they tried to get out of Swindon. A couple named Holt, from Reading. They arrived cautiously. Alice's great-great-grandfather, who had found a gun cabinet hidden in the back of a walk-in wardrobe in one of the master bedrooms and managed to crowbar the door off, greeted them with a shotgun in his hands, but they were too exhausted to make trouble, even if they'd been of a mind to, and they stayed.

None of them knew anything about farming – Alice's great-great-grandfather had been an advertising copywriter and Terry Holt had designed websites for a living, skills now long extinct – and they got by, that first year, mostly on tinned food looted from supermarkets, although that was an enterprise fraught with risk because the countryside was awash with starving, armed people. They hunkered down and waited, like everyone else, for the emergency to end and order to be restored, but it never did. The power never came back on. They sat it out, through the rioting and the mass starvations and the epidemics. Tucked away in the woods in this little corner of Berkshire, the long dieback of British society passed them by.

Eventually, it became apparent to them – and others had joined them at the house by now – that if they were to survive, they would either have to leave and try to find some vestige of civilisation, or make the best of it where they were. They'd already begun trading with some of the farms in the area – doing a day's work in exchange for some fresh food – and they asked for advice, and in time – and it took almost two decades – they had carved themselves a working farm. They expanded it beyond the original grounds, built new farmhouses and outbuildings. By then they were no longer Holts and Richardses and Barretts and Prestons. They were all one family. And when Harry married Alice, they had become his family too, the farm had become the Lyall farm.

Haunted, Alice, had said. Haunted by the original owners, by those early families. Haunted by the children she had lost. Haunted by Alice herself, whose cancer had consumed her in less than five months. And now haunted by Rob.

Harry found himself standing in front of the shed, tears pouring down his cheeks. He'd always done his best, and it had always seemed as if it wasn't good enough. The farm ticked over, but it still wasn't good enough. Alice was gone. Rob was gone. What was the point of going on, if the only point was to go on?

James, coming out of the house, saw his father standing there. A couple of the hands were standing a respectful distance away, watching. They saw him and drifted off, embarrassed to have been caught witnessing such a private moment. He stood on the doorstep, agonised. Finally, he turned and went back inside. Closed the door and left his father with his pain.

Harry opened the door of the shed and looked inside. At first, all his mind registered were the rows of agricultural tools hanging from the walls, most of them decades old. Scythes and sickles, rakes, spades, their handles worn shiny with years of use. Everything neat and in its place, the way his father had liked it.

The three bodies lay side by side on the floor, still covered with the tarps the Taylors had laid over them. He'd had some of the senior hands in here to look at the faces of the other two boys, to try and solve the mystery of who they were, although he had no idea what he was going to say to their family. It was the right thing to do, though. Someone had opined that they might be from up Risborough way, which meant they were a long way from home, but Harry remembered that a year or so ago Rob had been sweet on a Risborough girl he'd met at Goring market. Had she had brothers? He couldn't remember. He did know that Rob had been away a lot over the past twelve months, but he'd gone through a phase like that when he was Rob's age.

He sat on the floor with his back to the wall and hugged his knees to his chest, still turning it all over in his head. If Max and the boys had been attacked by bandits, he should have people out right now looking for them before they did any more harm. But he didn't because he knew it hadn't been bandits. Strangers passed through the Parish all the time, to trade or to do specialised work or simply to travel the old road of the Ridge Way which ran along the northern edge not so far from the Taylor and Lyall farms. But the Parish had its own fairly efficient bush telegraph, an informal word-of-mouth arrangement between the farms which went all the way back to the really bad days when refugees from the fighting in London had swept through the area, looting as they went. There had been no word of bandits or footpads or highwaymen. Harry knew in his heart that Rose was right. Max and the boys had had a fight out on the road somewhere, for whatever reason, and now Rob and the two strangers were dead and Max was fighting for his life, and Harry felt his life teetering on the edge of an abyss.

CHAPTER SEVEN

THE FIRST THING Frank said to him was, "Hullo there, I'm Frank Pendennis. Great to meet you."

The new arrivals were standing in ranks in what had once been the car park of Margate railway station. Looking a little way down the hill, Adam could see the sea, lashed by storms. He shook hands with Frank and said, "Adam Hardy."

Frank was a short, burly man in his sixties, all muscle and unruly grey hair. He was wearing a long overcoat with velvet lapels, over an old tweed suit, and a trilby. "Albie tells me you can do windows," he said.

"That's right."

"Good!" Frank was all grins and welcome, as if they weren't all standing out in the rain. "That's grand."

His review of the newcomers apparently complete, Frank walked back out to the front of the group, beside Albie, who towered over him. "We have a good place here," he addressed them in a loud voice. "It's a good place because people work hard. People here *want* to work hard, and if you don't want to work hard, there's no place for you in Thanet. We're building something special, rebuilding civilisation, and people are going to talk about what we achieve here for centuries. Now, Albie here and his boys will take care of you, find you places to bed down and settle in. Tomorrow morning you'll get your work assignments and you'll be part of our family." He beamed at them and then turned and walked away.

Uncertain of what to do now, the group shuffled their feet and started to talk among themselves, but Albie put a stop to that. "All right, everyone," he said. "I'm going to split you up into two groups. You in the first two rows, you go with Larry here." Larry was a tall, cadaverous-looking man with a rifle slung over his shoulder. "The rest of you, go with Jim."

Adam looked at Jim, who seemed to be aspiring to Albiehood, that same bulky shaven-headed look, trouser-cuffs tucked into his boots. There was a long wooden baton tucked through a loop on his belt. Nothing he had seen so far in Margate had inspired any hope in Adam at all. The place was a work camp, pure and simple, hundreds of thin and grey people toiling in the rain.

They'd managed a remarkable feat, clearing many of the roads around the town and dragging old cars out to a dump some miles away. Most of the shops and houses had been stripped of anything useful, and those which were not occupied were boarded up against future use. The place was swept by gales and storms howling down the North Sea coast. No one, apart from Frank and his enforcers and his favourites, looked particularly happy.

Jim gathered the back two ranks of newcomers – Adam among them – and without a word beckoned them to follow. They marched down the hill to the seafront and along the long curve of boarded-up shopfronts lashed with wind-driven salt spray. Decades of storms had scoured much of the paint from the buildings and they had a raw look.

Up another hill, and Jim led them to a big building with *THE*

SANDS painted in red on a big sheet of plywood mounted over the door.

"This is where you'll be staying," Jim told them. "Go on in. Mr Harper will assign you rooms, then come back down to reception and I'll give you the tour."

Inside, the hotel smelled strongly of damp carpet and mould. Mr Harper regarded the newcomers sourly and led them up three flights of stairs to a corridor lined with doors, each one secured by a padlock and hasp screwed into the wood.

Mr Harper had a big ring of keys, and he doled one out to each of the new arrivals in turn. As Adam opened his door, he heard his neighbour look inside their new quarters and mutter, "Fucking hell."

"Hot water for washing from the kitchens between five and six in the morning and seven and eight at night," Mr Harper recited. "You bring it up here yourself. Breakfast at seven. If you miss it, you go hungry."

Adam swung the door open. There were two single beds, a kitchen chair, a small table, a battered-looking wardrobe. Slug trails glistened on the carpet. Beyond a half-open door he could see what he presumed was the bathroom. The room was freezing and it stank of sweat and piss.

"Doors locked at all times when you're out," Mr Harper said. "Don't lose your keys. There's a laundry in the basement where you can wash your clothes."

Adam went into the bathroom. There was a bucket full of water by the toilet, for flushing, and two empty buckets in the shower. A hard sliver of soap on the handbasin smelled strongly of sheep. He put his hands in his pockets. Well.

Back in the corridor, there was an air of disgruntlement among the people who had arrived with him. He could see one or two of them considering leaving Thanet.

Maybe Mr Harper could see it too, because he said, "This is just a place for new bodies, until we can find you somewhere more permanent. There's a lot of empty houses in town; if you work hard and keep your noses clean, you'll be assigned a place of your own."

Newcomers at Guz were housed in a village of old modular accommodation units on the edge of town. They were a bit spartan, but they were warm and clean and there was hot running water and there were flush toilets – something Adam regarded, notwithstanding men on the Moon and space probes to other planets, as the height of human civilisation – and a twenty-four-hour canteen. People were expected to work for their keep, but that litany of 'if you work hard and keep your noses clean' was as disturbing as anything Adam had seen or heard here so far.

They all trooped back down to the foyer, where Jim was slouched in a threadbare old armchair. He clambered to his feet and said, "Right then, let's be having you."

Back outside, squalls of rain and spray blew in off the sea and broke against the buildings of the seafront. The group huddled down into their coats as Jim marched them around the town for the best part of an hour, calling out relevant landmarks. They saw people working, repairing some buildings, boarding up others, removing items from still more and loading them into carts and lashing tarpaulins over them. Nothing they did seemed to improve anything; the town still looked awful, looted in the first days after The Sisters and then mostly abandoned during the Long Autumn. The people were all working in groups of four or five, and each group was being watched over by someone like Jim or Albie.

The tour over, Jim took them back to The Sands and then went off on another errand. The newcomers stood around in the rain for a few moments and then, because there was nowhere else to go, went inside. Adam stood at the top of the steps, looking about him. He went back down onto the pavement.

On the seafront, the tide was in, and waves and spray were

breaking over the sea wall. Adam wandered along, hands in pockets, buffeted by the wind, until he encountered three of Albie's colleagues up near the station.

"Oi," said one, "where are we off to, then?"

Adam shrugged. "Just off for a walk. Have a look round."

"What work gang are you with?"

He shrugged again. "Just got here."

The enforcers – that was what they were, why not acknowledge it? – all gave each other long-suffering looks. "Well you can't just fucking wander about like that," said the first enforcer. "This isn't a fucking holiday camp, you know." And the others laughed. "Where are you bunking?"

Adam thought about it, as if the name had momentarily escaped him. "The Sands Hotel," he said.

Another exchange of looks, this time amused. "We'll see you back," said the enforcer. "In case you get lost."

"I'll be okay," Adam said. "I just wanted to have a look round."

All the amusement went out of the enforcers. "Nah. Best if you don't, eh?" And the enforcer's hand moved an almost imperceptible distance towards the baton hanging from his belt.

"Okay," Adam said. "Let's go back, then."

IF IT WAS run-down and impoverished, Margate did at least have one great resource – a complex of enormous greenhouses which had once produced vegetables in unimaginable amounts. Half of Adam's intake of newcomers had been sent to work there, and as the days wore on he first came to envy and then hate them. At least they were working indoors.

For him, and the work crew to which he was assigned, there were various jobs maintaining and renovating houses. A lot of this was outdoors, in the driving rain. And even when they were indoors, it wasn't much more pleasant. The whole town was afflicted by damp and mould, the buildings were freezing cold, and no one had looked inside many of them since the disaster. More than once, they came upon the remains of townspeople who hadn't managed to flee. Guz had a respectful protocol for this kind of thing, but Frank did not. They scraped the remains together into bags and dumped them on a huge pile of similar offerings rotting in the rain in a great open hole in the fields on the edge of town.

Days like that, Aggie, the permanently-angry middle-aged woman who led the crew, was more than usually hard to get along with and nobody talked much except Seth. Seth was in his sixties, a wiry grizzled man who limped quite badly because he'd fallen off a ladder and broken his leg and it had been set all wrong. Frank took a dim view of invalids, on the whole. If you couldn't work, he didn't have a lot of use for you. But Seth was a master carpenter and even Frank could appreciate the value of his skills.

"Why do you suppose they didn't get out?" he mused one particularly bad day while they were clearing a house of four mouldy skeletons.

"Maybe they were sick," said Adam.

Seth pulled down the piece of cloth covering his mouth and nose, spat on the floor, covered himself again. "I'd have been out of here like a shot," he said. "Sick or not."

"Where would you go?"

Seth looked round the room sourly. "Anywhere but here," he said.

"Are you two done yet?" Aggie said from the door.

"Almost," Adam told her, using a broken-off chairleg to scrape a skull and some arm bones into a bag.

"Well, get a fucking move on," she said, and she went back out into the hall, where the rest of the crew were repairing the front door.

"Yes, ma'am," Seth said. "No, ma'am. Three fucking bags full, ma'am."

"Heard that," she called from the hallway.

Seth, who had run out of fucks to give some considerable time ago, put two fingers up in the direction of the door and returned to helping Adam bag the remains. "What a fucking awful place to die," he said.

"Isn't everywhere?"

After three weeks in Margate, Adam had not seen Eleanor, or even anyone who resembled the sketch of her he'd been shown in Guz. He was more or less certain she wasn't on any of the crews working in town. The people out at the Glasshouses worked long shifts and didn't mix much with the others; he was still trying to come up with an excuse to go out there. He was conscious of having to do the job properly, but at the same time he was sick of this dreadful mouldy waterlogged corner of Kent, and he was sick of Frank.

Gossip among the work crews had it that Frank's family had come here in the first days of the Long Autumn from somewhere in South London, where they had been scrap metal dealers. They had found the town undamaged but almost deserted. Even after looters had been and gone, the shops were still full of food and tools and other supplies, the houses were mostly empty of living inhabitants. Weary and heavily-armed and – if Frank himself was anything to judge by – utterly without scruple, they had chosen to stay a while. Some locals, they discovered, had occupied a big out-of-town shopping centre a couple of miles away, and after a brief period of unpleasantness the Pendennises had turfed them out and begun living on the riches contained within.

Others turned up, wandering the sleet-lashed countryside. Frank's family offered them shelter, for a price. They began to work the Glasshouses, producing tomatoes and potatoes and other crops which were hard to grow out of doors in the sudden autumnal shock. And so, down the years, Frank's little kingdom had grown. His people worked to maintain the town and clear the roads along the coast as far as Ramsgate and Reculver, and some way inland. There was no one to stop them; this far corner of Kent belonged to them. They started to farm. They ranged far and wide and found more recruits, more weapons. In the early days, they still had motor vehicles and petrol to run them. Later, they raised horses.

In time, they performed a census, and discovered that almost three thousand people were living under their rule. Three thousand people was an army, and they set out to conquer the little fortified farms and settlements which had established themselves in Kent in the years after The Sisters. Well-armed and well-organised, they ranged down to Dover and Folkestone, and almost as far west as Maidstone.

And there they paused. The High Weald belonged to another family, and London was a nightmare not even the Pendennises would contemplate. It was, after all, the place they had fled. Sometimes, they looked across the Estuary and thought about Essex – the acres of rusting metal in the burned-out wreckage of the oil import terminal at Coryton were much on their minds, perhaps something about it called to a dim corner of race memory – but there was still a lot to do on their own territory. They bided their time.

There were stories, Adam had heard them more than once during his time in Margate, of interlopers from France or the Low Countries crossing the Channel in motley boats and trying to land at the dead of night on the beaches from Deal to Dover. He wasn't sure whether to believe it or not – multiple comet strikes in France had left it almost uninhabitable for nearly a century and much of Holland was simply drowned – but the accounts of pitched battles on the Kent beaches sounded in character. Frank's people were nothing if not patriotic.

The bag filled, Adam tied it at the top and stripped off his leather work gloves and wiped his eyes. In spite of the damp cold in the house, he was sweating.

There was a commotion in the hall, and a few moments later

Aggie looked around the door and said, "Adam. Someone wants you."

Adam and Seth exchanged glances. Adam handed his gloves to Seth and went to the door. Albie was standing in the hallway with two other enforcers. They were smiling, but Aggie was subdued and the rest of the crew was nowhere to be seen.

"Hallo, Adam" said Albie. "Frank wants a word."

"What's up?"

"Nothing at all, old son. Just wants a word. Now."

There was a horse and cart outside. The two enforcers climbed up onto the front seat and Albie indicated Adam should join him in the back.

They drove for about ten minutes, plodding unhurriedly up a long hill from the seafront and along narrow winding streets of houses being slowly unpicked by the weather. At one point, they passed the school where most of the workers from the Glasshouses were housed, and Adam looked about him incuriously in case he might see Eleanor. But there was no one about but enforcers guarding the gates. Frank prized gardening skills above all others and he didn't like his workers just wandering off.

Finally, they pulled up another steep street and stopped outside what looked like a small public library. Albie got down from the cart and beckoned Adam to follow him up the steps.

Inside, Adam found himself in the broken and scattered remains of a gift shop, Frank sitting on his own at a little table, smoking a pipe and watching the drizzle bead on the windows. Today he was wearing green whipcord trousers and jacket, over a black sweater. He smiled as Adam and Albie came in.

"Adam," he said happily. "How are you?"

"I'm all right, thanks," Adam said. There was a faint, but terrible, smell in here.

"Albie, get Adam a chair." Albie brought a chair from a haphazard pile and set it at the table and indicated that Adam should sit.

"So," Frank went on when Adam was seated. "How are you finding things here?"

Adam shrugged. "It's okay, thanks. Working hard."

"That's good." He waved at Albie, who went back outside. When they were alone, Frank said, "I understand you can read."

In one of the houses they'd worked in last week, Adam had found one room miraculously free of damp and mould, and in that room had been a wall full of bookshelves. He'd stood looking at them long enough for Aggie to shout at him, then he'd taken one book – a paperback Raymond Chandler – and slipped it into his pocket. He wondered who had seen him do that, who had told who, how word had got back to Frank. It was like catching a glimpse of the secret machinery grinding away under the run-down, broken surface of Margate, the machinery with which Frank ran things.

"That's right," he said.

Frank gave him a long, level look. "I like stories," he said. "My Ma could read, a bit, and she used to read stories to me."

Completely at a loss, Adam said, "Oh?"

Frank got up and said, "Let me show you something."

Adam followed him across the gift shop to a short set of steps ending in a heavy-looking door. Frank took a key ring from his pocket, selected a key, and opened the door.

The smell that billowed out was so awful that it was all Adam could do not to take a step back. Frank seemed not to notice, was fiddling about with an oil lantern. He finally got it lit and handed it over. "Take a look," he said. "Go on, nothing down there's going to bite you."

Adam held up the lamp and saw the stairs continued under the building, curving away out of sight. The walls were grey and looked strangely textured. He took a deep breath and went down a few steps. The walls, he saw, had hundreds of thousands of little shells embedded in them, and as he reached the bottom of the steps he could see more, set in the wall in simple patterns.

It was freezing down here. All of a sudden he had a terrible vision of Frank closing the door on him, and he retreated back up to the gift shop.

Frank was standing there nodding soberly and puffing on his pipe. "Don't know what this place used to be," he said. "Something for tourists, I expect, when there were tourists. Now it's where we put the bad folk. A few days down there, they're not bad any more. You'd be surprised."

Adam, who was fairly sure he was going to have to burn his clothes, shave off all his hair, and scrub off the top layer of his skin to get rid of the smell, would not have been surprised at all. He watched Frank close and lock the door again.

"Anyway," Frank said, taking the lamp from him and extinguishing it, "I miss those stories."

Adam stared, suddenly realising where this was going.

"So," said Frank. "You'll start tonight, then. Albie'll pick you up. You can walk back to your crew, can't you."

CHAPTER EIGHT

KATE MERCER HAD three sons. Alan, Graham, and Keith, who styled himself Big Keith after his late and, if local gossip was anything to go by, entirely unlamented father. He was nineteen that day he met them on the track, only a couple of years older than Morty and Karen, but he had a raffish, devil-may-care handsomeness about him. "A bit like a pirate king," his mother once said to Morty. "His dad was an ugly cunt, though."

They were pretty much on their last legs by then, thinking about turning back for Newbury. It was days since they'd found anyone who would give Morty work, the horse was sick, the weather had turned and the continual rain was only enlivened by the occasional shower of hail. Karen had begun to voice doubts about Morty's abilities in a wistful tone which would become grindingly familiar.

And then there was Big Keith, on his horse, riding down the track towards them, rifle slung over his shoulder, grinning.

"What have we got here, then?" he called. "Orphans in the storm?"

Morty felt Karen, who had been sitting listlessly beside him on the driving seat, stir. He said, "Looking for work, maybe somewhere to start over."

Big Keith's grin widened. "Well, we have all the work you can cope with." He was speaking to Morty, but looking at Karen, who was now sitting up attentively. "And there's plenty of places round here you could have that nobody else wants. Why not stay a while?"

"Yes, all right," said Karen, before Morty could open his mouth again. When he made to speak, she turned to him and said, "I'm sick of travelling, Morty." She put her arm through his and hugged him close. "Let's stay a while, eh?"

So they did. They pitched their tent in a corner of the Mercers' compound, and for a while, even though they didn't have a place of their own or any security at all, they lived happily. Karen pointed out, quite reasonably, that it was unfair to expect her to sleep rough any more when there was a spare room in the main house. It was just a box room, mind, and not big enough for the two of them, but it was important that she be well-rested because she was already planning their future in the Parish.

Karen moved into the Mercers' house, and Morty stayed in the tent. A couple of the other hands took pity on him and helped patch it up, so at least he was dry, and if he was honest, he was usually too tired to feel lonely out there because Kate Mercer worked her people hard. "No time for passengers, young Morty," she told him more than once.

Karen took to accompanying Big Keith on his trips around the Parish. Looking for somewhere to live, she told Morty, and lo and behold, one day, three months after they arrived, she came out to the tent and told him that she'd found somewhere.

"What happened to the last people who lived here?" Morty asked.

"Moved on," Big Keith said. "Couldn't hack it. Someone told me they went to Goring."

Morty, whose knowledge of the Chilterns was still only sketchy at best, had no idea where Goring was, but he thought that maybe they should think about going there too. The farm had been abandoned, and had clearly not been particularly successful even when it was occupied. The main house was damp and dirty, the henhouses filthy and deserted apart from half a dozen mouldy carcases lying in a sea of half-liquid droppings. Two painfully-thin sheep were listlessly cropping the grass in the yard, their fleeces matted and covered in mud and shit. Morty didn't realise it at the time, but this was his life from now on, summed up in one handy picture.

"It's brilliant," Karen said eagerly, giving his arm that little hug again. "A place of our own at last, Morty." And she beamed at him. And so did Big Keith.

That night, their horse died.

HE WAS UP on the roof, mending slates – the place leaked like a sieve, no matter how many repairs he did – when he saw two riders coming up the half-overgrown trackway towards the farm. He felt himself shrink a little inside. He knew that he occupied a space in the Parish somewhere between an object of pity and an object of fun, and he tried to avoid mixing with the locals unless he couldn't possibly avoid it. The day before, he'd done some handyman work at the Wren farm in return for a bit of bacon and a bag of vegetables, to shore up his lie to Karen, and he'd hated every moment of it, conscious of the way everyone was looking at him. But he'd put on his Morty Face, the cheerful one that said he was everyone's friend and always happy to help out, and he'd got through it. Watching from the slope of the roof, he willed the riders to pass by as most people did, but they came right up to the house and sat looking up at him.

"That you, Morty?" called one.

He called back, "That's me. What's up?"

Down below, he heard the scrape of the front door opening – he needed to sand it down or something, it was always swollen with damp – and saw the two riders tug the hoods of their coats respectfully as Karen came to the door.

Carefully arranging the Morty Face, he half-climbed, half-slid down the roof until he reached the ladder, and climbed down into the yard. Found himself looking at two men he barely recognised; he thought they worked for Harry Lyall, but he couldn't be sure. They were both carrying shotguns, and one had a crossbow over his shoulder.

"Hey, Morty," said one, rain dripping out of his beard.

"Hey," Morty said, still none the wiser about who they were. He looked at Karen, who was standing in the doorway with their shotgun in her hands.

"You heard what happened to Harry's boy?" asked the other rider, barely out of his teens himself.

Morty remembered meeting Tim Anderson on the Ridge Way. He said, "Yes?"

"There's some unpleasantness going on between us and the Taylors about it," said the bearded one.

Morty couldn't see any earthly reason why he should care, but he modulated the Morty Face into an expression of concern. "Oh yes?"

"Harry reckons people could get a bit excitable," said the younger one. "He doesn't want any more trouble."

Again, Morty had no idea what this had to do with him, but he said, "Absolutely."

The two riders exchanged a glance. The bearded one said, "So, no going out taking potshots at people."

Morty nodded enthusiastically. "Of course not."

The riders looked at him for a couple more moments, then they nodded to him, nodded to Karen, and turned and rode off without another word.

Morty turned to Karen, but all she did was hold the shotgun out to him. "You should have been taking care of me," she told him, without quite meeting his eye. "That could have been anybody." He took the shotgun from her, and she turned and went back into the house, closing the door on him.

THE NEXT DAY, another pair of riders turned up. Karen was out this time. Morty put on the Morty Face again and went out to meet them. He took the shotgun this time, just in case.

Again, he had no idea who they were. He just nodded hello to them amiably and said, "Lads. What can I do for you?"

"You heard about Max Taylor?" asked one.

"Yes. Yes, I did. Can I help at all?"

The rider was not in a mood for small talk, and neither, it seemed, was his friend. He said, "There's to be no retaliation. Rose's orders. Understood?"

Well no, not really, but Morty nodded. "Yes. Understood. Absolutely." And without another word the two men rode off, leaving Morty standing in the rain wondering what the fuck his neighbours were playing at.

CHAPTER NINE

"You should have sent for me right away," said Faye Ogden. "What were you thinking?"

Rose just sat there, clenching and unclenching her fists out of sight below the tabletop.

"That's the first thing. The second thing is, Max is very, very sick. John did his best, but there's infection and I don't have anything to treat it with."

Rose stared at her. Faye was a stout woman in her late sixties, untidy and permanently grumpy. Her family had originally been vets, treating farm animals in the area, passing their knowledge down generation by generation, learning how to treat people as well as they went. She was the closest thing the community had to a doctor.

"It's peritonitis," she said. "Do you know what that is?"

Rose nodded.

"I can operate – and I'm going to as soon as humanly possible, Rose – but I need antibiotics too."

Rose shook her head.

Faye sighed. "Rose. Listen. Max is going to die. I don't

know what problem you have with the Coghlans, but they can help."

Rose shook her head again.

Faye thumped her fist down on the table, making Rose and the cup and saucer in front of her jump. "Fucking *hell*, Rose!" She stood, pushed her chair back from the table hard enough to topple it backwards, and went out into the yard, where John Race was standing smoking his pipe and looking miserable.

"She's in shock," he told her.

"Yes, I can see that, John. Thank you for pointing that out to me." Faye rubbed her eyes. "What has she got against the Coghlans?"

"Nothing, as far as I know. She just doesn't want any help from anybody."

"Well, that's just fucking stupid. Why didn't you come and get me as soon as Max was wounded? Oh, don't tell me. Rose didn't want you to."

John shrugged.

"You poor fucking excuse for a man, John." She backhanded him across the chest. "You send somebody to Blandings this minute or I'm leaving here and never coming back."

"She said..."

"Are you not listening, John? I don't *care* what she said. I need antibiotics. Tetracyline, cephalosporin, ampicillin, I'll write it all down for you. I'm not interested in what's going on in Rose's head, we'll deal with that later."

"I'll go," he said.

"Don't be so fucking noble, John. This place needs you. Send one of the hands. If we're lucky, Betty will have what I need in stock. If not, we're going to have to wait a few days."

"Can Max wait that long?"

"I'll do what I can, but you'd better get a move on." She felt the anger drain out of her all of a sudden. "Max was the first baby I delivered. You remember the old Taylor place?"

John nodded. The old Taylor farm, a few miles away, had been absorbed by another holding when Max took over here. Max hadn't been sorry to see it go.

"Ramshackle fucking wreck of a farm; his dad couldn't farm to save his life. The house wasn't much better. Buckets all round the bed to catch water dripping through the ceiling, and my dad standing behind me the whole time, biting his lip to stop himself giving me advice about what to do. My hands were shaking so much, I cut the cord and dropped Max on the floor." She reached out again, and this time squeezed his upper arm. "I won't let him die, if it's within my powers, John. But you have to help me. You have to help Rose."

John looked at the house. "Fucking mess," he muttered.

"Let's all do our best for Max, eh? That way we're helping Rose too. And everybody here."

"Right," he said. And he set his shoulders and strode off across the yard to find someone to send to Blandings.

THERE WAS A graveyard, just beyond the original wall of the house, where the Lyalls buried their dead. Almost two hundred headstones now, which Harry didn't think was so bad for a century of hard lives, although some years had been far worse than others. His own immediate family were here, his father, mother and two brothers, all carried off together by an infection old Doc Ogden hadn't even been able to identify, let alone treat. Alice was here and beside their children – two of them stillborn, three dead of various accidents and illnesses. Alice had liked to come out here, when the weather allowed, and talk to them, chatting cheerfully about inconsequential things: something she'd seen that day, or something someone had told her. She said it helped keep her close to them, stopped her forgetting.

And now there was a new grave. Harry tried to picture himself talking to it.

The service done, three of the hands started to shovel earth into the grave, covering Rob's cloth-wrapped body. Harry thought he would be hearing the sound in his dreams for the rest of his life. The hands and other families who had attended the funeral – the graveyard was packed – started to drift towards the gate which led into the compound. Harry turned away and, James and Alan at his side, plodded slowly after them.

In the yard, a couple of the hands who hadn't attended the service were standing talking in an animated fashion. In Harry's experience this was never a good thing, and instead of heading over to the house, he wandered over.

"Now then, lads," he said.

Faced with their boss, the two hands – neither was much more than sixteen – became quiet and awkward, unwilling to say anything. Harry struggled to remember their names.

"Something up?" Harry asked, not ungently.

"There's a thing, guv'nor," said one. William?

"A thing, is there?" Harry said. "What kind of a thing?"

"One of the henhouses," said the other. "Something got in."

Harry sighed. Life went on. Except when it didn't. "You'd better show me then, hadn't you." He turned to his sons. "You go in the house and make sure everyone's fed and watered. I'll be back in a bit."

"Dad?" said James.

"Go on, son. I won't be long." He looked at the two farmhands. "Shall we?"

Down the years, the Lyalls had appropriated a lot of building materials from half-deserted housing estates in the general area, demolishing houses bit by bit for brick and wood and glass, building up and reinforcing the wall that ran around the house, constructing outhouses and sheds and sties. There were four big henhouses on the other side of the estate. Too large to fit inside the compound, which had grown cluttered with various outbuildings and storage sheds and extensions to the house over the years, they were surrounded by high brick walls to keep out foxes and feral dogs and cats and the occasional wolf. Mostly, the walls worked well enough, although one had constantly to make sure nothing had burrowed under them, but now and again something got in and carried away some stock. Last time it had been some monstrous bird of prey. They'd roofed the run over with chicken wire, but the fucking thing had torn several holes in it. Nobody ever saw it, and eventually it had stopped attacking the runs. Rob said it was a golden eagle. Rob had always been keen on birds.

None of this was surprising, then. But Harry wasn't prepared for what he saw when one of the hands opened the door to the run.

"Fuck *me*," he said quietly.

The run seemed to be carpeted in bloody feathers. In places, the wind had piled them into soggy drifts inches thick in corners and against the base of the wall. Here and there, among the fluffy carnage, lay a mutilated corpse.

"All dead," said the hand. Walter. That was it. Walter.

Harry put his hands in his pockets and stood, just inside the doorway, gazing across the run. They'd had forty hens in here, and a couple of very feisty cockerels. "All of them?" he said.

Walter nodded miserably.

Harry squatted down and brushed the covering of feathers away from the earth, hoping to find pawprints, but there was nothing. He looked at the wall, which kept out everything but the most determined predators. He stood up and walked out into the run, toeing feathers aside. Coming upon a dead chicken, he stooped and picked it up by one leg and looked at its wounds. He tossed the corpse aside and looked at the wall again. Looked up at the wire netting. They'd repaired the holes the bird of prey, whatever the hell it had been, had torn in the mesh, but something had forced its way through, leaving a big hole. Harry walked over and looked up, but he couldn't see any fur caught on the jagged broken ends of wire. Some of the ends seemed to have been carefully bent inward so as not to catch or snag or prevent whatever had forced its way in from leaving again. He thought about that for a while, then went back to the door of the run.

Outside, Walter and the other boy – Harry didn't have the first idea what his name was – followed him as he paced the wall, head down, scanning the ground. A couple of times, he squatted down again and examined places where the grass at the base of the wall had been trodden down by something, or possibly several somethings.

When he'd finished, he dusted his hands off and scratched his head. "Wolf," he said. "Must've been a big bugger, to get over the wall."

"This weren't no wolf, guv'nor," Walter said.

"Yes, it was, young Walter," he told the boy.

"But guv'nor..."

"It was a wolf," Harry said, gently but firmly. "I want the runs patrolled properly, day and night. If we get lucky, we'll catch the fucker in the act."

The two boys exchanged a glance. "Yes, guv'nor."

"All right," he said. "You lads get into the house. Tell Mrs Carter I've said you can have some beer and a sandwich."

The prospect of a beer obviously overwhelmed any doubts the hands might have had about whatever had killed the chickens, and they took off towards the house at a trot. Harry waited until they were out of sight and then squatted down and parted some of the long grass and spent a while looking at the deep bootprint in the soil beneath.

He brushed the grass back upright until it concealed the print and with a sigh he stood up, put his hands in his pockets again, and trudged away to his son's wake.

*   *   *

An hour or so later, James came out of the main house and walked across the compound to the gate. He asked one of the hands to let him through, and the hand swung the gate open far enough for him to slip out. His father had told everyone to stay near the farm for the next few days but James had no intention of obeying him.

The truth was, James hadn't even liked his brother very much. Rob could be a bully, self-centred and manipulative, and if he'd got himself killed doing some fucking stupid thing that was really all he deserved. What did hurt James was how his father was taking it. He seemed hollow, uncertain, distant, almost broken, and that made James angry. It made him angry at Rob, and it made him angry at whoever had killed him. Alan, who was only ten, was uncomplicatedly distraught, and Charlie, the youngest, was too young to understand, upset by the atmosphere in the house more than anything else. Four Lyall boys, and now there were three.

He walked along the side of the compound until he reached the henhouses, looked in through the open door of the one which had been attacked. Looked at the broken wire netting. He too swept his toe back and forth in the layer of sodden bloody feathers on the ground, and this time he saw a deep bootprint. He went back to the door. It only locked from the outside; there was a simple latch on the inside to let yourself out after you'd collected the eggs or fed the chickens or whatever. He'd used it himself hundreds of times without noticing.

Back in the house, his father and some of the family and people from the neighbouring farms were in the lounge, drinking beer and eating sandwiches. James went down the hall unnoticed. At the far end was the family's gun room, a locked windowless room that had once been an airing cupboard. James popped into his father's office for the key and opened the door, stood looking at the racks of shotguns and rifles and crossbows. He stood there for quite a long time, thinking, listening to the quiet conversation from the lounge, and no one ever noticed he was there.

CHAPTER TEN

"Never heard of it," Seth said, turning the book over and over in his hands in a way which suggested that he, in common with almost all of Thanet's population, could not read.

"It's about ships," Adam said. "And a whale."

"Yes, well, I can see that," Seth told him, looking at the cover. He handed it back. "And he makes you read it to him?"

"Don't spread that around," Adam said. "I don't think Frank wants people to know."

Seth made a rude noise. "As if thinking he can read would make people hate the wanky little cunt any less."

They were sitting in the lounge of Seth's house. There was a fire in the grate and the curtains were drawn against the rainy night. There was a curfew in Margate, but it was fairly straightforward to break it if you were careful and confident. The enforcers were keen but there were not enough of them to be everywhere. The house was small and neat but shabby, the furniture worn and stained and mismatched, as if it had come from two or three different houses. Seth had half a bottle of whisky, which was illegal in Margate unless you were an enforcer or someone Frank considered a special friend. Adam presumed reading to him didn't qualify, because no alcohol had come his way yet.

"Why doesn't everybody just *leave*?" he said.

"Where would they go?"

We can't take in every raggedy Bob and tattered Brenda. Adam drank some whisky. It wasn't very good whisky, but it was at least whisky. Seth wouldn't say where it had come from. If someone here was running a black market in things like whisky and tobacco, they were playing a dangerous game. They might, Adam thought, be worth getting to know, because it was the first real sign of resistance he had seen here.

"A lot of people don't have anywhere *to* go," Seth said. "Back out into the countryside to starve or be killed by bandits or dogs. At least here they're safe."

"They're really not."

Seth looked at him. "What are you doing here, son? You're a smart lad. Too smart to fall for Albie Dodd's bullshit, anyway."

Adam thought about it. "There was a girl, back home. Eleanor."

Seth nodded sympathetically. "Dumped you, did she?"

Adam blinked at him. "No. No, she came here. To work."

"Oh. Right. Eleanor, you say?" He shook his head. "Don't know the name."

"I've been keeping an eye open, but I haven't seen her. Thought maybe she might be out at the Glasshouses."

"Why'd *she* come here? Have a row?"

Adam found himself unable to come up with anything better, so he nodded sadly.

"Well, if she's in the Glasshouses, you'll not see her," Seth mused. "They don't get around town much; Albie's boys take them to and from their dormitory to work, don't let them out of their sight."

"I know. Any way I can get out there? Have a look for her?"

Seth shook his head. "They don't like us mixing. You could get in a lot of trouble doing that." He sighed. "What on earth were you thinking? Find your girl and leg it back home with her?"

Adam shrugged. "How hard can it be?"

Seth gave him a long hard stare, shook his head again. "They'll notice you're gone, you and your girl, and they'll come looking for you and they'll make an example of you."

"They'll have to find us first."

"They're good at that." Seth drained his glass. "What does this Eleanor look like? Have you got a picture or something?"

"Not with me, no." Adam gave him a quick recital of the description he'd been given before he left Guz. "But don't ask about; I don't want to attract people's attention to her. Just keep an eye open. Please."

The old man sighed. "Word to the wise, son. Love will fuck you up every time. You're better off without it."

HE WAS STARTING to go native, he realised. There had been one morning, not so long ago, when he'd woken in his room at The Sands and Guz had seemed unreal, a distant land over the rainbow. His life here was real, the days of hard labour in the wind and the rain, the evenings sitting by the fire in Frank's study reading to him. It was a dangerous feeling; he'd had it before, and he needed to watch out that it didn't overwhelm him.

He was also becoming aware, through continued close proximity, just how dangerous Frank was. Frank was a living demonstration of the corruptive nature of power, a man who literally had the power of life and death over everyone in his world. It came off him like a bad smell, and it infected everyone around him. As if the town was slowly revealing itself to him, Adam started to see enforcers beating workers more and more often. Usually a quick slap with a baton was enough, but more than once he saw someone lose control and start to rain blows down on their cowering victim. Not out of anger, but because they *could*. One afternoon, walking from one job to the next through the never-ending drizzle, he looked down a side street just in time to see Albie Dodd flooring someone with a single punch.

"You're quiet tonight," Albie said.

Adam glanced at him sitting in the front seat of the cart with the reins dangling easily from his big meaty hands. "Tired," he said.

"Well, you'd better buck your ideas up for Frank."

Adam nodded. "Yes. I will."

At Frank's house, the door was answered by Rhoda, the worn-out, pinch-faced girl Frank used as a maidservant and cook, and, rumour had it, much else besides. There was supposed to be a Mrs Frank, but so far Adam had not seen her and he hadn't been able to find anyone else who had.

Frank came out of the study, all rubicund bonhomie, wearing cord trousers and a smoking jacket. "Adam, my friend," he said, smiling broadly. "Come on in. Rhoda, make us some tea, there's a good girl."

Like everything else in Margate, Frank's family had simply walked in and taken this house as their own because there was nobody there to stop them, and their presence seemed to have frozen it in time. The original wallpaper – a discreet pattern of roses climbing a vertical trellis – was still on the walls, and much of what appeared to be the original furniture was still here. It was always warm in here, and it did not smell of damp. It was as if the previous owners had just popped out for a walk and would come back through the door at any moment. Although if they had, Albie would have beaten them and thrown them in the Shell Grotto until they stopped being bad.

There was a fire burning in the grate in the study, as ever, and two comfy armchairs pulled up to it, facing each other across a little table.

"You're looking well," Frank said as they sat.

"Thank you." Frank actually had very few conversational gambits; Adam thought he would have been perfectly happy not to say anything at all, just point at things he wanted or at things he wanted done or at people he wanted hurt or killed. But Frank had some strange body-image of himself as a prosperous man of civic probity, all hail-fellow-well-met, and this meant having to come up with small talk which his brain seemed unable to cope with, so he just had a few phrases memorised.

Adam picked up the book and opened it to the bookmark. They were barely a hundred pages into it, the rest of the novel a desolate path leading away into the distance. He pictured himself still sitting here months from now, finally closing the book, Frank producing another one and saying, "How about this, old son...?"

He was about to begin when Rhoda came in carrying a tray on which were a teapot, two cups and saucers, a milk jug, and a sugar bowl. Sugar was rare, even in Guz, but down the years Frank's family had rationed the supplies they had found in Margate and the big shopping centre outside town, and for tobacco and alcohol they had control of the old ferry terminal at Dover and its bonded warehouses and their contents. Adam looked down at the page.

Perhaps Rhoda caught her toe in a little ruck in the carpet; more likely she was just exhausted, but she stumbled and the tray and its contents went flying, spraying milk and hot tea and sugar cubes everywhere.

The girl gave a little cry that was half anger, half despair, and immediately went to clean up the mess. Adam sat where he was, feeling himself tense up, ready for the inevitable loss of control from Frank and this time ready to do something about it.

But to his surprise, Frank just shot him a long-suffering look and went to help Rhoda clean up. When they had all the bits of broken teapot and shattered cups on the tray again, and had blotted up the worst of the tea and milk stains with damp cloths, Frank helped Rhoda carry everything back to the kitchen. He was gone some time, and when he came back, he seemed to have been exercising hard.

"Sorry about that, old son," he said, settling himself back into his armchair. "Do you want to start?"

So Adam read the next chapter, but Frank's mind wasn't on it. He kept asking Adam to go back and read paragraphs again.

Eventually, he sighed and said, "Tell you what, let me introduce you to Gussie."

He led the way out of the study and up the stairs, and as he followed, Adam heard a single choking sob from the direction of the kitchen, saw Rhoda, her face covered with blood, closing the door so that no one would see or hear her.

ONE NIGHT A couple of weeks later, Albie took him back to The Sands as usual, waited until he had walked up the steps and gone inside, then drove off. Adam plodded tiredly up the stairs, hearing Mr Harper locking the front door behind him.

Up in his room, he took off his coat and sat on one of the beds and took off his boots. But he didn't undress and climb under the covers. He sat there, in the dark, for over an hour, thinking. Then he got up, put his coat on again, and with his boots in one hand he went to the door and quietly let himself out.

In one direction, the corridor led to the stairs down to the lobby. In the other, they led to a heavy wooden door. Adam opened the door and stepped out onto a darkened landing, pulling the door shut behind him and listening for a telltale scrape of boots on concrete or a quiet cough which would signal that the stairwell was guarded. Once upon a time, this had been an escape route in case of fire, but the hotel was so damp these days that there was nothing in here which would burn.

He felt his way down the stairs, counting flights, until he

came to a landing with another heavy door, this one locked. He picked the lock with a bit of wire and the tip of a penknife he'd found in one of the houses he'd worked in, and slipped out into the yard behind the hotel, pausing only to put his boots on.

It took him the best part of an hour to walk to Cliftonville. There was no street lighting, but the rain had abated and a half-moon shone weakly down on the town through rushing, broken cloud. Once or twice, he heard enforcer patrols, but it was easy enough to hide in overgrown gardens or down alleyways until they passed. Enforcers made up in muscle what they lacked in professionalism.

Cliftonville was an area of vaguely genteel housing to the east of Margate proper, a place most of the population could aspire to but never attain. The houses were in good repair because Frank's extended family – which numbered well over a hundred – and his trusted favourites lived here. Frank's house had a stone with MON REPOS carved into it set into the wall beside the front door, and the garden was as well-maintained as any garden could be considering the weather.

Here, the enforcer patrols were thicker on the ground, and more careful, and Adam took a long time working his way through various back gardens before he reached Frank's house, where he sat behind a huge old rhododendron bush for some while. The back of the house was dark, no sign of any movement, and he moved up onto the patio. Examining the back door in the fitful moonlight, he took off his boots, picked the lock as quietly as he could, slowly opened the door, and slipped inside.

It opened onto a little vestibule containing an old washing machine and drier, neither of which could have worked for almost a hundred years, piled high with bits of assorted rubbish. On the other side of the room, another door led into the kitchen. Adam left his boots in the vestibule and stepped inside the house.

Moonlight picked out the kitchen furniture, the sinks, the huge range which had been retrofitted in by Frank's parents or grandparents. Adam started to move towards the door to the hallway.

"Have you come to kill him?" asked a voice from a corner of the kitchen.

He whirled around, biting back a cry of surprise, ready to fight and then flee, but he saw, in the fitful moonlight, a little old woman sitting on a kitchen chair. She was wearing an old parka over a thin cotton nightdress.

"Have you come to kill him?" she asked again, and for a moment he thought he was going to have to kill *her*, to prevent her bringing someone to check what was going on in the kitchen. But she said, "He won't hear us. He's upstairs, stinking drunk with one of his whores." She brushed her long brown hair back from her face, and he realised she wasn't old at all. No older than Frank, anyway. He started to move towards the hallway.

"I tried to kill him once, myself," she said, and he paused and looked back at her. "I put a knife under the bed and when he was asleep, I stabbed him." She turned her head back and forth as if looking for something, and he realised she was blind. "I didn't stab him hard enough. All I did was wake him up and then he took me to see Albie." She shivered. "I hope you've come to kill him. I can't do it myself."

He stood where he was for a few moments, quite still, breathing slowly through his mouth, deciding what to do next. Scrubbing it and coming back another night was a real possibility, but he didn't know if he'd have the nerve to do it again. He walked slowly out of the kitchen, down the hall, and up the stairs. When he came back down, the woman was gone.

HE HAD NO idea what time it was when he got back to The Sands, weary, footsore and soaked through. The moon had long since set, and the sound of waves crashing against the seafront was audible all over town. He let himself in through the back door and locked it behind him, made his way up the stairs until he reached his landing, opened the fire door a fraction, and looked down the hallway. It was only lit by a single oil lantern at the far end, but to his night-adapted eyes it seemed almost too bright.

Boots in hand, he padded slowly down the corridor, feeling slugs burst under his feet. What the fuck was it about this place and slugs?

He reached his door and slipped the padlock silently out of the hasp, turned the handle, and stepped inside, and suddenly the adrenaline of the night drained out of him and he was exhausted. He dropped his boots on the floor and flopped onto the bed fully-clothed and closed his eyes.

Some time later – he hoped it was at least an hour but suspected it was more like five minutes – one of the hotel workers came down the corridor beating a large saucepan with a ladle to summon everyone to breakfast.

CHAPTER ELEVEN

MAX DID NOT die. Or as Faye put it, "The operation was a success but the patient survived. Sorry. Doctor humour."

They were walking across the compound towards Faye's horse. It was the first time Rose had been out of the house since Max came back from Blandings.

"We still need those antibiotics or he's not going to make it," Faye said.

Rose glowered across the yard, where John Race was supervising a wagon wheel repair and intently pretending she wasn't there.

"Did your hand give you any idea when they'd be here?" Faye asked. "Rose? *Rose.*"

Rose looked at her, a little bemused. "No. A few days is all he said."

"Don't you dare blame John for this, Rose," Faye told her. "I made him do it. When Max is well again, you can be as angry as you want with me, but John did the right thing."

Rose stared at her.

"You're not thinking straight, Rose. You're so worried about

Max that you can't make proper decisions. And I'm worried *you're* going to get sick, in a way that I can't treat."

"I'm okay."

Faye gave her a long-suffering look.

"When will you be back?"

Faye turned and started to pack her medical gear into the horse's saddlebags. "Tomorrow morning, if all goes well. Keep him warm and comfortable and make sure he takes some water." She swung herself up into the saddle and looked down at Rose. "And for Christ's sake try to get some sleep. You're no good to anyone like this."

Rose watched her ride away across the compound and pause in front of the gate. One of the hands cranked the handle and the gate slid aside, and suddenly Rose was running, shouting, "Shut it! Shut it! Shut it!" Faye, the hand, everyone in the yard, turned to look at her. She was the only one who saw the figure outside the gate step forward, raise a shotgun to its shoulder, and fire, and then Faye was tumbling from the horse and the figure was gone and the hand by the gate was running to catch the bridle of the startled horse, Faye still dangling from it by one foot caught in a stirrup.

"WE SHOULD GO over there right now and torch their fucking house," said Patrick.

"No one's doing any torching," Rose said. "And don't swear in front of the children."

"We don't know who did it," said John Race. The hands patrolling the wall hadn't seen anyone approaching the compound, but after the shooting they had seen a figure running away into the screen of trees a hundred yards or so away. They'd fired on it, but failed to hit it.

"It's obvious," Patrick told him. "Who else would be waiting out there to shoot someone coming out of our gate?"

Rose felt utterly calm. It was as if she was watching the world from the other side of a window, warm and safe. Nothing could hurt her in here, nothing was real. She said, "I want everyone armed when they go outside. No exceptions."

John looked at her.

"Someone should go and tell Faye's family what's happened, take her body back to them," she went on. "Would you do that please, Patrick? Don't go alone; take some hands with you. Show Faye some respect; she was always a friend to us."

"Yes, Ma."

John leaned forward across the kitchen table. "This is going to get out of control."

She looked him in the eye. "It was out of control the moment Max left for Blandings," she told him calmly.

He sat back, staring at her.

"Who was supposed to be on watch?" she asked Patrick.

"Jim and Andrea."

She nodded. "I want them gone. Give them some clothes and a couple of days' food, but I want them out of here before sundown and I want them shot if they ever come back round here."

"Jesus..." said John.

"No more mistakes, John," she said. "No more sloppiness." She turned to Patrick. "And no torching. Is that understood?"

"Yes, Ma."

LATE IN THE afternoon, as the light was starting to fail, a group of hands came back to the farm. They had a boy with them, his arms bound behind him and his face bloodied and bruised. Rose went out to meet them.

"Found him a couple of miles away, missus," said one of them. He held out a rather shabby twelve-bore. "He had this with him."

She walked up to the boy and put her hands on her pockets. "What's your name, son?"

The blood on the boy's face was streaked with tears and snot. "Walter, missus," he sniffled.

"Do you know what happened here today?"

"No, missus."

She took the shotgun, broke it, extracted the cartridges and sniffed the breech. "Have you been out shooting, Walter?" she asked, not unkindly.

"There's a wolf, missus," he blurted. "It got in our henhouse and killed our chickens. I've been out looking for it."

"Did you find it?"

"Thought I saw it, over to Pennywise Wood."

Rose looked at the boy for a while. Then she turned to the hands. "Hang him," she said. "Then take him and dump him at the Lyalls'."

The boy started to sob uncontrollably.

CHAPTER TWELVE

HE DIDN'T SEE a lot of Karen. She stayed at the Mercer farm while he worked to get their place fit for human habitation again. "I'm working," she said when he mentioned that he seemed to be doing everything on his own. "I'm planning for our future. It's not easy, you know, Morty."

So he did it himself, mostly. Some of the Mercer hands came over, from time to time, to help out, but he kept seeing them exchanging knowing smirks and he was glad when they left and he could get on with it on his own.

It took him over a year to get the house ready, but Karen refused to move in. She was busy planning, she needed to be close to the Mercers, she'd be there soon. "You understand, don't you, Morty," she said, giving him the little arm hug, and for the first time he found himself putting on the Morty Face and saying that, yes, he did understand and it was okay.

She did turn up, eventually, and gave the house a critical once-over before listing all the things he'd done wrong and would have to do again. He nodded and weathered it and did the things again.

*   *   *

AND SO HERE they were, five years later. Karen was mostly at home, although she spent a lot of time over at the Mercer compound, discussing things with old Kate. Morty tried and could not make the farm work, but it wouldn't quite fail either. There was some livestock and somehow enough of that survived to sustain them, and a few vegetables he managed to grow in the chalky soil. For the first few months here, he had been constantly alert for signs that his family or hers had come looking for the runaways. When those signs failed to materialise, he started to relax. Clearly, the folks back home had accepted that he and Karen loved each other and wanted to start a new life together. Although a tiny little doubt kept running back and forth through his mind that, actually, their families were simply happy to be rid of the pair of them.

"Keith says something's going on between the Taylors and the Lyalls," she said one morning, putting on her coat to go out. "You should go and find out what it is."

"One of the Taylors got hurt," he said. "One of the Lyalls got killed. It's none of our business. Where are you going?"

"Keith says people have started fighting," she said. "It might start being our business."

"The Lyalls and the Taylors are miles away." And really, if they wanted to knock seven bells out of each other that was fine by him; they'd never lifted a finger to help him.

"I want you to go over and see the Lyalls or the Taylors, one or the other," she told him, her hand on the handle of the front door. "Find out what's going on."

"If they're having a scrap, they won't take kindly to strangers rocking up at their front gate," he pointed out.

Karen came over and gave him the old arm-hug. "I'm just thinking of you," she said. "You've put so much work into this place, almost killed yourself, and you've made it really nice for us. I don't want someone coming here and ruining all that if a quiet word somewhere could avoid it."

It was the kind of suggestion which was not, of course, a suggestion. So later, after she'd taken the wagon and gone wherever it was she was going, he saddled up their remaining horse and went for a ride.

Apart from the visits by the Lyall and Taylor hands a couple of days ago, he had never had any contact with the Parish's two largest families. Their farms were quite some distance from his, and apart from Market Day he rarely strayed far. The Mercers excepted, he barely knew his closest neighbours. Even the Wrens didn't want to have much to do with him if they could help it.

So he was left with something of a dilemma, as he rode along through the drizzle. Who should he visit? Taylors or Lyalls? As he passed the nearest farms, he saw armed people patrolling on top of their walls. At the Wrens' compound, he stopped at the gate and waited until someone noticed him.

"What do you want?" they called down from the wall.

"It's me," he said. "Morty Roberts."

The figure on top of the wall seemed to think about it. "Oh, right. What do you want, Monty?"

"I heard about the Taylors and the Lyalls."

"What about it?"

"Wanted to know what's going on."

"*I* don't fucking know. People shooting at each other, is what I heard."

"I was going to go and see them."

"Who?"

"The Taylors and the Lyalls."

The figure thought about it again. "Yeah," it said finally. "That's grand, Monty. You do that." And they disappeared from view.

Morty sat where he was for a minute or two, but nobody else came to talk to him, and eventually he urged the horse away from the farm.

It didn't occur to him until much later that he had ridden through the early days of a war that morning. Everything seemed quite peaceful, save for the occasional shot in the distance, and that could have been someone hunting rabbits or taking care of a pack of dogs. The drizzle hissed down onto the trees and the undergrowth, dripped from the hood of his coat. Someone – he couldn't remember who – had told him that ten or twenty years ago this had been a dangerous place to travel alone, beset by bandits and wild animals, but now it seemed tranquil and rather pretty. It was certainly better than Southampton. Morty fancied himself a country boy at heart.

All the farms he passed seemed to be locked up, their gates closed and armed patrols moving in the distance, but no one bothered him. He rode on, and the drizzle finally dried up and the birds sang. It was nice to just be riding along, not a thought in his head.

Eventually, more by accident than design, he found himself on a trackway leading to the Lyall farm. The gate was shut, people with rifles and shotguns stood on the parapet watching him approach, and when he drew up outside, a stout, harassed-looking woman called down, "Who the fuck are you?"

"Morty Roberts," he said.

The woman seemed surprised to see him, which was a first for Morty. Most people barely noticed him. She said, "What do you want, Morty Roberts?"

"I heard about the trouble."

"Yes?"

"And I just..." And words failed him. It was all right Karen telling him to come here and talk to the Lyalls, but what on earth was he supposed to say? "I..."

"Yes?"

"I've got a farm over there." He waved in what he hoped was the right direction. "Down on the south side. By the Mercers."

"Right...?"

"And it's just me and my wife, just the two of us."

"Okay...?"

He'd been hoping that the woman would fill in the blanks, but that obviously wasn't going to happen. He said, "We don't want any trouble."

The woman glared down at him with a mixture of wonderment and annoyance. "Well, here's what you do then, Morty Roberts," she said. "You go back home and you lock your doors and don't come out until things settle down, okay? No one's going to make trouble for you unless you make trouble for them."

"Right."

"Now, I've got a fuckload of stuff to do and you're stopping me doing it, so if you don't mind...?" And with that she vanished out of sight, to be replaced by two armed men who just stood there looking at him until he rode away.

Plodding along, he wondered if this was going to be sufficient for Karen. *Lock your doors and don't come out until things settle down* sounded like excellent advice to him, but it really wasn't the guarantee of safety and security that she seemed to want, and reaching a crossroads, he halted the horse and sat there in an agony of indecision. He imagined himself passing on the Lyall woman's message, imagined the disappointed shake of the head from Karen, imagined her telling him to go out again and make sure they weren't going to get involved in whatever the hell was going on here.

Eventually, instead of turning left towards home, he turned right.

The Taylor farm was a fortress. It was the first time he'd seen it, and he couldn't help but be impressed by the ring of old freight containers surrounding the compound, or the neat, tidy, well-tended fields and outbuildings beyond the wall.

He never managed to get close to the gate, though. As he approached someone on the wall fired a shot into the air and then pointed their rifle directly at him. "That's close enough!" they shouted. "What do you want?"

"I'm Morty Roberts," he shouted back, reining in the horse. "Over on the south side."

"What?"

"We heard there was some trouble up here."

The figure on the wall had a brief consultation with someone standing next to them. "Morty Roberts? Down by Mercers?"

Morty sighed. "Yes."

"What the fuck are you doing up here?"

"I came to see if there was anything I could...do..." The words were out of his mouth before he was quite conscious of thinking them. Volunteering was the last thing on his mind right now, even if he'd known what he was volunteering for.

The two figures had another consultation – quite a long one this time. He saw one shake its head, and he saw the other's shoulders move in a way which suggested suppressed laughter.

"Nah, you're okay, Morty," shouted the first one. "We're good. Go home and stay there. Now fuck off."

Morty sat where he was.

"Fuck off, Morty Roberts," the figure shouted, "or I'll fucking shoot you myself."

That seemed unequivocal enough. Morty turned the horse, and as he did, he saw a group of people coming down the track towards him. They had a boy with them, shaken and dishevelled, and as they passed by, Morty saw that his arms were tied behind his back and he was practically being carried along. The gate opened just far enough to let the group bundle their captive inside, then closed again and Morty heard shouting from the other side of the wall, then there was silence.

Nothing much seemed to be happening here, so he turned and rode away towards home.

HE'D BARELY GONE half a mile before he came upon a group of men standing in the middle of the track, all of them pointing guns at him. Morty was not a brave man, but this seemed so peculiar, on top of all the other peculiar things which had happened to him today, that he didn't feel particularly alarmed. This was the Parish, it was his home. What could possibly happen to him here?

The horse didn't need to be reined in. He had the feeling that it had had enough for one day; it just plodded to a halt and didn't seem upset when one of the men stepped forward and took the bridle.

"This your horse?" he asked.

"Yes, it is," Morty said.

"No, it's not," the man said. "It's mine."

"Who're you with?" asked another. "Taylors or Lyalls?"

"I'm not with either," Morty said. "I'm from the south side, down by Mercers. And this is my horse."

"No, it's not," said the first one again.

"Lads," Morty said, arranging the Morty Face for maximum effect. "I don't want any trouble. I'm not armed."

"You're a fucking idiot, then," someone called from the back of the group.

"What brings you all the way up here on my horse if you don't want any trouble?" asked the man holding the bridle.

"It's not your horse."

"Oh, yes it is." He didn't seem angry or threatening, more amused than anything else.

"I know this bloke," said another of the group. "It's that Monty Roberts. The one from Wiltshire. Him with the wife."

Morty weighed the pros and cons of correcting his name and place of origin in front of a large group of armed men, and decided against it.

"Poor fucker," said someone else. "Leave him alone, Fred."

Fred – the one holding the horse – looked over his shoulder. "Who's running things?"

"Not you, that's for sure, you cunt," someone called, and

Morty suddenly, finally, felt a thrill of alarm. This wasn't an organised group. It was a mob.

Fred turned back to him and said, in a low, reasonable voice, "Get off my horse, Monty."

Morty thought about it. There was never any question of giving up his life for a horse, that would have been absurd, but there was a principle here.

In the end, the principle lost. He climbed down, suddenly almost nose to nose with Fred's sneering grin. "Good lad," Fred said, and actually reached out and patted him on the head.

Morty felt a strange sensation at the touch, and it took him some moments to realise that it was anger, and some moments more to realise that actually there was rather a lot of it and that it had been there for a very long time and he really quite liked it. Years of embarrassment and ridicule, working his heart out only to receive, at best, the pity of his fellows. He thought of Big Keith Mercer, with his pirate king's swagger and his easy charm, and something burned away to ashes inside him and when it was over, there was nothing left but a howling emptiness and the Morty Face, looking out on the world, eager to help and shrug off all slights. It was that simple.

Fred, maybe, saw it happen, because he withdrew his hand and seemed momentarily uncertain. Then he recovered himself and said, "Good decision, Monty Roberts. No need for any unpleasantness."

Looking out at the world from behind the Morty Face, Morty heard his voice – or something that sounded like his voice – say, "No. That's right. No need at all."

THEY WERE SITTING in the kitchen when he got back. Karen and Big Keith. He closed the door behind him and looked at them.

"Where've you been?" Karen said. "You should have been back hours ago."

"Someone stole the horse," he said.

"What?" She and Keith exchanged glances – more of a smirk, on Keith's part, to be honest. "Who?"

"Fred," he said. "Fred stole the horse. I had to walk back." He supposed he was tired and footsore, but they were distant sensations, like smoke on the horizon.

"Have you any idea how much that horse cost?" she said, her voice a near-shriek.

"Yes," he told them. "Yes, I do, because I bought it. I'm tired. I'm going to bed." And he navigated himself past them and into the hallway, and as he walked upstairs, the howling void inside him performed what would once have seemed like an impossible calculation, based on their body language and their faces, the way they had been sitting leaning towards each other as he opened the door, and he realised that they hadn't expected him to come back.

CHAPTER THIRTEEN

THE SIGN SAID *DREAMLAND*. It jutted vertically from the face of the building, towering over the promenade. Once upon a time, it had been picked out in hundreds of lightbulbs, but they were all broken now, rendered brittle by decades of frosts and shattered by howling hailstorms. Adam had almost stopped noticing it, unless he was feeling particularly tired and miserable, when it took on a satirical meaning.

It was raining again, and veils of sleet occasionally swept across the town, blending with the breaking waves that lashed the seafront so that half the time the rain tasted of salt and stank of rotting seaweed. Adam and the others huddled near the entrance of the old amusement park, sharing cigarettes and bitching about whatever came into their heads. Looking along the front, he could see a long curve of shops as far as the clocktower, where Frank and his family traditionally hanged those who displeased them. Beyond that, it was hard to make out details through the rain, but he thought he could see the angular shape of the old Turner Gallery and the dark band of the harbour arm.

"Smoke?" asked Seth, limping up and offering a damp rollie.
Adam shook his head. "No, ta."

The old man tucked the cigarette behind his ear and pulled up
the hood of his coat again. He turned and glanced at the little
group of men and women hiding from the worst of the wind
and rain. "How long have we been doing this?"

"About a hundred years," Adam said.

Seth chuckled wetly. "Must be lunchtime by now, surely."

Adam glanced at the sky, but there was no clue there, just low,
driving clouds. He shrugged.

"Watch out," one of the others said.

Adam and Seth looked back along the promenade and saw a
small group of enforcers coming along the pavement towards
them from the direction of the station. As they drew level with
the workers, they stopped and their leader said, "Oi, shirkers."

"Who's shirking?" Seth demanded loudly. "We've been at
it since first light." Seth tended to overestimate the value his
carpentry skills brought to Margate. He thought they gave him
a certain latitude to talk back to the enforcers. Sometimes it
did, sometimes it didn't; it was always somewhat fraught to be
standing next to him when he got into a slanging match with
them.

Today was another lucky day for everyone, it seemed. The
enforcers were just as wet and miserable as they were; it was
just too much trouble to stand in the rain beating people up.

"Get back to work, you daft old bastard," the enforcer said.
"We'll be back this way in a bit; if you're still here, you and me
can go and have a chat with Albie."

The mention of Albie's name was enough to make the rest of
the working party shuffle their feet in a manner which suggested
this break was none of their fault and they would have been
happy to keep working until midnight if it wasn't for *those* two
blokes. Seth just curled his lip and spat his cigarette onto the
wet pavement at the enforcer's feet.

The two of them looked at each other for a few moments. Adam fought the urge to take one step away from Seth.

The enforcer shook his head, gave Seth a final hard stare, and walked away towards the clock tower, followed by the others.

Adam and Seth watched them go. There were various sounds of qualified relief from the work party, but Seth was unrepentant. "Fucking arseholes," he muttered. He took the roll-up from behind his ear and lit it, bending over and cupping his hand around the match. "Fascists."

Adam glanced at him. He doubted there were more than a thousand people in the entire country who understood the proper use of the word 'fascist'. He said, "You're going to get yourself in trouble one day."

Seth snorted. "I'm not afraid of those jumped-up little shits."

The crew reluctantly picked up their toolboxes and set out again into the rain. They had spent the morning boarding up broken windows in a big old hotel overlooking the beach near the station, the tail end of a job which had occupied them for several days. Adam had to wonder why they'd bothered. The place had been overwhelmed by damp and mould; it would take years to make it habitable again, and even then no one in their right mind would want to live there because decades of storms beating at the coast had started to undercut its foundations.

For lunch, they trooped into one of the community canteens in the maze of little streets just behind the seafront. They sat in what had once been an artisanal chocolatier's shop and ate thin, watery mutton stew. You could tell a person's place in Thanet's hierarchy, more or less, just by looking at them. The general populace were thin and grey and weary, managers and overseers a little more sleek, enforcers generally fit and muscled. Frank and his family looked as if they had never missed a meal in their lives. Seth and some of the others muttered darkly about the quality of the food, but the two women who ran the canteen just shrugged. "You're welcome to go somewhere else, lovey," one of them told Seth.

Aggie's crew had been together for the best part of a year, going wherever they were sent, doing whatever they were told. They had been pig-sick of it long before Adam joined them, and now they were just going through the motions in return for food and shelter, just like everyone else. Frank and his family had Thanet well-organised, but they were not making it happy. Which Adam thought was a vaguely heartening state of affairs. It was far from being an atmosphere of rebellion, but it was a start.

That evening, he wearily climbed the steps of The Sands, pushed open the door, and stepped into the foyer, was greeted by the familiar Margate smell of seawater and damp, occasionally mixed with a powerful whiff of decay drifting up from the harbour. Some days, when it wasn't raining, one could stand at the windows of the dining room and watch Frank and members of his extended family taking the air or inspecting their troops. Adam didn't know what to make of it all; there was an element of grim comedy about things here.

He plodded, bone-tired, up the stairs to his room and unlocked the padlock on the door. The padlocks were a nod to privacy, but the enforcers had duplicate keys to almost every lock in the town, in the name of 'security', so it was best not to keep any secrets in your room.

Adam actually shared the room with two other people, but by a quirk of scheduling, he had never seen them; they were always out while he was there, and vice versa. The only evidence he had that they existed at all was various bits of detritus which appeared mysteriously; discarded clothing, a single boot with a split sole, sandy footprints on the sticky carpet. At first, he hadn't known what to do about these seemingly phantom manifestations. Then he had tidied them up. Now he just left them where they lay and eventually, after a few days, they went away again.

He sat down on one of the beds and unlaced his boots, then lay back with his eyes closed and wiggled his toes. It was not, he thought, that he was exactly unused to hard physical work. It was just that he didn't enjoy it very much. When he first arrived in the town and Mr Harper had shown him the room, he'd had to fight an instinct to just leave again. But that had never been an option, and anyway he barely noticed the place any more. All he did was sleep here because most of the time he didn't have the energy to do very much else.

The door opened and Albie poked his shaven head into the room. "You ready?" he said. "Time to go."

Adam sighed.

SETH CALLED CLIFTONVILLE 'the chav ghetto', a term Adam was not familiar with but presumed was not complimentary. Albie allowed him a quick wash and change of clothes and then drove him out to Frank's house, and all the way tried to slow his racing heart, adrenaline fighting exhaustion. It was two days since his nocturnal visit to Mon Repos. The following morning there had been something of a fluster among the ranks of the enforcers and he'd readied himself to flee, but nothing had happened, and that evening Frank had seemed as avuncular as ever. The same the next evening; Frank had even become mellow and expansive enough during the reading to offer Adam a glass of whisky. The safest, the most professional, thing to do would have been to get out of Margate as soon as possible. But his job still wasn't done, and anyway he'd abandoned professionalism when he let his temper get the better of him and he broke into Frank's house. He was just going to have to wing it, pretend nothing had happened, and hope for the best.

Frank answered the door himself, recently-bathed and smoothly-shaved, wearing his tweed suit with a cravat tucked into the neck of his shirt. "Adam!" he said cheerfully. "Mate! Glad you could come! Please, come in."

Adam stepped into the hallway and stood dripping on the

carpet. The house was well-lit by oil lamps and there was an almost unbearable smell of cooking. "Hello, Frank," he said.

"Here," said Frank. "Let me take your coat. Do you want to dry your hair? Rhoda!"

Rhoda came to the kitchen door, not nearly as happy and well-nourished as her boss. She was wearing an apron and holding a tea towel, and the bruises on her face were poorly-hidden with make-up. Her nose was swollen and one of her lips was split. "Yes, Mr Pendennis?"

"Fetch Adam a towel, there's a good girl."

"It's okay," Adam told them both. "I'm fine. Really."

"You're not," Frank said. "Just look at you. You'll catch your death." Which seemed unlikely; the house was heated to within an inch of its life. "Get him a towel," he told Rhoda.

"Yes, Mr Pendennis." The girl went upstairs, came back a few moments later with a fluffy white bath towel, which she handed to Adam without looking him in the eye. Adam stood there with the towel in his hand, momentarily unsure what to do with it, as Rhoda returned to the kitchen.

"Thought we'd have a bite of dinner before we get started tonight," Frank said amiably, leading the way towards the dining room.

"All right," said Adam. Just another normal evening at the Pendennises'.

"So," Frank said. "How are you doing? Everything going all right?"

Adam unfolded the towel and rubbed it over his hair. "Yes, I suppose so," he said. "Thanks for asking."

"I like to look after all my friends," Frank said amiably. He also liked to look after his enemies, although not quite in the same way. Adam fought to remain calm.

After weeks coming here, the dining room still looked absurd. The curtains were drawn against the wind and the rain and the night, there was a fire burning in the hearth, and there was another young woman, this one dressed as a waitress, standing to attention beside a table set for two. Adam had a very strong urge to grab a fork from one of the place settings and stab Frank repeatedly in the face with it.

But instead he allowed himself to be seated at the table, and sat there, overheated and damp, while the girl managed to serve steaming bowls of oxtail soup without looking either at him or at Frank. He wondered where the blind woman was, what she had told Frank, if anything.

"So," Frank said between slurped spoonfuls, "what have you been up to today?"

Adam, who hadn't tasted anything remotely as good as this soup for longer than he could remember, took a moment to realise he was being spoken to. "Sorry, Frank?"

"Work-wise. What have you been up to?"

"Oh. Boarding up windows in that big hotel near the station."

"You're quite pally with that old sod Seth Godden, aren't you."

"We're on the same crew. I wouldn't say we're 'pally'."

Frank chuckled. "He's going to get you all in trouble one day, talking to my lads like that."

"I told him that."

"I bet he told you to fuck off."

"Something like that, yes."

Frank chortled. "I remember when he first turned up, you know," he said. "Must've been, what, twelve, fifteen years ago. My dad was still alive back then; he liked to have a quiet chat with all the newcomers, if he could."

Adam wasn't sure whether to believe some of the stories he'd heard about Frank's father, the monstrous Leonard, but if only a fraction of them were true, the thought of him welcoming new arrivals was actually quite scary.

"So Seth turns up," Frank went on genially. "Scruffy as fuck; he'd walked from...oh, I don't know, Hampshire or something. Half-starved. And my dad says to him, 'You know what? I like the look of you, young Seth. You can stay here so long as you work hard and keep your nose clean, and we'll do right by you.' And do you know what Seth told my dad?"

Adam looked down at his soup bowl. He had somehow managed to empty it without being consciously aware of doing it. "Of course I don't, Frank. I wasn't there."

"He said, 'Fuck you, I don't work for no man.' Imagine that." And he chortled again.

"That sounds like Seth, all right," Adam agreed.

Frank sat back and clasped his hands across the smooth swell of his belly. "That tickled my dad, that did. So he broke Seth's leg with a lump hammer."

Adam laid his spoon down beside his soup bowl. After a few moments he said, "He says he fell off a ladder."

"Well, he would, wouldn't he?" Frank shook his head. "Always a hands-on sort of chap, my dad." There was a tiny little bell on the table; he picked it up and tinkled it and put it back down. "Anyway, once he'd done that, Seth didn't have any choice but to stay here and play nice." He beamed.

The girl came into the room and tidied away the soup bowls. A few moments later, she returned from the kitchen with plates, which she set in front of them.

"What's her name?" Adam asked, when she had gone back to the kitchen.

"Her?" Frank looked surprised. "Dunno. She's new."

Adam nodded and looked at his plate. Slices of dark meat, potatoes, green beans. Two days' meals for one of the people in his work gang. He frowned at the food.

Misreading his expression, Frank said proudly, "Venison. Bet you've never had that before."

Frank would have been surprised. The New Forest was full of deer, and a lot of venison made its way west. Adam cut a morsel of the meat and chewed it. Not bad. Not great, but not bad. Frank's family had made good use of the Glasshouses. They were not farmers, but even they could appreciate just how valuable the place was, in a world where crops were failing and people were starving.

"Where's Gussie?" Frank asked.

Adam looked at him, silently counted to three. "What?"

"Gussie," Frank said calmly, spearing venison, potato and beans with his fork. "Where's Gussie?"

"I have no idea."

"Oh, come on, son." Frank put the food in his mouth, chewed, swallowed. "You can do better than that. Tell me where Gussie is and we'll forget all about it."

"I don't even know who Gussie is, Frank."

Frank put his knife and fork down on his plate and crossed his arms. "You know," he said reasonably, "it's a shame to spoil a nice dinner like this."

"To be fair, Frank, I'm not the one spoiling it."

Frank looked at him for a few moments more. Then he reached out, picked up the little bell, and rang it again. This time, instead of the girl in the waitress's uniform, Albie stepped into the room.

"So," Adam said. "No dessert, then?"

"YOU KNOW WHAT your problem is?" asked Frank.

"I have a good heart and a trusting nature?" tried Adam.

Frank chuckled. "Well, that too, I don't doubt. But no, no. Your problem is you don't know when you're well-off. Do you want something to drink?"

"No, thank you."

Frank got up from the table and walked over to the window. He stood with his hands clasped behind his back and looked out over the vista of rooftops and houses. "Don't know when you're well-off," he repeated, half to himself.

They were sitting in a room in the Barracks, where Frank quartered his enforcers. It was a big old apartment block almost on the seafront, and it towered over everything else. Adam had lost count of the number of times he'd walked past it, but he had never stopped seeing it. It was just one more visible manifestation of Frank's power. The room itself was almost bare of any furniture; just the table and a couple of chairs and a filing cabinet, which probably didn't contain much of anything.

"My grandad built this place eighty years ago," Frank said without turning from the window. "Came here from London, walked out with his mum and dad and some friends."

Adam was weary of hearing about Frank's family history, but he wasn't in any position to complain. He looked down at his feet, which were bound by the ankles to the legs of the chair, and he thought *that* was the real answer to the question, 'You know what your problem is'? He looked at Frank, all unruly grey hair and badgery eyebrows. He looked at Albie.

"You could just let me go," he suggested.

Frank looked at him, a surprised expression on his face, as if the thought had never occurred to him. Which of course it hadn't. "Nah," he said eventually.

Worth a try. Adam flexed his wrists, but the cords binding them to the back of the chair didn't give. At least no one had hit him yet.

Frank returned to the table and sat down again. The sleeves of his shirt were rolled up above the elbows, and for the first time Adam noticed the knots of muscle in his forearms. The two of them looked at each other for quite a long time.

Finally, Frank said, "This isn't a good situation, you know."

"I had noticed."

"Oh, I don't mean for you," Frank said irritably. "I don't care about you. It's not a good situation for me."

Adam sighed.

"I can't have any fucker just swanning in here and taking stuff from me," Frank went on. "It makes me look stupid. It makes me look weak."

"Yes, I can see that."

"If I look stupid and weak, people are going to start wondering what the point of me running things is."

"It's a difficult one, Frank, I agree."

"Don't patronise me, son. I'm not the one tied to the chair."

"I was just thinking that, Frank."

Frank glared at him. "I want Gussie back," he said.

"I don't know where Gussie is, Frank. How many more times?"

"You were seen."

Well, *that* hadn't happened. Unless the blind woman had been a lot less blind than he'd thought. Frank was fishing, although to be fair he was fishing for the most recent person he had introduced to Gussie. "Whoever told you that is lying."

Frank sat back and regarded Adam. "Why? Why would anyone do that?"

Because they're shit-scared of you and they'll say anything at all if it means you giving them an extra square meal a day. "I don't know, Frank. Maybe they don't like me."

"Well, I can see how they'd feel like that. *I* don't like you." He ran a hand through his hair. "I don't know," he said. "Did we treat you badly or something?"

"I haven't done anything, Frank."

"You've stolen from me."

"No, I haven't."

Frank looked past Adam, who heard a shuffling of feet behind him and tried to tuck his head entirely down between his shoulders. He wasn't fast enough; there was an enormous concussion on the side of his head which left his ear ringing. He blinked away the pain and stared at Frank and Albie hit him on the other side of the head.

"So," said Frank. "Where's Gussie?"

* * *

THE BARRACKS MUST have seemed ridiculously out of place, even before the disaster; it was a huge concrete and glass block, far taller than any other building in town. From its upper floors, on one of the rare clear days, you could see along the coast to Sheppey, but the room where they put Adam had no windows. They didn't bother untying his hands and feet, just dumped him on the floor and locked the door as they left.

He lay where he was, counting the aches and pains. It took a while. He didn't think anything was broken, but a couple of his teeth felt a bit wobbly. Maybe it was his imagination.

After some time, he rolled over on his back and managed to sit up. Pushing with his heels, he managed to hutch by degrees over to the wall and rest against it. The room was small and shelved on two sides, some kind of storeroom. It smelled of mould and cobwebs. The whole fucking town smelled of mould and there were slugs everywhere. There was a vent in the door, near the bottom, and the faint lamplight coming through that from the corridor outside was the only illumination.

Escape never even crossed his mind. Before he did anything else, he was going to have to free his hands and feet, which was much harder than people tended to assume. If he managed to do that somehow, he was going to have to get out of the room. He'd managed a glance at the door as they bundled him inside, and it didn't look particularly solid, but without a key his only option was kicking his way through it. Which was going to be noisy enough to bring the whole town running. After that, he was going to have to get out of the Barracks, which was full of armed people. And after that, he was going to have to get away from Margate somehow, with no supplies and no weapons. No, escape was not, at the moment, a realistic possibility. He leaned his head back against the wall and closed his eyes.

Hours passed. He was deep within the building and the only sounds he could hear were the footsteps of people walking along the corridor outside, the occasional quiet conversation.

He dozed uncomfortably, woke up, dozed again.

Eventually, someone came down the corridor and stopped outside the door. The key turned in the lock and the door opened.

"Time to go," said Albie.

"THE GAFFER'S GOING to give you one last chance," Albie said in a low voice as they headed for the stairs leading to the ground floor. When Adam didn't respond, he said, "Do yourself a favour, son. Tell him where Gussie is."

Adam put his head down and concentrated on putting one foot in front of the other. They'd untied his ankles and then retied them with a short length of cord. Just enough to shuffle along, not nearly enough to save himself if he lost his balance.

"We had someone like you last year," Albie went on. "Outsider. Ella, she called herself. Said she was from Lincolnshire, but who knows? She just walked in one day, like you did. Good girl, hard worker, good with her hands; the Gaffer put her to work helping to do up some houses in Canterbury – you know what it's like there. Mind your step." They'd reached the top of the stairs. "Wouldn't want to take a tumble and hurt yourself. Anyway, someone saw her making notes and hiding them outside town. A spy. The Gaffer was livid, of course. We hung her."

Adam jumped over the banister.

Had he actually taken time to think about it, it would probably have occurred to him that jumping into a stairwell of uncertain depth with his ankles tied and his wrists bound behind his back was not a terrifically good idea. On the other hand, they were going to hang him anyway, or put him in the Shell Grotto to starve to death. He hopped briefly up onto the banister, took a fraction of a second to balance himself, and jumped out into the stairwell, concentrating on keeping his balance and praying there was no rubbish at the bottom.

It was a drop of about thirty feet onto a flat hard floor. He bent his knees and rolled, used the momentum to bring himself to his feet again. Two flights up, there was a racket of running feet and shouting.

Now what?

He was in a short corridor lit by a single oil lamp. At the end was a blank wall with what looked like a big metal door set into it at around chest height.

Ah, fuck it.

He shuffled quickly down the corridor to the door – they were almost at the bottom of the stairs now – and nudged it with his shoulder. It hinged up slightly and he thought for a moment. *They're going to hang me anyway.* He shouldered the door up and threw himself through.

And found himself falling again, sliding down a steeply-angled metal chute that dropped him, after a few panicked seconds, onto a pile of musty mouldy cloth with a force that drove the breath from his lungs and almost dislocated his shoulders.

No time to pause. Tucking his knees up to his chin, he managed to bring his feet between his bound wrists and get his hands in front of him and stand up.

Right. Now what? He was in a large, echoey concrete-walled room strewn with masses of rubbish and illuminated by dim light coming in from a line of narrow, filthy windows set high up near the ceiling. He glanced around as he tried to loosen the cords around his wrists with his teeth. Some kind of storeroom? There were doors at either end, and a line of shelves along the opposite wall, piled high with junk and ancient boxes. Dust and cobwebs everywhere, and the place stank of rodent piss. It didn't look as if anyone had been in here for a very long time.

There was a thunderous rattling in the wall behind him, and with a bang one of Frank's enforcers dropped out of the hatch and thudded onto the pile of cloth in a cloud of dust. Adam looked desperately around the floor near his feet, saw a length of piping sticking out of a pile of rubbish, grabbed it, half-turned, and hit the enforcer squarely in the face as he stood up. The man crumpled and lay still. There was a knife strapped to his calf; Adam took it and cut the cords binding his wrists and ankles, then he scooped up the enforcer's fallen shotgun and looked around the room again. A minute had passed since he jumped down the stairwell; maybe two. Albie had sent one of his men down the chute just in case, despite it being a poor tactical move. The rest of them would be running downstairs to the basement and any moment now one of those doors was going to fly open, and then there would be a brief period of shooting, after which Adam and a number of enforcers would be dead.

He went over to the opposite wall and looked up at the windows. They looked almost too narrow to squirm through, but he climbed up on the shelves for a look anyway and saw that the windows weren't built to open; they were set into solid frames. He thought about it briefly, then jumped down, ran over to the enforcer and stripped off his waterproof waxed jacket. Going back to the shelves, he climbed up again, swung the shotgun, and smashed one of the windows.

A minute or so later the door at the far end of the room burst open and Albie and half a dozen of his men ran into the room. They were sloppy about it; anger had made them careless, and a single man with a shotgun could have taken down half of them before they had the chance to gather their wits.

As it turned out, it didn't matter. There was no one here. They searched the room, overturned boxes, looked under piles of cloth. They checked their fallen comrade, noted the missing shotgun and knife. Two of them carried him out of the room. Albie stood looking at the broken window. He scanned the shelves, noting where dust had been disturbed by someone climbing up, then climbed up himself and looked at the window again, peered out into the loading bay beyond.

Eventually, they left. An hour or so later, Frank and a couple of enforcers came into the room. Frank glared around him, kicked a box so hard that it disintegrated in a cloud of mouldy dust, and left again. There was the sound of the door being locked behind him.

Another hour passed. Then the hatch in the wall slowly lifted up and Adam dropped quietly onto the pile of cloth. He lay there for a while, contemplating his aching muscles and listening. It was very quiet here, in the unused depths of the building. Not even the scrape of a footstep or a cough to signal that someone had been stationed outside the door. Why should they? They thought he'd gone.

Frank's men were not necessarily stupid, but they were angry and they were terrified of what Frank would do to them for letting the prisoner escape. They were acting, for the moment anyway, on automatic pilot, and little details – such as the chute – were going to pass them by. That wasn't going to last.

He got up stiffly and walked over to the far door, tried it carefully to make sure it was locked, then went to the other door. Once upon a time, this door had had an electronic lock – the keypad, almost invisible under layers of grime and dust, was still mounted on the jamb – but it was a long time since there had been mains electricity in this building, or anywhere in this part of Kent, and some considerable time ago someone had compromised by fitting bolts to the top and bottom of the door. Adam gently eased them back and opened the door a fraction.

It was pouring with rain. The building's loading bay was a sunken yard connected to the street by a steep ramp, and water was streaming down the ramp and puddling in the yard. Windows looked down on all sides, some with lamplight in them, most of them dark. Dusk was collecting in the far corners of the yard, and under a line of wagons drawn up along one side. No one was about.

Adam stepped out and pulled the door closed behind him. Shouldering the shotgun, he walked across the yard and up the ramp. The secret was to look as if he belonged here, as if he didn't have a care in the world. At the top of the ramp, he turned right, and walked calmly away down the street.

MARGATE WAS NOT a large town, but it was still impossible for Frank to cut it off entirely from the outside world. He operated checkpoints and tolls on the main roads, and the family had, down the years, blocked off many of the minor roads by the simple expedient of dragging old cars and buses across them. But the town was a warren of alleyways and footpaths, and in places it was possible to cover a surprising distance by traversing overgrown back gardens, and there simply weren't enough people to keep watch on all these byways.

Having said that, Frank had tried. Patrols were sweeping the streets, checking long-abandoned houses and shops. Some of the patrols were being supervised by enforcers, but most were just ordinary members of the public, hurriedly pressed into service, soaked to the skin, and miserably resentful about it. In the rainy dark, it was fairly easy to tag along with one of these groups. In the dark and the pouring rain, and with the hood of his coat pulled up, the chances of anyone recognising him were slim.

As they walked, they occasionally heard other patrols. There was some shouting in the distance, and now and again the sound of gunshots in the night as someone or other succumbed to excitability.

"Fucking idiots," muttered the woman walking beside Adam at the back of the group.

Against his better judgement, Adam asked, "Do you know what's going on?"

"Nah," she said. "Some fucking stupidity of Frank's."

"Susie said they'd found a spy," said one of the men in the group.

The woman snorted. "Who in their fucking right mind is going to want to spy on us?"

"Maybe you should keep it down, Sonia," one of the other men said nervously.

"Fuck off," Sonia told him. But she lowered her voice a little. "Frank," she said. "I knew his dad. He was a wanker too."

They wandered around in the dark and the driving rain for another couple of hours. Now and again they met other little groups, each carrying a single lantern. Adam hung back out of the light, but nobody challenged him. The obvious assumption would be that he was either in hiding or heading out into the countryside, not joining in with the search effort. People generally saw what they wanted to see.

Nearing the southwestern part of town, Adam gradually dropped behind until, as the search party turned a corner – he could still hear Sonia grumbling in the distance – he ducked down a path between two houses. The path led to a row of garages, their doors pried off by long-ago looters and never repaired. At the far end was another path that became narrow and overgrown and eventually disappeared altogether, and he was finally out in the open countryside.

THE TWIN TOWERS of St Mary's Church at Reculver stood on a low headland overlooking Herne Bay, three or four miles west of Margate. The first time Adam had seen them, he'd thought the church had been demolished by The Sisters, although the neighbouring village was intact, merely deserted. Apparently, though, the church had been a ruin even before the disaster, cackhandedly-demolished in the early Nineteenth Century, and the towers had later been repaired for use as a navigation landmark for ships.

It took him most of the night to get to Reculver, moving slowly and carefully, alert for patrols. It was starting to get light when he saw the towers of the church through lashing veils of rain. He was tired and hungry, and any anger he had set out with had been washed away by fatigue.

There was a cottage near the edge of the village, almost lost within its overgrown garden. Adam fought through the grass and brambles and rose bushes until he reached the front door, then he felt his way along the front of the building until he found the living room window. He got his fingernails in the gap between the window and the frame and pulled slowly until it opened far enough for him to squirm through and drop into musty dimness.

Working his way carefully around the room, avoiding rotten pieces of furniture, he went out into the hallway and along to the kitchen at the back of the cottage. Here, he grabbed a wooden chair and took it back into the hallway and set it down. Standing on the chair, he put his finger through a tarnished brass ring set into the ceiling and pulled. He'd oiled the hinge the last time he was here, and the trapdoor opened smoothly and silently, and he was able to pull himself up into the roofspace. Just inside the roofspace, beside the trapdoor, there was an oil lamp. He lit it, held it up by his head and looked for signs that someone else had been in here.

About halfway along the space there was an old water tank, long empty. He lifted the lid and took out the rucksack he'd stashed here weeks ago, on his first recce of Thanet.

He stripped, dried himself as best he could, and dressed again in clothes from the rucksack. There was a bag of dried meat in one of the side pockets, and he chewed a couple of pieces while he rummaged about for various items of clothing, pulled out a long waterproof coat and the radio.

Sitting on one of the ceiling joists, he turned the radio over and over in his hands, thinking. Finally, he pulled out the handle and cranked it carefully. He pressed the button and a crackle emerged from the little speaker.

He thought again. Pressed the button and said, "Hello." Let the button go.

Almost immediately Chrissie's voice said, "Well, you took your time."

"I've been busy," Adam said.

"How's it going?"

"Oh, it's going about as well as it ever does. Have you been sitting waiting for me to call?"

"I was just going past on the way to the loo."

That made him smile, for the first time in what felt like a very long time. "If there was some way you could get me out of this place, I would be eternally grateful," he said.

"Are you safe?"

"For the moment. I don't know how long that's going to last. Not very long, probably."

"We could pick you up off the beach, but it'll be a week or so before we can get a boat to you."

"Well, that's no good, Chrissie."

"We've been busy."

"I've got a thing for you."

"A thing?"

"Something you'll like."

"Sorry, that's not going to get you a boat any sooner. What kind of thing?"

"You'll have to wait until I see you."

There was a silence at the other end. Then Chrissie said, "Have you seen Eleanor?"

Adam looked around the cluttered little attic, decorated with cobwebs and old pigeon skeletons and mouldy mouse corpses. He sighed. Pressed the button. "They hanged her."

Another silence. "Bollocks."

He let her think about that for a little while. Then he said, "So, what am I going to do? I can't sit here for a week."

"Can you get out of there on foot?"

"Probably," he said, not liking the sound of this at all.

"There are some people who'll give you shelter until someone can come and collect you."

"I might as well walk the whole fucking way, Chrissie."

"Of course," she said. "If you feel like doing that. Or you could just sit tight for a week and wait for us to send a boat."

He shook his head. "I can't stay here." He *could* – the area was large and sparsely-populated and there were many places to hide – but he didn't see any reason why he should tempt fate. And he was sick of the place anyway.

"Get out of there. Make contact again in four days and I'll give you the details."

Adam sighed. "All right."

He put the radio back into the rucksack, repacked it, and then he sat where he was on the joist for a few minutes, chewing some more dried meat and not thinking about anything much at all.

Finally, he sighed and stood up. He shouldered his rucksack, then bent down and reached into the water tank again and took out an ancient and badly-stained nylon carrying-case. He looked at it for a few moments, then he slung it over his shoulder and climbed back down the ladder.

Outside, the rain was easing off. He stood for a moment on the edge of the village and looked out to sea, watching squalls dance along the wavetops. For a few seconds they drew apart, and in the morning light he could see a forest of great pale columns rising out of the sea a few miles offshore. They seemed eerie, otherwordly, the pylons of a great wind-farm shorn of its rotors by years of storm-force winds and metal fatigue. Then the veils of rain closed again and they were gone, but Adam was already trudging away from the coast.

CHAPTER FOURTEEN

MORTY OPENED HIS eyes to grey light filtering through the thin, threadbare curtains. He felt perfectly calm and rested, and he lay on his back looking up at the cracked and uneven plaster of the ceiling for some time. The other side of the bed was empty, had not, it seemed, been slept in. This was normal. Karen often slept on the sofa downstairs when she was angry with him. Those times, he always woke to anxiety, a fidgety sense of needing to stabilise things between them before he could go on. But today the anxiety wasn't there. It was as if something within him had been redrawn during the night.

Eventually, he dressed and went downstairs, to find that the house was as empty as the bed. In the kitchen, the range had been allowed to go out. He opened the front door and stood on the step, looking around the farmyard. Most of the houses round here had had outbuildings of some kind – extensions, sheds, garages – arranged in a roughly square plan, and the people who came after The Sisters had used these as the basis for their defensive walls. In the case of the larger properties which already had high walls, these had been strengthened and built up. The Roberts farm had been a modest place, with only a garage, and whoever had lived here down the years had not had the manpower or the skills to loot building material from other properties and build a wall. It had remained defenceless, open to whoever or whatever decided to come and plunder it. It had been an act of madness to come here and expect to make a success of it, but the void within him was still performing calculations and he realised now that Karen had never expected him to succeed.

He walked round the back of the house to the stable, and saw what he knew he would see. Their remaining horse and the cart were both gone.

Once, he would have gone after her, stood in front of the locked gate to the Mercer compound and begged her to forgive him and come home. Now he just went back in the house and closed the door.

An hour or so later, he emerged again, dressed for the weather, an old rucksack on his back with a tent and bedroll strapped to the top. He locked the front door, then he walked away from the house without looking back. Had he done so, he would have seen smoke starting to wisp out of the open windows, flames licking at the curtains. But he didn't need to see what he already knew was there.

An hour or so after leaving home, he came upon one of his neighbours walking down the track. A Wren, possibly, someone he barely recognised, anyway. They were carrying a shotgun, and a big satchel was slung over their shoulder. Walking towards the Wren, he composed the Morty Face. It was still a bit of an effort, and he found himself grimacing and gurning as he brought the muscles under control.

"Is that yourself, Monty?" asked the Wren, when they were close enough.

"Yes," Morty said. "It's me."

"You don't want to be walking around here on your own right now," said the Wren. "There's all kinds of shit going on up north."

"I know," Morty said. "I was there yesterday."

They were almost toe-to-toe by now, and the Wren was looking at his face as if uncertain of what he was seeing. "Someone shot Doc Ogden; everyone's kicking off."

"I don't know who Doc Ogden is," Morty said, putting his hand in his coat pocket.

"You're kidding, right?" But the Wren saw that he wasn't kidding. "You need to get back home, Monty."

"My home burned down," Morty said, and in one movement he took the kitchen knife from his pocket and stuck it in the Wren's left eye up to the hilt. He felt a crunching sensation run up his arm as it went in. The Wren didn't have time to cry out or run or anything. He just dropped straight down, boneless, like a puppet whose strings had been cut.

"My name is Morty," Morty told him.

THERE WAS GUNFIRE in the distance, shotguns and rifles, but it seemed unimportant. He moved further and further into the uncleared overgrowth between two farms until he found a cluster of little buildings behind a high brick wall. There was a sign on the wall with some words and what looked like a jagged bolt of lightning, but he couldn't read. He shinned over the wall and found himself in a little compound with a line of large rusty metal objects behind a corroded wire fence. No way of knowing what they were. The three little buildings – more like sheds, really – were all locked. He examined the lock on the door of the first one for a while, then poked at it with the Wren's survival knife, but either it was rusted or jammed or something, so he just shot it a couple of times, blew a hole the size of a dinner plate where the lock had been, and dragged the door open.

Inside were a number of metal cabinets, these not so rusted because the door had kept out the worst of the weather. He pried the front off one, and was rewarded with an impossibly dense tangle of wires in various faded colours. There was also a big toolbox over in one corner, far too large to carry. Inside were trays of hammers and screwdrivers and other, less identifiable, objects.

With a hammer and a screwdriver, he opened the other two sheds. They were in a surprisingly good state of repair; much better than his house had been, obviously overlooked for decades because they were hidden by vegetation. They would do, he thought.

He stashed most of his gear in one of the sheds, took the shotgun, and moved out again.

He saw Big Keith riding along the track between the Mercer farm and the Roberts farm, all alone, master of all he surveyed. Hidden in the undergrowth at the side of the track, Morty watched him pass and then worked his way through the trees until he could see the Mercer compound. The wall here was a mixture of brick and stone, cemented together long ago by some Mercer ancestor. It was taller than he was, but the Mercers thought they were invulnerable and down the years they'd become lax about cutting back the vegetation at the rear of the property. Several trees grew close to the wall, and one draped its branches over the yard.

He waited until dark, then carefully climbed the tree, shinned along the branch, and dropped quietly into the compound. The back of the house – an old single-storey home – was dark, but as he watched from the shadows at the base of the wall someone came into one of the rooms and lit a lantern, hung it up, and moved on to another, illuminating what seemed to be a sitting room. Morty watched and waited as more lamps were lit. He could see, through the windows, a kitchen and what might have been a study.

Karen and Big Keith came into the sitting room, talking animatedly. There was a strange sense of distance, watching them from the dark outside like this, unable to hear what they were saying. Kate Mercer came in, walking with a cane, and she said something too, then they were all talking at once. Karen appeared to be shouting, but he couldn't make out a sound apart from a distant gunshot carried on the breeze. He'd been hearing gunfire all day, some of it quite near by but most of it far away, and he wondered what was happening between the Taylors and the Lyalls now.

He moved along the wall so he could see past the house and into the rest of the compound. A few figures were moving about, but not many. The Mercer farm was not a large one and most of the hands lived on neighbouring holdings. He estimated that no more than six people were inside the compound at the moment. Clearly whatever was happening further north didn't worry Big Keith.

Over in the corner of the yard there was a brick-built storage shed. He scuttled through the shadows at the base of the wall until he reached it, sat behind it, and settled down to wait.

A few hours later, he looked round the side of the shed and saw nobody about. Going back along the wall, he saw that the house was in darkness again. He walked up to the big windows of the sitting room and examined the lock in the moonlight. It was a simple latch, and by working the tip of his knife between the window frame and the jamb he was able to spring it open with barely a sound. He slid the door open a little, slipped inside, closed it behind him.

He stood in the sitting room for a minute or so, letting his eyes become accustomed to the darkness inside the house, then he moved soundlessly to the door and looked out into a long hallway. Moving unhurriedly, he listened at each of the doors opening off the hall. From two of the rooms, he heard snoring. Listening at a third, he heard quiet conversation, a man and a woman, their voices too low to make out what was being said. He moved on.

In the study, he found what he was looking for. A metal gun cabinet standing in the corner, like a tall narrow wardrobe. It was unlocked, because who would dare steal from the Mercers? Inside were racked three hunting rifles and, miracle of miracles, an ancient semi-automatic rifle of a kind he had only heard about in stories. It looked alien and efficient. Carefully, he lifted the rifles out of the cabinet and laid them on the carpeted floor. At the bottom of the cabinet were boxes of ammunition, and clips for the semi-automatic. He opened the study window and placed each of them outside, then climbed out after them and carried them behind the shed.

Going back into the house, he found his way into the kitchen. Lighting a spill from the range, he lit one of the oil lanterns hanging from the wall, then another, then another. He moved into the sitting room again and lit the lanterns there and carried them out into the hallway. And here he paused.

There was, perhaps, still a dim corner of the old Morty left, the one who would absorb any punishment and insult thrown at him because giving up was easier than fighting back. It was that faint remnant which waited, savouring the quiet, the peace. There was a surprisingly sexual thrill about knowing that he could stop right now, leave the farm, and he delayed acting for long, long moments, finally in control of something. Then he picked up one of the lanterns and pitched it underarm down the hallway.

It smashed and instantly burst into a ball of flame, but he was already moving, opening a door, throwing a lamp inside, moving to the next, throwing another.

In a few moments the hallway was full of smoke and

screaming. One of the doors opened and a figure lurched out. Morty lifted his shotgun and fired and the figure collapsed. He moved on, pitching lamps into the study and the sitting room and finally into the kitchen before opening the front door and walking out into the yard.

The house was already on fire; it had taken a surprisingly short time to catch. Morty saw someone come round the side of the building, and he shot them and reloaded unhurriedly. More shouting and screaming in the house. The front door flew open, and he saw, silhouetted against the flames, the figure of Big Keith.

If this were a story, he would have a last line to say, something pithy and amusing. But this wasn't a story. He took two steps forward and Big Keith had just enough time to register who was standing in front of him before Morty emptied both barrels of the shotgun into his face.

Moving quickly now – the shots would carry a long way on the night air and someone would be coming to investigate – Morty collected the rifles and the ammo and carried them across the yard to the gate. A last look back – the house was completely ablaze now – and he unlatched the gate, opened it a little, slipped through, and was gone.

CHAPTER FIFTEEN

"OH, FOR FUCK'S sake," Harry said.

The Mercer farmhouse was still smouldering, smoke rising into the drizzly air from broken windows and the collapsed roof. He could see a couple of bodies lying in the yard. It was hard to be certain from here by the gate, but one seemed to have no head.

"It's the second one in two days," Tony Khan said. "Someone burned the Roberts farm too. Monty Roberts and his wife are missing."

"Morty," said Gary Wren.

Tony shrugged. "Whatever."

Harry was at a loss for words. Since Faye Ogden's death and the delivery of Walter's body to the Lyall farm – dumped in the mud outside the gate like a sack of vegetables – his people and the Taylors' people had been taking potshots at each other in the woods and along the trackways that laced the Parish. Nobody had been hurt so far, though. And it was all local, around the two respective farms. The Mercers were miles away from any trouble.

"We want your protection," Gary said.

"You want my what?" said Harry.

"We know who did this," said Tony. "Big Keith had a row with Max Taylor last year."

Harry hadn't known the Mercers very well, but he suspected it was more likely that Big Keith would have been responsible for any retaliation, not the other way round. He said, "And your William's missing too?"

Gary nodded. "Haven't seen him since the day before yesterday. Ma's going frantic."

Harry was having a hard time connecting this atrocity with his own problems; it was a completely new level of madness. He said, "You know, this is just as likely to be bandits."

"Strangers came through here and did this, we'd have noticed," Tony said. "Big Keith was no fool; must've taken fifteen or twenty people to get into the compound and kill everybody."

Harry wasn't so certain. He said, "If fifteen or twenty of the Taylors came through here, you'd have noticed too."

"Locals?" Gary said. "Moving at night?" He spat on the ground.

"Did nobody hear anything?" Harry asked.

"We heard some shooting, came over to see what was going on, but the house was already on fire and everybody was dead."

"It's got to be the Taylors," Tony said. "Who else could it have been?"

Harry walked out into the yard and stood with his hands in his pockets, a sick feeling in the pit of his stomach. "Look," he said, "I can't tell you lads what to do, you don't owe me anything, but if I was you, I'd be really careful about spreading rumours about who did this. Things are bad enough right now as it is. We don't need a war on our hands."

"What if they come back for us?" asked Gary. "We were friends of Big Keith's."

Harry rubbed his forehead as if massaging away a spike of pain. "Trust me," he said, "the Taylors have got their hands full at the moment without coming down here and giving you grief."

Gary and Tony looked at each other. "So you won't help us?" said Tony.

Harry thought about it. The southern edge of the Parish had always been a peaceful place; they traded more with the community in Lambourn than they did with the farms along the crest of the ridge. He said, "If you need my help, *really* need it, I won't leave you hanging. But there's no earthly reason for the Taylors to have done this." He watched the two men exchange glances again, and knew it was pointless.

AFTER WALTER'S FUNERAL, Harry and the senior members of his family retired to the house. Harry refused to think of it as a council of war, but really that was the only difference. He still had a couple of bottles of whisky his father had bought from the Mortons up in Wycombe, back in the day, and he poured everyone a glass and sat them down around the big dining table. Everyone here was a cousin, either by blood or marriage, although some were more recent additions and Harry didn't know all their names. There seemed too many of them.

"Well," he said. "There seems no reason for someone to be hanging round the Taylors' gate waiting to take a potshot at someone coming out unless it was one of us." The story of what had happened at the Taylor farm had come via two Taylor hands, exiled and looking for shelter. After hearing their story, Harry had given them some food and sent them away. He didn't need to be harbouring two more people with a grudge against Max and his family.

"Walter didn't do it," said an angry, teary woman he didn't know but assumed was a relative of the boy. "It wouldn't have crossed his mind to hurt anybody."

Harry felt he had to bear the lion's share of the blame, for putting the idea of a marauding wolf into Walter's head. But he was going to have to bear it on his own. He said, "I don't want any reprisals for this." And he rode out the angry muttering of his family. When it had subsided, he said, "Someone shot Faye Ogden, for fuck's sake. If it *wasn't* Walter and I find out who did it, I'm going to shake them by the fucking ears myself."

"We can't just sit on our hands while they kill our own, Harry," said his cousin Barbara.

"We can, and we will." He looked around the table. "Unless you really *want* a war." The lack of agreement was dispiriting, at best.

"So, what," said Neil Brookes, his second cousin Ruth's husband. "We're going to carry on as normal?"

"No, we're not," said Harry. "We're going to be very, very careful not to annoy anyone. Not just the Taylors, but any of the other families."

"What if they do this again?" asked someone whose name he didn't know.

"They won't," he said. "I'm going to make sure of that."

It WAS, WHEN he thought about it later, an act of quite considerable bravado. He'd known these paths and roads and fields and woods all his life – had played in them with Max when they were boys – but now the landscape seemed fraught with danger as he rode slowly down the path towards the Taylor farm in the drizzle.

As he came round the last bend, he saw dozens of people patrolling on top of the wall around the Taylor compound and for a moment he faltered. He drew the horse to a halt and sat there looking at the gate, the clusters of heads peering over the parapet at him. There was still time to turn and go home. He might make it.

Instead, he clucked his tongue and shook the reins and the horse plodded contentedly up to the gate.

"Taylors!" he called.

Patrick, Max's eldest, looked down at him. "Go home, Harry."

"I want to talk to your mother," he said.

"Not going to happen. Go home before I shoot you." And he lifted a crossbow to his shoulder.

"I'm not armed," Harry said. He shrugged out of his long coat, sat there in the drizzle in his pullover and jeans.

"I don't care, Harry. You're not coming in here."

"Let him in," called a voice from the other side of the wall, down in the yard.

Patrick turned and looked down. "No."

"He's come here, on his own and unarmed," said the voice. "Don't you know how much balls that takes? Let him in, let's hear what he has to say. While we still can."

For a moment, Harry had a dizzying sense that the past few days had not happened, that he was here again to collect Rob's body. He wondered if any of this could have been avoided if he'd done things differently.

Patrick leaned over the wall and looked in both directions. Then he nodded down into the yard, and after a few moments the gate slid open, just far enough for Harry to walk the horse through. Where he faced a semicircle of heavily-armed people. He noted crossbows and longbows and shotguns and various pieces of edged and serrated agricultural equipment. The gate clanked shut behind him.

The semicircle opened, and John Race stepped through and took the horse's bridle. "Harry," he said.

"I'm here to talk to Rose, John. I don't want any trouble."

"I think things have gone way beyond that. Get down; we'll look after the horse."

Harry dismounted. "Can I put my coat back on?"

Patrick came down a set of stairs built against the inside of the wall. He patted Harry down, then took his coat from where it was draped over the horse's neck and inspected the pockets. He threw it at Harry and earned a look of rebuke from John. He beckoned Harry.

"You've got guts, I will give you that," he said, as they walked across the compound.

"I didn't see there was much choice," Harry said, shrugging into his coat and pulling up the hood. "Where's Rose?"

"She's with Max. I can't let you see her, Harry. I don't know what she'd do if she knew you were here."

Harry glanced at him. "This has got to stop, John."

"It's not me you have to convince. Did that lad kill Faye?"

Harry shook his head. "I don't know. I don't think so, but I don't know."

"Well, miz is sick. Faye said it would happen."

"Sick how?"

"In shock. Exhausted."

"So who's running things?"

The old man shrugged.

Harry stopped and looked round the compound. "Well," he said, "*this* is good."

"I've known you and Max since you were boys; you're not bad men. *Nobody* here is a bad person. But bad stuff is going to happen. Half the people in this yard would give you a good kicking if you gave them the slightest reason. The other half would shoot you."

"Have any of your people been down on the south side lately?"

"What? No. Not that I know of, anyway."

"Someone burned out Big Keith Mercer's farm last night, killed everybody. And another farm." He couldn't remember the name.

John scowled. "Fucking hell," he said. "Bandits are all we need right now."

"The locals down there say Max and Big Keith had some sort of grudge going on."

"Oh, come on, Harry. You know Max; he never held a grudge against anybody in his life. I'm sorry to hear Big Keith's dead, but seriously, he was a twat."

"So he wasn't making trouble? Taking advantage of the situation?"

"No. No, not that I know of, anyway. We don't even know what the situation *is* yet." He reached out and grasped Harry's forearm. "Whatever's going on down there, it's got nothing to do with us. We've got enough trouble here."

There was a commotion across the yard and Patrick came striding towards them, crossbow in hand. "What are you two plotting?"

"We're plotting a way for nobody else to die," John said.

"And how's that going?"

Harry and John exchanged glances.

"Time for you to go, Harry mate," Patrick said.

"We haven't finished having our conversation," said John. The tone of his voice suggested that he wasn't talking to his boss's son; he was talking to a sixteen-year-old boy who had interrupted two men trying to do something important.

If Patrick noticed, he gave no sign, and that, more than anything he had seen here, made Harry's heart sink. "Yes, you have."

John turned away, looked around the yard. Harry willed him to carry on, to make Patrick know who was running things while his father and mother were unable. But he didn't. He sighed, and Harry saw his shoulders slump a fraction, and he knew it was all over.

He reached out and touched John's arm. "I'll go," he said.

"That's good, Harry," said Patrick.

He turned to face the boy and took a step towards him, saw out of the corner of his eye every single person in the yard tense up. He leaned forward until their faces were inches apart. "Don't do this, Patrick," he said quietly.

Patrick looked startled for a moment, then he smiled and stepped back. "Off you trot, Harry," he said, waving his bow in the direction of the horse. "I'll be seeing you."

Harry paused a few seconds, then he nodded to John, who looked as if he was in agony, and set out across the yard. The crowd parted silently, no one threatened him, but it was still the longest walk he had ever taken.

CHAPTER SIXTEEN

THE MOSTLY LEVEL country between the coast and Canterbury was so waterlogged and overgrown as to be almost impassable. Frank's family had opened two of the roads from Margate – quite an achievement in itself – but they were patrolled by enforcers even at the best of times, so trying to get out of Thanet that way was likely to be a bit of a grind ending in a firefight he couldn't win.

He could go back the way he had come, that first time, looping south back into Sussex before turning north again, but that was a fuck of a long way, and he was going to have to do most of it on foot because he didn't dare beg for rides on passing wagons.

There was, however, the old railway line between Margate and London. Slightly elevated above the surrounding land in most places, swamped by trees and washed away by floods in others, it was useless as a trade route or for moving large numbers of men. But looking at it from the branches of a tree about half a mile away, Adam thought it might work. It would at least take him up onto the Downs, and the further he got from Thanet the more sparsely the countryside was inhabited. Frank's people couldn't be everywhere; there just weren't enough of them and the territory they controlled was too large. They would be concentrating themselves on and around the obvious roads in and out of the area and hoping he was too stupid not to use them.

Four days out from Reculver, Adam found himself a hiding place in a ruined house and cranked up the radio again.

"How certain are you that they don't have radio?" asked Chrissie.

"If they had it, they'd be using it," he reasoned, looking out at the drenched landscape. "I didn't see anyone with a radio. They're not technical people; brute force works just as well."

"Hm." Chrissie didn't sound convinced. "Okay." She read out a map reference.

"I presume that's some distance from here," he said, writing down the numbers.

"Call us when you get there and I'll give you a final set of directions. Take care."

"Mm," he said.

It took him three days to walk the fifteen miles or so to Canterbury, moving carefully along the old trackbed by night and hiding up during the day. It rained every single day. Where the line ran through villages he stopped to watch the area for some time before moving on. He trapped rabbits for food, going some distance from the track to cook them, and by the time he'd skirted the city and begun to climb out of the drenched landscape onto the Downs, he would have been happy never to see another rabbit as long as he lived.

Just west of Shottenden, some presentiment stopped him pitching his tent one evening; he climbed up into a tree, hauled his gear up after him, lashed it to a branch, made himself secure, and fell asleep. In the depths of the night, he was woken by the sound of several figures moving about in the undergrowth below the tree. Animals? Frank's men? He had no idea; he sat very still, barely breathing, for what seemed like an hour while they crunched about in the bracken and twig litter, and eventually they went away.

When the overcast finally brightened, he started to make a move to leave the tree, but again something stopped him. Careful not to move too much, he peered through the foliage at the surrounding woodland. He couldn't see anything obvious, but there was still a sense that something was not quite *right*. So he spent the day in the tree, moving as little as he was able, and then only to relieve himself or get dried meat or water from his pack, and that night he was rewarded with the sound of voices and something moving through the undergrowth on the other side of the wood. He couldn't make out what the voices were saying. Some of it seemed like swearing. The sounds moved off into the distance until he could no longer hear them.

Frank was many things, few of them pleasant, but he was not a fool, and neither, with some notable exceptions, were his people. His pursuers' departure had been just a little bit too obviously noisy. So Adam stayed where he was. Chewed some beef jerky, drank some water, pissed discreetly over the side of the branch he was resting on, and sometime around the middle of the afternoon he was rewarded with the smell, ever so faint, of tobacco smoke wafting on the breeze, and he knew he was going to be all right.

They didn't know he was here. All they had was a suspicion. They'd searched the area, come up empty, then departed to look somewhere else, making as much noise as possible, but they'd left someone behind, just in case. Probably not someone too bright; just somebody to hang around for a bit and raise the alarm if they heard anything. Probably none too willing, either; the others had bribed them with a bit of tobacco from one of the old bonded warehouses Frank controlled in Dover.

And here they came, crashing petulently through the undergrowth, muttering to themselves. As they passed beneath the tree, Adam leaned over the branch and looked down, saw the figure of Sam Dodd, Albie's younger brother, wading through the bracken and brambles, swinging a stick angrily in front of him. That was Sam; always getting the shitty jobs, always resentful about it. Adam watched as the furious little man stamped away into the distance, listened to him for a while longer. Presently, peace returned to the wood.

He gave it another couple of hours, then he cautiously lowered his gear out of the tree and climbed stiffly down after it.

By nightfall, he had picked his way carefully out of the wood. By the end of the next day, he could see Leeds Castle in the distance. He was right on the edge of Frank's kingdom here, but it was another day or so, climbing the rising ground onto the Weald, before he stopped looking over his shoulder.

The Wealders had centred their base of operations on Tonbridge Wells, some distance to the north, and though there were almost as many of them as there were people in Thanet, and very nearly as aggressive, he didn't see a single soul until a week later, skirting the ruins of Crawley, when he spotted a group of scavengers in the distance, toiling their way home through the rain.

Beyond Crawley, he followed the old road signs towards Woking and Reading. Both towns looked burned out, almost completely reclaimed by vegetation, only the tallest buildings peeking over the treetops. He found himself following the Thames along a narrowing gap in the surrounding hills, and finally, footsore and exhausted, he reached Streatley.

The town was a tax operation, he realised when he saw the ferry. He was carrying several things of value, but he didn't feel inclined to give any of them up just for the sake of a hot bath and a soft bed and a decent meal... well, he did, but he wasn't going to. He walked upstream for several miles, but the river was broad and swollen with rain, its roiled rushing surface rich with debris. There was nowhere to cross. Nowhere even to try.

He walked back to the ferry crossing. The ferry itself was a big flatboat, large enough to carry two or three wagons and a few dozen people. It was winched back and forth along a cable stretched between the banks, using what appeared to be an ancient and fucked-off steam engine. The engine was remarkable enough for him to want a closer look at it, but there were a couple of lads standing guard and they looked miserable enough to make him change his mind.

Half a dozen wagons and a group of about thirty people were waiting on the slip road. He sidled unhurriedly up to them, walked up and down the line of wagons, dumped his gear in the back of one that was stacked with cages of scrawny-looking chickens, and swung himself up into the seat.

The driver, an old woman wearing camouflage gear and what seemed to be half a dozen sweaters, looked him up and down and said, "Bugger off, sonny."

"Give me a lift, please," he said quietly. "I need to get across the river."

"Sod off. You're not half as charming as you think you are."

"I'll pay," he said.

She snorted. "With what?"

He put a hand in his coat pocket, brought it out holding a short length of brass chain. At the end of the chain was a battered old pocket watch. The woman looked at it. "What the fuck do I want with that?"

"You could tell the time with it," he suggested.

"I don't need a watch to tell the time," she said. "I know what time it is. It's time you got off my wagon."

"You know," he told her, putting it back in his pocket, "there are places where you could get a good meal and a bed for the night for this watch."

"It's a shame you're not in those places, then. How about your gun?" She nodded at the enforcer's shotgun that he was carrying.

"Well, now *you* can fuck off."

"What about that thing?" She half-turned and pointed at the nylon carrying-case sitting with his rucksack and tent among the chicken cages.

"No."

She sniffed and looked out across the river. Adam sighed. He reached into the other pocket of his coat and took out an automatic pistol. Shielding it from view, he wiggled it hopefully. The old woman looked at it and said, "Ammo?"

"Two full clips and a hundred rounds."

She sighed. "What's your name?"

"Adam Hardy."

"Not from round here, are you, Adam Hardy."

"Not by quite a long distance, no."

"One thing we have no shortage of here is guns," she told him. "I'm Margaret Oakley. Where are you going?"

He told her, and she nodded. "I'm going by there."

"I only need a lift across the river."

She looked at him. "Do you have a problem noticing when someone's doing you a fucking favour?"

"It doesn't happen very often, it's true," he admitted.

"Well, someone's doing you one now; you might want to remember it, so you can recognise when it happens again."

Adam considered getting down and trying one of the other wagons, but all of a sudden it seemed like too much work.

"Put your little pop-gun away, sunshine," Margaret told him, and she shook the reins and the horses moved forward towards the ferry. "Welcome to the Chilterns."

THE SIGN SAID *BLANDINGS. FUCK OFF.* It was fixed to a wall beside two high gates at the end of a long driveway. Margaret had dropped him on the main road and given him two cages, each containing a chicken. "Tell her Margaret sends her regards," she said, and drove off without looking back.

Adam stood in front of the gates with the cages at his feet and looked at the sign. He looked left and right along the wall, and then behind him. He put his hands in his pockets.

"Hello," said a voice. "Don't know *you*."

Adam considered the pile of sandbags on top of one of the gate pillars. "Your boss is expecting me."

"My," said the voice. "Aren't *we* grumpy this morning. Miss our breakfast, did we?"

Adam smiled, the way one does when one is trying to be patient with someone who is pointing a heavy machine gun in one's direction. "I've come a long way," he said.

"Indeed you have," said the voice. "And you're late; I was expecting you last week."

Adam thought about that. He thought about walking along the old railway out of Thanet. He thought about the hours he'd spent up a tree waiting for Frank's men to decide to leave. Frank's father had built a gallows from old scaffolding poles by the clock tower in Margate; it could accommodate fifteen people at a time. He thought about that, too.

"I've come a long way," he said again, a little louder.

A head bobbed up over the sandbags. Grey hair, broad grin. "What's the password?"

"What?"

She stood up, a tall woman in early middle-age, broad-shouldered and ruddy-cheeked. "Quite right. There isn't one."

He stared at her. "I've brought chickens," he said.

"Just a sec." She dropped down out of sight, and a few moments later the gates started to clank aside. "Come on in!" she called from out of sight. "But stop just inside the gate. Don't want you exploding when you've only just arrived."

He picked up the chickens and walked through the gate. On the other side, a broad open strip of gravel ran along the wall as far as he could see. Directly in front of him, another gravel driveway curled through overgrown grounds. In the distance, over the treetops, he could see the chimneys of a large country house.

The gates closed and the woman walked up. She was wearing a black duffel coat and jeans and she was smiling. "Betty Coghlan," she said. "You'll be Mr Hardy, then."

"I will be, yes." They shook hands.

"You don't sound too pleased to be here."

"I've had one of those weeks."

"Yes, so I understand. I'm sorry about that. You'll have to tell me all about it over dinner."

"Dinner sounds nice."

"It should do; you brought it with you." She picked up the cages and set off, not along the drive, but down a well-trodden path towards a little copse. "Stay right behind me," she said. "Don't stray; the place is mined."

"Margaret sends her regards," he said, following carefully.

"Margaret Oakley? Are these *her* chickens? And here was me thinking you'd brought me a present. How is she?"

"Is everyone around here so angry?"

"Margaret? Angry?" She chuckled. "Margaret's a little ray of fucking sunshine compared to some of the locals. We went through some rough times in the early days."

"Didn't everyone?"

"We had a lot of refugees from London. Some of them stayed, most just passed through, but things were very difficult for a while. Turn left here. Don't touch these trees."

He looked at the trees they were passing between. "You've mined the trees as well?"

"Old habits die hard. Like I said, we went through some rough times."

It took them about fifteen minutes to follow the winding path to a point at which the trees and undergrowth suddenly ended and another huge area of gravel began. Right in the middle of it sat one of the ugliest houses Adam had ever seen. It was as if a Tudor mansion had been built by someone who only had a sketchy verbal description to go on.

Betty saw the look on his face. "I know," she said. "But it's home."

"Do you mind if I ask who you are?"

She smiled at him. "Didn't anyone tell you?"

"I was just told to stand in front of your gates and wait until you let me in."

"Hm. Is your work always quite so... ramshackle...?"

"No, sometimes it's *utterly* chaotic."

"Well," she said, leading the way across the gravel to the front door of the house, "we're an oasis."

The front door opened onto an entrance hall panelled in dark wood. The walls on both sides were lined with doors, and directly ahead a carpeted stairway rose to the first floor. Betty turned and flicked a switch on the wall next to the door, and lights came on along the walls.

"Well," said Adam.

"Wind generators," she said.

After months in Thanet, where the most technological form of lighting was an oil lamp, the lights in the hall seemed bizarre and mystical. Frank and his family were too busy keeping control over their kingdom to worry about electricity.

"My great-grandparents," she said. "They were pretty well self-sufficient even before The Sisters. We've got two wells on the estate, we've got electricity."

"You've got mines."

She laughed. "Oh yes. Go on upstairs; first door on the right down the corridor, we've got a room made up for you. Have a rest and a bath, there's plenty of hot water. We'll talk this evening. Okay?"

He thought he felt a terrible weight lift off his shoulders. "Okay."

She nodded. "Good to see you," she said. "I'm glad you're here." And she walked away across the hall towards one of the doors.

Adam watched her go, thinking. It had been quite some time since someone had told him 'I'm glad you're here'.

THE ROOM WAS three times the size of the one at The Sands. There was a fire burning in the grate, heavy velvet curtains, solid furniture, a bed of miraculous comfort. There were no slug trails on the carpet. It was, it occurred to him, the first time in more than eight months – apart from his visits to Frank and Seth – that he had been in a room which did not smell of mould and damp.

The bathroom down the hall contained a massive claw-footed bath with a complex shower-tap arrangement that looked like part of an old rocket engine he had once seen. There was soap, and it did not smell strongly of lanolin. He filled the bath – it took some time – and was glumly unsurprised by the amount of grime that washed off him. He drained the bath, rinsed it, and filled it again, woke suddenly some time later almost submerged in lukewarm water.

Drying himself, he looked in the mirror. He was covered in cuts and bruises, some of them old, rather more of them recent, and he'd lost a lot of weight, but now the dirt was gone it didn't seem as bad as he'd expected. He did look tired, though. More tired than when he got back from Wales. Maybe everything was catching up with him.

Dusk had fallen while he was in the bath. The windows of his room looked out on a rainswept dimness full of the uncertain shapes of trees and bushes. Someone had laid clean clothes out on the bed; a pair of jeans, a baggy homespun hooded shirt, underwear. They'd guessed his sizes, reasonably accurately. He dressed, sat on the bed and undid his rucksack, took out the radio and wound it.

"Are you there?" asked Chrissie.

"I am," he said. "I am here."

"Good. Well, you'll be safe and sound there for a while. We'll send someone to collect you in a bit."

"I might as well just keep going," he said. "I could be there in a couple of weeks."

"Are you seriously telling me you'd rather set off walking again?"

He towelled his hair, one-handed. "Now you mention it," he said.

She laughed, her voice tinny from the radio's speaker. "You stay put; we'll come and get you." Debriefing over the radio – notwithstanding that radio communication was still rare as hens' teeth – was frowned upon. There was no way of knowing who was listening. "And be nice to those people. We've done each other some favours in the past; it'd be good if we stayed friends."

"They're already my best friends," he said, looking around the bedroom. "Have we decided what to do about the thing?"

"Not yet. We'll wait until we've spoken with you."

The people who ran Guz – in particular the people he worked for – were not, generally, in favour of snap decisions. He pressed the button and said, "Roger that."

"We'll deal with the thing," Chrissie said. "One way or another."

He thought about it. Pressed the button again. "Roger that. Got to go; I'll check in later."

"Try to get Andrew to cook dinner for you; he's really good."

He turned the radio off and sat looking at it for a while. Then he tossed it onto the bed and got dressed.

HE WANDERED DOWNSTAIRS, followed the smell of cooking to the kitchen, where a tall young man was clattering pots and pans around on an impressive-looking wood-fired range.

"I won't shake hands," the young man said, smiling. "Been chopping onions. I'm Andrew."

"Word of your cooking has reached Devon," Adam told him.

"Has it?" Andrew laughed. "That's good to know, if I ever need somewhere else to live."

"Is that likely?"

"Not a chance."

"Ah, good, you've met," Betty said, coming into the kitchen. She looked Adam up and down and nodded. "The clothes suit you."

"It's nice to wear something clean."

"Come on through and sit down," she said, heading back up the corridor towards the hallway.

The dining room was down another corridor, in another wing. As they walked through the house, Adam caught sight of other people in other rooms. "How many people live here?"

"A dozen in the house, seventy on the estate. There are a couple of farms a mile or so from here that we've sort of been responsible for since The Sisters. About two hundred people."

Adam suspected the number was a lot higher than that. "Your family was here, even before The Sisters?"

"Oh yes. We've been here for two hundred years. We have a certain stake in the area." She smiled brightly at him. "Where are you from, by the way?"

"Guz. Born and bred."

"I've always wondered. Why do you call it that?"

He shrugged. "It's an old nickname for the naval base. Why?"

"I'm interested in the way society's starting to come back together. Here." She showed him into the dining room, a long, narrow wood-panelled room with a big table set for three. "Sit down. Anywhere'll do."

Adam sat. "Is society starting to come back together?"

"Here and there." Betty sat opposite him and leaned her elbows on the table. "I think Plymouth – sorry, I can't call it 'Guz,' it sounds ridiculous – may actually be the capital of the country. If we had a country to have a capital of."

"We don't want to be," he said. "I don't think."

"You might not have a choice."

He thought about the last time he'd sat in a dining room, in Margate. "I don't know what the Committee's planning. If they're planning anything."

"Of course not. But if I was your Committee, I'd be thinking very hard about stuff."

"Oh, they do that all right."

Andrew came in pushing a small trolley and started to serve dinner before sitting down at the third place setting. Betty poured wine for them. "My great-grandparents kept a pretty good cellar," she said. "Most of it's ruined now, but this isn't too bad. Or we have beer, if you'd prefer."

He tried the wine. "No, this is good, thank you."

Dinner was individual steak and kidney pies, roast potatoes, a mixture of vegetables. "I thought we were having chicken," Adam said, trying a bit of pie.

Betty chuckled. "A little joke. Margaret sent me a couple of layers; we're always losing hens to foxes or dogs."

"This is very good," he told Andrew.

"I don't get the chance to cook with steak very often," the younger man said. "The farms round here tend to raise pigs."

"A pig's very economical," Betty said. "Turns rubbish into meat. Your cow's a bit more labour-intensive. There are a few dairy farms around here, but they tend not to slaughter their stock until they absolutely have to."

It occurred to Adam that he was being given a lot more information about Blandings and its environs than he strictly needed. But the food *was* very good.

When they'd finished, Andrew cleared away the plates and took them into the kitchen. Adam said, "I hope you don't mind me asking, but 'Blandings'?"

Betty sat back and beamed at him. "Why, Mr Hardy," she said. "I do believe you can read. And in fact *have* read."

He shrugged.

"I think you're the first person who's come here and appreciated the reference," she said. "My great-great grandfather was a big fan of Wodehouse, apparently. He renamed the house. It used to be called The Limes, although god knows why; there aren't any lime trees around here." She got up from the table and said, "Come on; let me show you something. You can bring your wine, if you want."

He picked up his glass and followed her back along the corridor to the entry hall, then through another door and down a long flight of stairs that ended in a small square brick-lined room with doors on three sides. Betty opened one and stepped through, Adam right behind her. There was a click, and all of a sudden the room was filled with light.

"Oh my word," said Adam. The room was full of guns.

"You can look, but don't touch," Betty said with a smile. "Oh, go on. You can touch too."

He walked out into the room, looking at the racks of shotguns and hunting rifles and pistols and assault weapons and machine guns. Propped up against the wall were several old RPG launchers, alongside boxes and boxes of ammunition.

"Where did you get all this?" he asked.

She shrugged. "Here and there. Police stations, mostly. Army camps. We traded for some of them. Others, we made."

He glanced at her.

"We had some original RPG rounds," she went on, "but we had to get rid of them. They were unstable; too old. We've been making new ones, but it's slow going. Andrew wants to try knocking together a flamethrower, but fuel's scarce." She smiled at him.

"How would you feel about moving to Guz?" he asked.

Betty burst out laughing. "Oh, we're happy where we are, thank you. I couldn't live in a place called *Guz*, anyway."

He took a last look around the room. "Let me introduce you to Gussie."

* * *

He went up to his room, collected the nylon carrying case, and brought it down to the study, where Betty was rummaging in the hearth with a poker.

"I shouldn't have done this," he told her. "It was stupid."

"We're all of us victims of strong passions, from time to time," she said, hanging up the poker and sitting in the armchair.

He took the rifle out of its case. It was almost six feet long and someone had carved the word *GUSSIE* into the stock.

"That's very nice," said Betty. "Heavily modified. Looks like it started out as an H&K PSG1. In good condition, too." She slipped the gun's scope out of its pocket in the side of the case and turned it over in her hands. "Hensoldt ZF 6x40. Nice optics." She put the scope down on the table. "We should have some ammunition for this, you know. It takes 6.72 NATO but a lot of specialist police firearms teams used them so there's still ammo lying around, if you know where to look."

"I wasn't really planning on firing it at anyone," Adam said.

"No," she said thoughtfully. "No, it's more important as a *template*, isn't it." She sat back. "I'd have thought your people would have all the weapons they could cope with, though."

In the very early days, there had been some discussion about firing up the turbines of one of the three Type 45 destroyers which had been caught in Devonport by the disaster. Adam wasn't entirely certain what the purpose of this would have been, but as it turned out it never happened, and the old warships had become the core around which civilisation had started to rebuild itself in the West in the following years. They were never going to go anywhere now, and their guided missiles were useless, but they – and the surrounding naval base – had impressive stockpiles of supplies and weaponry.

"We don't have anything like this," Adam said. "I don't know why." Frank had said Gussie could hit a rabbit in the eye from more than a mile away.

"But what you do have is armourers who could copy it," Betty said, nodding. "Although you didn't walk across the country just to steal a *gun*, did you?"

Adam looked at her. He said, "We lost someone."

Betty raised an eyebrow, and Adam sighed.

"You needn't be embarrassed," she told him, getting up and going over to a cupboard in a corner of the study. "Spying's been a noble occupation in this country all the way back to Walsingham." She opened the cupboard, took out a bottle and two glasses, closed the door, and came back to the fireside. "Single malt," she said, putting the bottle on the table beside the rifle. "A hundred and fifty years old."

Adam looked at the bottle. "There isn't much left."

She shrugged and poured them each a measure.

"There are some people in Kent," Adam told her, taking his glass from her. "Thank you. We've been hearing about them for years now, but just recently we've started to wonder if they might be a problem."

Betty nodded. "I've heard of them too. So you sent someone to take a look?"

Adam sipped his whisky. "When we didn't hear from her, someone had to go and see what was going on."

"Did you find her?"

Adam looked at his glass.

"I'm sorry." Betty took a drink. "Just how dangerous are these people in Kent?" When he didn't answer, she said, "Think of it as intelligence sharing. One day we may have a common enemy."

"How organised are people round here?" he asked.

She shrugged. "Not very. Just farmsteads. Most of the trading that goes on is informal, there's no real governmental structure. Hardly anyone can read. We get by all right."

"If Frank decides to move west, he'll walk right over you as if you weren't here."

Betty looked into the fire, thinking. "He might get a surprise," she said finally. "A lot of the farms round here were settled by old-style Preppers. Survivalists. They were better-prepared than most people when The Sisters came, although I suppose even they were expecting some sort of warning that the world was going to end. Some of our farmers are pretty hard-nosed."

"Frank's got an army," he told her. "They're well-armed and they're well-organised and they're shit-scared of him. One day the whole South's going to belong to him or his kids."

"So why doesn't he just take over?"

"The Nassingtons," he said. "On the High Weald. They're not much better than Frank, but at least they're content with their lot for the moment. If he wants to go anywhere, he'll have to go through them, and they won't be a pushover." He sipped more whisky.

"It would be good," Betty mused, "if Mr Frank and the Nassingtons cancelled each other out."

"Frank's waiting until he's strong enough, or he can talk enough of the Wealders into coming over to him." Adam leaned back in the chair, suddenly aware of just how utterly weary he was. It would be very nice, he thought, if he could just stay here for the rest of his life.

Betty looked at Gussie. "And this belongs to...?"

"Frank. It's Frank's gun. And before him it was his dad's. And before *him* it was his grandad's."

"A family heirloom, then."

"He showed it me one night. He'd just... well, never mind. He was like a little kid, so proud of his fucking gun. I could have broken his neck there and then."

"But instead you decided on something more subtle."

He grunted. "Subtle. I fucked everything up."

"As I said, strong passions."

It had been more than that. It had been a strong urge to hurt Frank, to ridicule him, to make him look a fool in front of his own people. He shook his head. "Stupid."

She smiled at him. "Well, since you're here, would you mind if we took a look at Gussie? A sniper rifle might come in handy."

"You don't have one of your own?"

She chuckled. "Custom work is always interesting; it might help us improve our own weapons."

"Go ahead."

"Thank you." She put the sniperscope down on the table and sat back in her chair. "We still don't know how many people there are in the country, you know," she said. "First there were The Sisters, then the Long Autumn. Famine, disease; my great grandparents' generation barely had time to have children; they were too busy just trying not to die."

Adam sipped his whisky.

"You and me and Andrew are the only people who can read, pretty much, within a radius of about twenty miles. That first generation after The Sisters..."

"Too busy trying not to die," he finished.

She nodded. "And when *their* children started to have children, there was hardly anyone around who could teach them to read. We've lost a lot of things. Oh, stuff gets handed down from generation to generation, hands-on stuff, but there are whole libraries of technical information still in the cities and we can't use them, by and large."

"This is what you meant about being an oasis."

She raised her glass to him. "My great-grandparents realised that if anyone survived the Long Autumn, there had to be something afterwards, otherwise there was no point in surviving at all. Times were very hard round here, as I said, but we've started teaching some of the locals to read and write. We're thinking of opening a school next year."

"Am I being softened up for something?"

Betty beamed at him. "Bless you," she said, "you're not nearly as dim as you look, are you?"

"I've come a long way."

"Yes, you said." She looked at her glass, looked at the inch or so of whisky still in the bottle, then reached out and topped up both their glasses. "There was a chap named Billy Morton; he's a bit of a legend round here. He's gone now, and so are his family, but once upon a time they lived like kings. They arrived in Wycombe just after The Sisters and they found a Tesco superstore, just abandoned. Packed with goods. So they fortified it, fought off other people who wanted the stuff in there. That store kept them supplied for *years*. Canned and bottled food, water, medicines, clothes." She looked at her glass again and smiled nostalgically. "Booze."

"What happened to them?"

"They were parasites and they killed their host. They ran out of stuff. One day that Tesco was just a big empty building, and then the Mortons weren't special any more and they upped sticks and moved out, probably looking for another store to colonise."

"And the punchline is...?"

She gave him a long, steady look. "Maybe you *are* as dim as you look, now I think about it."

"Everyone comes to that conclusion, sooner or later."

"We need to organise, or in another fifty years or so we'll be back to feudalism. We can't keep leeching on the past. Those boots you were wearing when you arrived, I'm willing to bet they're almost a hundred years old. Probably came out of stores at Devonport. Am I right?"

"They were a present."

She waved it away. "We can't make boots like that now, because those boots were made by *machines* and nobody knows how to make the machines that made them. We're living on the carcass of a dead civilisation; the only reason we haven't run out of stuff yet is because there aren't enough of us and there's still plenty to go around. But it *will* run out." She nodded at his feet, at the moment clad in a rather fetching pair of slippers. "No more boots."

There were probably people in Guz who could knock together a machine that made boots, he thought, if they put their minds to it. "It's not our responsibility," he said. "We just want to be left alone."

"But you just walked a very long way to check out what's going on in Kent."

"We're not stupid."

"No," she agreed. "No, you're certainly not."

"And you really ought to be saying this to the Commodore and the Committee, not to me."

She grinned. "Oh, without a doubt. But you're here and they're not."

He sighed and curled up in the armchair, tucked his feet under him, closed his eyes.

"How bad was it?" she asked. "Margate?"

"Pretty awful."

There was a long silence. He opened his eyes. Betty was sitting staring into the fire, holding her glass against her cheek, lost in thought. She looked at him and her expression brightened. "I'm sorry," she said. "You must be exhausted and all I'm doing is interrogating you."

"To be honest, after that dinner I'm happy to tell you everything I know."

She shook her head. "Sometimes I forget how hard things are everywhere else."

"I find *that* hard to believe, somehow."

Betty looked across the room to the curtained windows. "This is a good place, you know. It's not *Plymouth*, but we get by. There's a lot of possibility here now. I'd hate anything to threaten that." She smiled at him. "Go to bed, Mr Hardy."

*   *   *

LATER – MUCH MUCH later – it occurred to Adam that Betty actually waited several days before making her suggestion. Eventually, he came to admire that, in a grudging sort of way, but it took him a long time.

He was having breakfast in the kitchen one morning – bacon, fried egg, sausage, fried potatoes – and vaguely wondering whether all this luxury was going to make him soft when Betty came in and sat down across the table from him.

"So," she said. "How's it going?"

"It's brilliant," he said, indicating his plate. "Thanks."

"You know," she said, "it'll take Andrew another week or so to work on the rifle."

Andrew had dismantled Gussie and was examining it in minute detail in a workshop easily as well-equipped as anything in Guz. "Yes, we had a chat about that yesterday."

"And another week or so for your people to turn up."

"That's my understanding, yes." During their most recent contact, Chrissie had been vague about exactly when someone would reach him. It was already more than a month since he left Margate; he would, he thought, have been better off just hiding out in Reculver until a boat could reach him after all.

"How do you feel about making yourself useful?"

Adam put his knife and fork down and looked at her. "I *am* making myself useful." He'd spent the previous day mucking out the stables, the day before that helping to mount new blades on one of the estate's wind generators.

"I need someone to pop over and see some friends of mine, and I can't spare anybody."

He sat back and crossed his arms.

"They live a couple of days' ride from here. There's been some kind of accident and they need antibiotics."

He raised an eyebrow.

"No, we don't make them here," she told him. "And no, I'm not going to tell you where they come from."

"This is a very interesting place, you know," he said.

"I've had a good relationship with your people for quite a long time," she said. "But we don't tell each other everything. That's life, right?"

"If I take this stuff to your friends, will you tell me where it's from?"

Betty shook her head. "But it would go some way towards bringing forward the day that I do."

Adam rubbed his eyes. "What kind of accident?"

She shrugged. "I don't know, and that's irrelevant, really. They need the antibiotics, that's what matters."

He sighed. "All right."

"They should be arriving sometime this evening. You can leave in the morning; you can take one of our horses and you'll be back here by the end of the week."

"I'll walk, thanks."

"Best you ride," she told him. "You *can* ride?"

He sighed. "Of course I can."

THE HORSE WAS named Roderick, and it was the size of a small cottage. Adam eyed it cautiously as Andrew walked it round the stable yard.

"Good as gold, is Roderick," Andrew told him with a smile. "Not a bad bone in his body."

"That's good to know," Adam said.

Andrew fed the horse a carrot. "Loves carrots."

"That's good to know, too."

"You've never ridden a horse, have you?"

Adam looked at the young man. The horse twitched its head alarmingly against its bridle, bared its teeth at him. "Yes," he said. "Yes, I have."

"How can you never have ridden a horse?"

"Boats," Adam said. "I do boats. And I *have* ridden a horse."

"Long way from the sea, here," Andrew mused.

"Yes. Isn't it." Adam took a few steps forward and tentatively patted the horse's neck. "Good horse," he said. The horse looked at him and he got the impression that it was considering which part of his face to bite off first. He took half a step back.

Andrew guffawed. "City boy."

Adam turned and fiddled with his gear. There wasn't much, he didn't expect to be gone long, but the Coghlans had lent him a very nice semi-automatic rifle. Belgian, Betty had said. "One of a kind, probably," she'd said. "No more rifles coming from Belgium now."

He'd had a long conversation with Chrissie the previous night, weighing up the pros and cons of the trip. Chrissie had been enthusiastic about it.

"Sure," she said. "Take a look at the area, it's all intelligence."

"And what about the intelligence about Thanet?"

"There won't be anyone there to debrief you for days," she said.

"Maybe I should write it down. Just in case."

"No. No, you don't do that. Not around Betty Coghlan, anyway. She's probably listening in to this conversation as it is."

He looked around the bedroom. Pressed the button on the radio. "I thought we were friends."

"There's friends, and there's friends you leave intelligence with, and Betty isn't one of those. Not yet, anyway."

He wondered what *that* meant. "If you don't mind me saying," he told her, "this is quite an unusual way of doing things. Even for us."

She chuckled, a hundred and fifty or so miles away in her nice office in Guz. "When was there ever a *usual* for us? Listen, it'll be a nice trip, nothing's going to go awry. Deliver this stuff to Betty's friends, have a poke around, come back to Blandings.

Four days, tops. And if you could find out where she's getting antibiotics from, that would be good too."

"I thought you said she's probably listening to us."

"Doesn't matter. She'd try to find out if *we* had antibiotics."

"Just for the record, and because *someone* ought to say it, I don't think this is a very good idea. We should be working out what to do about Frank Pendennis rather than playing postman."

"And we will. Just *go*, Adam. Nice relaxing ride, meeting new people. How can it hurt?"

HOW CAN IT hurt? Well, it could involve riding along on what was basically half a ton of mildly dangerous muscle and teeth. He felt himself swaying alarmingly as Roderick plodded along, every now and again craning its neck around to try and bite his leg.

"I swear on my mother's life," he told the horse, "if you keep doing that, I'll shoot you." The horse whinnied but otherwise took no notice.

On the other hand, it *was* quite a pleasant trip. The rain had stopped, the sun was fighting its way unenthusiastically through the clouds. He rode past fortified houses and farms nestling in the countryside, other houses abandoned and half-demolished for building materials. For all that there was no central organisation, the people here seemed to have their act together pretty well. When he encountered someone – on foot or horseback or in a wagon – they nodded hello cautiously but without threat. After Margate, it was nice to find people getting along without the encouragement of armed guards.

There were a lot of people in Goring, apparently getting ready for market day or something. He stayed overnight at a boarding house recommended by Betty, pressed on across the river the next morning. He remembered how exhausted he had been when he came the other way, days before. Now he was rested and well-fed and even Roderick, who seemed mostly to know the way for himself, had given up trying to bite him.

On the other side of the river, he climbed up into the hills again, following a broad path which Betty had told him had been a trade route as far back as the Bronze Age. He passed carts and wagons heading for market. The view out over the Vale of the White Horse was extraordinary, a vista of flooded fields and woodland that seemed to fade out into infinity. He pulled Roderick to a halt and sat in the saddle examining the distance through his binoculars. He could see buildings, farms, grey patches he presumed were old towns. In a few places, he saw smoke rising into the breezy air, what he thought might be large groups of people on the move down old lanes. Further off, there was a large pall of smoke hanging over what seemed to be a town. He wondered what was going on down there.

The path he was using was obviously well-travelled and cared for, important to the locals for trade and travel. Betty had told him that it had once stretched from Dorset to the Norfolk coast, which seemed hard to believe. Here and there, at the side of the track, were black signposts, amazingly not toppled over by wind and hail, their white lettering all but worn away. He kept an eye out for the signs until he found one indicating the distance to something called Wayland's Smithy, and he turned off the track.

A mile or so further on, he noticed a group of people standing in the path. He'd been riding along more or less contentedly for the best part of two days, and the group didn't seem particularly threatening, so he kept going towards them. It was only when he saw their weapons that he unslung his rifle, cocked it, and held it across his body.

There were about ten of them, dressed in a motley of rain gear and old camouflage clothing. Some of them had shotguns, others had crossbows. None of them looked particularly welcoming.

He rode up to them, drew Roderick to a halt. Sat looking down at them. "Hello," he said.

One of them, presumably the one in charge, looked up and said, "Who are you?"

"My name's Adam. What's yours?"

"Where are you going?"

Adam told him. "I don't want any trouble," he said, suddenly conscious of the flask in his saddlebag containing the antibiotics which had been delivered to Blandings from who knew where. He shifted slightly in the saddle, making sure everyone could see his rifle.

"Get down."

"No."

CHAPTER SEVENTEEN

HE FINALLY CAUGHT up with them not far from the Wren farm. Five of them, walking along the track laughing and joking, like they didn't have a care in the world, Fred walking in front, shotgun slung over his shoulder. He watched them pass from the undergrowth beside the track, then he stepped out into the open.

They didn't hear him, didn't notice him. He could have taken them all down and they would never have known who did it, never known what hit them. But he didn't want that, so he carefully arranged the Morty Face and said, "Hey."

That got their attention. They stopped and turned. A couple of them unslung their rifles, but they relaxed when they saw it was just one man standing in the middle of the track in a rain poncho that was too big for him. He pulled the hood of the poncho back so they could all get a look at him.

"Hey," said Fred, a big grin on his face. "It's what's-his-name. Monty. Monty boy who had my horse."

"My horse," said Morty. "Not yours."

Fred shrugged. "Too fucking late now, anyway. Sold it. Didn't

185

get much for it, either, worthless pile of bones." He stepped forward, starting to bring up his shotgun.

Morty lifted the semi-automatic from under his poncho and fired. The rifle had quite a kick; it was a struggle to keep the muzzle down, but the effects were quite miraculous. All he had to do was pull the trigger and wave it back and forth a couple of times and everyone was dead or dying.

It made a miraculous sound, too, echoing through the trees and off into the damp morning. Someone would be coming to see what had made that noise. He rifled the bodies for any useful items – food, ammunition, little bits of gear – and looked at their faces. One of them was a Wren, he was fairly sure of it. Another looked like one of the younger Khan boys – and that was all they were, really, just cruel boys out for a day's fun, not caring who they hurt. There had been lads like this in Southampton, but that seemed so far away and long ago.

Fred was still alive, barely. He was lying on his back, bloody foam on his lips and two holes in his chest, eyes blinking desperately and fists clenching and unclenching.

Morty knelt down beside him and went through his pockets. Some shotgun shells, a roll of string, a ham sandwich wrapped in brittle old brown paper. Morty put them all in his satchel and then he looked down into Fred's eyes.

"*My* horse," he said, and he let the Morty Face slip, let Fred see what he really looked like now, and Fred's eyes widened and he died.

A minute or so later three men came riding along the track. Morty shot them from cover, tumbling them out of their saddles and sending their horses cantering away in terror. Then he set off through the trees towards the Wren farm, a spark of cold joy in his heart that he had, finally, discovered something he was good at.

*   *   *

AT A DISTANCE of almost two hundred yards through the trees, the scope of Big Keith Mercer's hunting rifle made the figures patrolling along the top of the wall of the Wren compound seem almost close enough to touch. Morty rested the crosshairs on the forehead of one, breathed in, breathed out, and squeezed the trigger, was rewarded with a burst of reddish-grey mist. He sighted on a second and fired again, and a third, and then he was moving to another position.

The people on the wall didn't know what was going on. Several of them were just standing there, looking out into the surrounding woods, firing at shadows. Morty shot two more and moved on, and two more from another position, and by that time someone in the yard had seen some sense and called everyone down off the wall.

Morty moved around until he was in cover beside the track leading to the farm. A few moments later the gate opened and four or five heavily-armed men emerged. Morty brought the first two down as they stepped out, killed a third as the others ran back into the yard and the gate closed behind them. Someone popped their head up over the parapet and took a shot into the undergrowth before popping down again. Morty fired but this time he wasn't sure if he'd hit them.

The last of the gunshots echoed away into the trees. Morty heard distant shouting from inside the farm, but couldn't make out any more movement. He settled down in his nest of weeds and bracken. He reached into the satchel round his neck and took out the sandwich he'd taken from Fred, unwrapped it, and took a bite.

He'd just finished the sandwich when he heard horses coming along the track towards the farm. Four riders. He waited for them to pass, then stepped out for a moment and shot them with the semi-automatic before plunging into the undergrowth again and making his way around the wall of the farm. At the back, he found three ladders and signs that a number of people had made their escape in a hurry.

Morty climbed one of the ladders and looked down into the compound. Not a soul about. This was really too easy. He climbed over the wall onto the walkway, and from there down the steps into the yard.

Ten minutes later, as he let himself out through the front gate and vanished into the woods, the house was already burning.

BY THE TIME Morty was safely back in his bolthole, the survivors of the massacre at the Wren farm had reached the safety of the Khan compound and told a breathless story of being attacked by at least fifteen men armed with long guns and possibly automatic weapons. The Khans listened, and then sent out word to the neighbouring Thompson and Walsh farms, and before nightfall fifty heavily-armed riders set out northward.

They didn't really have a plan, as such, but they came upon the Croker farm, a small, lightly-defended place half a mile or so from the Taylor compound. Because the Crokers worked for the Taylors, and because it was an easier prospect than a direct assault on the Taylor farm itself, they burned it and killed everyone they found, and then they rode home.

By the time the sun rose the next morning, five days after Max Taylor had returned home wounded and four days after Morty Roberts set fire to his own farm, the Parish was in a state of war.

Wayland

CHAPTER EIGHTEEN

"Don't move," said a voice. "It'll hurt if you do."

He did, and it did. He thought he went away for a moment.

"Can't say I didn't warn you," grunted the voice.

He was an island of pain, out of which rose mountains of agony. His face felt huge and swollen, like a balloon overfilled with water. He tried to speak, but his lips wouldn't work properly and the only sound that emerged from the awful ruined unknown country of his mouth was a faint sigh.

"At least you're not dead," the voice said. "Although they did try. I'm Theresa Abbot. This is my husband, Paul." A vaguely-sensed presence on the other side of him. "You're at our place and you're safe. For the moment, at least."

He couldn't open his eyes. Or maybe he could. Maybe he already had and he was blind. It hurt just to breathe.

"I'm not going to tell you how badly you're hurt," said Theresa's voice. "That can wait; you'll find out yourself, soon enough. Rest now."

Panic overtook him. He tried to raise his arm and the pain swept him away.

* * *

"HELLO." THERESA'S VOICE. "Are you awake?"

Truth was, he was no longer certain, but he managed to force his right index finger to stir slightly in response.

"Good. Okay. We're going to sit you up a little bit and it's going to hurt a lot, but you need to eat something. All right?"

He thought about it, softly grunted.

"I'll take that as a yes. Okay. Here we go."

Strong hands grasped him under the armpits – her husband? what was his name? – and lifted him. The mountains of pain shifted and there was a great ringing noise in his head.

When he came back to himself, he was sitting up, his back supported by something soft. "You don't have to do anything," said Theresa. "I'll hold the mug. Here comes the straw."

A smell of something hot and meaty below his nose. Something gently slipped between his swollen lips. He sucked gently, was rewarded with a teaspoonful of broth. He swallowed, choked a little. The straw was withdrawn, replaced with a softly-dabbing cloth.

"Again?"

He grunted and the straw returned. He sipped again, this time managed to swallow without mishap. The broth tasted very good. He sipped again.

"Not too much at once," said Theresa. "That's good." She let him sip the broth for a while in silence. "I'm sorry this happened to you."

He tried to turn his head and open his eyes to look at her, but the pain was too great.

"Just eat," she said. "Paul found you out on the road. I expect they left you there to die, if they didn't think you were dead already. You picked a bad time to come here."

He let the straw slip from his lips and managed to murmur,

"Horse." The effort of that single syllable seemed almost impossible.

"You had a horse? Well, that's gone, I'm afraid. And any gear you had, too. I'm sorry."

"Who?" It was barely an exhalation, let alone a question.

"Who did this? I don't know. Right now it could have been anyone. Had enough?"

He took a final swallow of broth, let the straw fall from his lips, and relaxed back against the pillows, exhausted.

"I don't know who you are, and I don't know what you're doing here," she told him. "I'm going to assume for the moment that you're not here to do us any harm because we're taking care of that quite nicely for ourselves. So you're welcome to stay, so long as nobody finds out you're here."

This seemed an odd thing to say, but he was too tired to unpick it. He managed to whisper, "Thank you," and fell asleep.

HE LEARNED, BY cautious experimentation, that if he lay very still, propped against the pillows, he could minimise the level of pain. Cautious experimentation also revealed that his chest was tightly bound and that his left forearm – a flaring knot of pain if he moved too abruptly but a sullen throbbing ache if he remained motionless – was splinted. His face was too painful to touch, but he brushed his fingertips across it enough to establish that it had taken on a new and frightening shape and that he now had the nose of a stranger.

In time – he had no idea how long it took – the swelling of his eyelids subsided enough for him to be able to open his eyes, and he found himself looking at a small, neat bedroom with cheerful curtains and an oak wardrobe in one corner. He looked at his arm, splinted with lengths of wood, and his bandaged chest. He managed to lift the covers enough to see the bruises covering his legs.

"Where are you from?" Theresa asked him one day, sitting by the bed while he ate a bacon sandwich one-handed.

"I'm just passing through," he said.

She looked at him for a long time. She said, "Do you remember what happened?"

"Some people stopped me and told me to get off my horse. That's all."

"Would you recognise them again?"

He thought about it, shook his head.

"We used to get on all right round here," she said after a few moments. "The people round here are good people."

"Not convinced," he said. "Sorry."

"I don't know the full story. A chap from a farm a few miles from here came home one day with a crossbow bolt in his gut and three dead boys in his wagon. One of the boys was the son of another farmer. Nobody really knows what happened because Max – that's the wounded chap – Max has been at death's door ever since."

Adam thought of the antibiotics he'd been carrying, wondered where they were now.

"Things were quiet for a few days," she went on. "Then all of a sudden everyone was shooting at each other."

He'd ridden into a war. He put the half-eaten remains of his sandwich down on the plate resting on his knees. "This has nothing to do with me," he said. "I'll be leaving as soon as I'm able."

"That could be a little while," she told him.

"How long have I been here?"

"A week."

He was overdue returning to Blandings. "And no one's been through looking for me?"

Theresa shook her head. "Not that I know of. Not that they'd have got very far; the Lyalls and the Taylors have more or less cut us off from the outside world."

Someone from Guz would be arriving at Blandings soon, if they hadn't already. A detachment of Marines, probably, with a senior officer from the Bureau, tasked to debrief him about Thanet. Betty would tell them where he'd gone, and then things here could only get worse.

"I need to get word to someone," he said.

"Were you not listening? There are almost seven hundred armed people wandering around the countryside, shooting at anything that moves. The few of us who haven't taken sides have barricaded ourselves in our compounds until they either come to their senses or wipe each other out. Have you finished this?"

He looked at his sandwich, not feeling remotely hungry any longer. "Yes. Sorry."

Theresa took the plate and stood up. "You need to get your strength back."

"I know. Sorry."

After Theresa had gone, he settled cautiously back against the pillows and stared at the wall beyond the end of the bed. Getting out of here was going to be no problem. Being physically able to before someone turned up looking for him was going to be more difficult.

THE NEXT DAY, there was no word of heavily-armed strangers marauding through the area calling his name. Or the next. Paul, a tall, rangy, taciturn man in early middle age, periodically visited some of the other farms to talk with other families, returned with no news.

Paul and Theresa's farm was one of the smallest in the area; just fifteen people living in a little compound, jumpy and heavily-armed at all times in case either the Taylors or the Lyalls suddenly took offence at their non-aligned status.

"I keep wondering if this was there all the time, under the

surface," Theresa told him as she joined him on a walk around the compound one day – as much to make sure he didn't overdo the exercise as for the conversation. "The Taylors and the Lyalls have been friends for years, but it makes you think."

Adam, for whom the family and interpersonal politics of the Taylors and the Lyalls were irrelevant beyond the fact that they were keeping him stuck here, grunted and kept loping along. "You said people died."

"Max is still alive, as far as I know. At least, nobody's heard otherwise."

He paused and tried to catch his breath. His broken ribs still hurt and his face was still a grotesque landscape of swelling and bruising and cuts, but he was feeling stronger every day. His arm... well, he could *use* it, but he had a sense that the break wasn't knitting as well as it might. That was going to be a problem.

"How many people did you say? Seven hundred?"

"At least. Could easily be more; we don't exactly keep an accurate headcount."

Now he thought about it, that was actually quite a lot of people for such a relatively small area. That many people would have been lost in Thanet's drenched landscape, or the hundreds of square miles controlled by Guz. He looked around the compound, the high wooden wall that had kept out wild animals and wilder people for decades, the house and its outbuildings and extensions.

"I really have to get out of here," he told her.

"You're not nearly well enough yet."

"I can walk."

She gave him a long-suffering look.

"I've done this before," he said.

"With three broken ribs, a broken arm and borderline concussion?"

Well, there had been that time in Cornwall... He scowled.

"I'd have got our doctor over to look at you, but someone shot her. *That's* what this place is like now. I can't force you to stay. I'm not going to tie you to the bed and lock the door. But for Christ's sake be sensible."

He took to walking round the farmyard every day, doing circuits of the wall. At first he got curious looks from the farmhands, but soon nobody paid him very much attention beyond nodding hello. Everyone had other things to worry about. No one dared go outside to tend to the fields; they'd brought as many of their sheep and pigs inside the compound as they could, but a lot of their livestock was now wandering the countryside, fair game for anyone who felt like some chops.

At night, he lay awake staring at the ceiling, still unable to turn on his side because his ribs and arm hurt too much. Sometimes he heard gunfire in the distance. When he did sleep, he dreamed of Margate and Frank Pendennis's patient expression as he asked about Gussie. He dreamed about the cave covered in seashells, the place where he put bad people until they stopped being bad. The smell in there had been like a punch in the face.

"Sounds a rum old place," Paul said, when he described Thanet to him.

"Thing is, it works," Adam said. "Frank's getting things done. There aren't enough people there to do everything at once, but he's fixing up the town, running farms, going out into neighbouring towns and stripping them for supplies."

"We get things done," Paul pointed out. "With about a quarter of the effort and none of the unpleasantness." He glanced at the window. "Used to, anyway."

Adam shook his head. "You and Frank, you're doing two different things. You're farming, you've put down roots. Frank's thinking about *conquest*."

"Why?"

"I don't know. Because that's what he does; it's the way he is. His family's been pushing out into the countryside for years, absorbing farms and little communities. And the Wealders have been doing the same."

"Sounds to me," Paul said, "as if everyone in Kent is fucking mad."

"You've kept yourselves to yourselves ever since the start of the Long Autumn," Adam said. "Bunch of little farms hidden away in the countryside, making do, surviving. That's not enough for Frank. He wants more. He wants civilisation, and he wants to be the one running it."

"Civilisation got us in this fucking mess in the first place."

Thinking that, like the people he had met in Wales, the farmers of the Parish believed there had been a nuclear war, Adam said, "No. It was a comet. A broken-up comet."

Paul looked at him. "Oh, I know that. Know it's what people say, anyway. No, I didn't mean that. We were too reliant on *civilisation*. I've read about it. Motor cars, aeroplanes, electricity, *television*. Can you imagine television?"

Adam could – and had, on occasion – but he couldn't see what purpose it had served, apart from transmitting news across great distances, and anyway it had been among the first things to go when The Sisters came and it had never come back.

"We were soft. *They* were soft. Didn't know what to do when *civilisation* went away."

"This is not the way Frank is thinking," Adam said. Or Guz, for that matter. Or, now he thought about it, Betty Coghlan.

"Frank or the Wealders come here, we'll give them some trouble," Paul said.

Adam opened his mouth, about to give his little speech about Frank rolling over the Parish as if it wasn't there, but he thought better of it. "You've got to sort out your own trouble first," he said.

Paul nodded. "Aye," he said. "You know the history of this area?"

Adam shook his head.

"Story is that years and years ago, before the Romans came here, the whole country was covered in forest, pretty much, from the south coast all the way up to Scotland. Dangerous place, full of wild animals and scary things. It was safer to travel on the high ground, where the tree cover was thin."

"The Ridge Way."

Paul nodded. "You do know about it."

"I heard some stories."

Paul laughed. "That's all we've got left, stories. Anyway, folk round here call it the oldest road in the world. Traders used it to transport goods down into Dorset and up into East Anglia." He got up and went over to a bookcase and took down a large old book with a tattered cover, handed it to Adam. "That's all the civilisation we need."

The book was full of colour photographs of a neat, tidy, tamed landscape quite unlike the one beyond the wall around the Abbots' compound. It seemed impossible that the country had once been like this. In most of the photographs the sun was shining and the sky was blue, full of fluffy white benign clouds. He turned a page and saw a photograph of a series of stones arranged in the middle of a clearing.

"What's this?"

"Wayland's Smithy," Paul said, glancing at the book. "It's really an old tomb, but the story is that Wayland the Smith lives there. Sort of a god of mischief and horseshoes. The Saxons named it – a lot of people have been down this way and settled, down the years."

"I saw a signpost for it, not far from here."

Paul nodded. "It's a few miles along the ridge. You're in Oxfordshire by then, or near as makes no difference these days. Anyway, that makes my point, really. That tomb was thousands of years old before the Saxons ever came here and put a name to it. People have made a life for themselves here for a very long time and for a lot of that time they didn't need cars and television."

Adam smiled. "Your god of mischief and horseshoes sounds as if he would have liked television and cars."

CHAPTER NINETEEN

ROSE'S FATHER HAD died when she was sixteen. He'd cut his hand while working in the yard and he'd washed and cleaned the cut and bound it up and for a few days everything had seemed fine. Then he came down with a bit of a temperature and after a day or so he seemed to fight that off. Then it came back and he couldn't keep any food down, and a few days later he was gone.

She remembered her father as a big, strong man. Max wasn't nearly as strong as he was; he got through life on common sense and charm rather than physical presence. But he refused to die. He was unconscious – had been, more or less, since he'd come back – and his temperature was frightening and his breathing was laboured, but he hung on. Rose didn't know how much longer she would be able to stand it.

She and Nell sat shifts by his bed. At least, that was the plan; in reality Rose stayed with him most of the time, even when Nell was there.

"You need to get some sleep, Ma," she said one evening.

Rose shook her head. "No."

Nell came round the bed and held her hand, and together they sat looking at Max, who was snoring almost loudly enough to mask the wet rattling noise his chest was making.

The door opened and Patrick looked into the room. "Ma?"

"Bugger off," Nell snapped. "Don't you dare come in here."

Rose reached out and put her hand on her daughter's arm. "What is it, Patrick?"

"The little ones are playing up. They won't go to bed."

"Well, why don't you sort it out, big man?" said Nell.

Rose squeezed her arm. "Nell. You go and take care of them, lovey. I'll stay with your father."

Nell glared at Patrick for a few moments, then got up and left the bedroom, brushing past him.

He caught up with her on the stairs and took her arm, propelled her complaining down to the kitchen and closed the door behind him.

"What's wrong with you, you stupid fucker?" she hissed, punching him in the chest. "Haven't you done enough damage?"

"Look," he said quietly. He turned and opened a cupboard and took out a black metal flask.

"If this is one of your stupid games, Patrick..."

"It's the antibiotics Faye sent for," he said. "For dad."

She looked at the flask. The name *Taylor* was written on the side in bright orange paint. "When did they get here?"

"Just now," he said. "One of Betty Coghlan's hands brought them."

"You're lying," she said. "I can always tell. Where did you get them?"

"Someone just brought them," he protested, but she could see there was something he wasn't saying. "I don't know what to do with them; Ma could just throw them away if I give them to her."

Nell looked at him, and for a moment, under the shell of bravado that he had put around himself, she saw a frightened little boy. Looking around the kitchen, she saw a rifle leaning against the wall by the door. Not like any rifle she'd seen before. "What's that?"

He didn't take his eyes off her. "What's what?"

She pointed. "That thing. Where did that come from?"

He looked over his shoulder, trying hard to be nonchalant. "Betty's bloke brought it for us."

She walked over to the door and stood looking at the gun. "What have you done, Patrick?"

"I've got the antibiotics dad needs," he said, suddenly angry. "Do you want them or not?"

For a moment – just for a moment – she almost said no. Almost told him to take them away and throw them down one of the composting toilets in the yard, let his conscience suffer for whatever he'd done. Except his conscience wouldn't be the only thing to suffer. "Silly sod," she said, taking the flask from him. "I'll give them to dad." She uncapped the flask, looked at the vials inside, the syringes in their packages. More valuable than anything in the world. "When she goes to bed."

"Do you know how?"

"It'll be in Ma's medical books. I'll look it up." She sighed. "Where did you get them, Patrick?"

"Betty's bloke," he said, but he wouldn't meet her eye.

"Fine," she said. She closed the flask, hefted it in her hand. "I suppose it's too much to hope that you're going to stop being a twat now."

"About what?" He straightened up, and the frightened child was gone again.

"I know Harry Lyall was here, trying to make peace. And I know you threw him out."

He snorted. "You sound like old John."

She punched him in the shoulder again. "If you had half the sense you were born with, you'd listen to Mr Race."

"I'm not the one that started this, Nell. I didn't kill Faye. The Lyalls are killing our people out in the woods because dad killed

Rob. You want me to just stand by and do nothing about that?"

"You deserve to get yourself killed," she told him. "I'd shoot you myself if you weren't my brother. Fuck, I'd do it anyway if I thought it would do any good."

He leaned forward and said quietly, "Dad's hurt, Ma's... you've seen what Ma's like, John's just *weak*. Someone's got to stand up for this family."

She turned away from him and started to walk across the kitchen to the door. "I'm just hoping that there's going to be a family left to stand up for."

THE TWENTY OR so farms and homesteads in the Parish were scattered in a rough square about four miles on a side. The Lyall farm was in one corner, the Taylors in another, and around them was a complex web of family and allegiance going back, in some cases, all the way to the early days of the Long Autumn. Most of the farms mucked in together and helped each other out when necessary, but in general those closest to either compound had the strongest ties, with eight or ten stuck in the middle. No one had ever done a proper headcount, but Harry reckoned there must be around a thousand people in the Parish.

"Oh, Harry," said Catherine Wright. "What the bloody hell do you think you're doing?"

Harry almost found himself saying, 'we didn't start it,' and then remembered that they had. Or seemed to have.

"I don't know, Cat," he said instead. "That's the truth."

"We had Patrick Taylor here this morning," she said. "Same sodding reason you're here."

He looked at her. He'd known Cat Wright his whole life, they'd played together as kids, their families visiting each other, and now he felt like a stranger. He'd felt that way with the other families he'd visited today.

"I don't want anything to do with this, Harry," she said.

"This thing between you and the Taylors is between you and the Taylors; it's got nothing to do with us."

Of all the farms in what Harry was starting to think of as the no-man's-land between himself and the Taylors, the Wright farm was the largest, almost a hundred people living around what had once been a ranch-style executive home but was now a scatter of buildings and smaller holdings.

"That isn't going to last, Cat," he said. "Unless this thing stops soon, everybody's going to get dragged into it, one way or another."

"So make it stop."

"I tried."

She grunted. "Heard about that. What Patrick needs is a good slap. I told him that, when he was here."

They were sitting in the living room of the main house, looking out across the farmyard at outhouses and smaller buildings through windblown curtains of drizzle. Cat's hands and family were going about their business, doing repairs, looking after animals. It was a scene of such normality that it made Harry's heart ache.

He said, "You've talked to him. You know he won't stop. He won't listen to anybody, not even John Race. He'll keep poking and prodding at anyone he thinks is siding with me, and they'll poke and prod back. This is going to go on for years."

"You could apologise."

He blinked at her. "For what?"

"For what Rob did."

"I don't know that Rob actually *did* anything, Cat."

She gave him a long-suffering look. "See how easy it is, Harry? They're wrong, you're right. And they're sitting up there at the farm thinking they're right and you're wrong."

"I'm sorry, Cat, I'm not going to apologise for something that might not have been our fault in the first place. Rob's *dead*."

"Well, until one of you backs down, this business is just going to go on and on." She shook her head. "Bloody men. Where's Rose in all this?"

"John says she's sick too. Patrick's running things."

She snorted. "John Race always was a balless waste of space."

"He's a good foreman," he said. "And if I'm any judge at all, he's one of the few people round here with any sense."

"He's letting a sixteen-year-old boy push him around."

"His gaffer's son," Harry pointed out. "Backed up by all the other hands."

"You're starting to whine, Harry. Be a man and stop this stupidity."

"So you don't have to make a choice?" She gave him a hard stare, but this time he stood his ground. "What are you so afraid of, Cat? Having to choose between us or the Taylors? Easier to tell someone else to sort it out than get involved, right?"

"I should punch you about a bit and then throw you out, Harry Lyall," she told him. "But I'm not going to do that. You lost your boy and you're angry about that, and your family wants some kind of revenge for it. And Max is probably going to die, and the Taylors are angry about that, and their family wants some kind of revenge for it. I don't see how any of that's my business."

"Did you tell Patrick that?"

"I might have used some different words, but yes, pretty much."

"And how did he take it?"

She got up from her armchair and went over to the window. "He said the time was coming when we'd be involved anyway, whether we wanted to be or not. He said it was better if we made a choice now, while there was still time. We might lose fewer people that way than if we were caught between the two of you." She regarded him sourly. "It's a little boy's argument, and it's the same argument you're using, Harry."

"I just want your help, Cat. That's all. We've always helped each other out."

She shook her head. "The business with Faye Ogden, that lost you a lot of friends. I know you didn't order it, but that doesn't matter because everyone else thinks you did."

The truth was, Harry no longer had any clear idea what had happened. Why would Walter have done such a thing? And if it wasn't him, who was it? And Cat was right. It didn't matter. It was like having a lightning strike kill all your sheep and then wondering what caused the lightning. The sheep would still be dead; you had to deal with it.

He said, "Please, Cat. Maybe if we all get together, Patrick will see sense and stop this."

Cat shook her head again. "He's got maybe a third of the Parish on his side – the Lakes, the Tomlinsons, the Cybulskis – not to mention his own family. He's a little boy, Harry. He wants to win."

"He's a little boy with a lot of guns."

She turned her back on the window, the scene of normality that Harry knew was going to become a distant memory very soon. "The best thing you can hope for is that Max pulls through."

WENDY, HIS FOREMAN, was waiting out in the yard. She fell into step beside him as he walked over to the stables to collect their horses.

"Well?" she said quietly.

Harry didn't say anything.

Wendy sighed. "The hands want to help out," she said. "Some of them, anyway."

Harry shook his head. "They won't do anything unless Cat tells them to, and I wouldn't want her to. I don't want to cause her trouble with her own people; she's going to have enough trouble soon as it is."

In truth, most of the families he'd spoken with had felt the same, a sense of quiet horror about what was happening in the Parish, an unwillingness to become involved. At the Fenton farm, he'd found Colin and Louise Fenton and their hands loading wagons. "Going to stay with Colin's brother in Goring," Louise told him. "Sorry, Harry, but we've got kids." She didn't sound remotely sorry, and he couldn't blame her, but he had an awful feeling in his heart when he thought about what would be left of their farm if they ever did come back.

At the stables, two of the Lyall hands, heavily armed, were waiting to escort them back home. After the initial flurry of massacres, the war had settled down into a series of skirmishes in the woods and the fields, hit-and-run ambushes between families he was increasingly finding he had no control over. It was all slipping away from him. Nobody would listen to reason; he was rapidly being forced into a corner where he would have to fight, simply in order to defend what his family had taken so many hard years to build. It had crossed his mind, watching the Fentons preparing to flee, to do the same, but that wasn't really an option. The Lyalls and the Taylors had been in the Parish a long time, since before it had been the Parish. Neither of them was going anywhere.

Wendy had done a quick inventory of their available weapons. Mostly crossbows and hunting bows, a few shotguns and sidearms. They had enough ammunition to last weeks under normal circumstances, but there was no telling how long they'd have to stretch it. Late one night, Harry had sent two hands out with a wagon to travel to Robert Mason's, up by Wycombe, to trade for more. They'd returned several days later with less than half the supplies he needed and the news that the Taylors had been there first and virtually stripped Mason's stock of firearms. The same with the other weapons traders in the Chilterns. He'd hoped that he could stop this by appealing to reason when he should have been arming himself, and now it was too late.

He was learning to see the Parish with new eyes. For decades he and his family had been used to being in control. They had one of the biggest farms, they took care of a lot of people, and it had given them the illusion of being in control. But they'd been wrong. *He'd* been wrong. When push came to shove, he was no more in control than anyone else. He had no right to order people about, and even if he did, they weren't of a mind to pay him any attention. They *wanted* to fight. Years of hard life in the Parish had piled grievance up on grievance, small petty things that under normal circumstances would not have mattered much. Until an excuse came along to act on them. He had started to think that, beneath the surface of good-hearted cooperation, the people of the Parish actually hated each other.

Meanwhile, there was much to do at home. He increased patrols in the area, warning them not to fire unless fired upon and knowing that was a forlorn hope. He had the undergrowth around the compound cleared, reinforced the wall. He took to walking circuits on the parapet, looking out over what had, until recently, been home and now seemed like an alien landscape. He started to stockpile food and water.

Approaching the Lyall compound, the drizzle stopped and the sun broke weakly through the clouds, and Harry said, "Looks like the weather's starting to pick up."

"Don't kid yourself, Harry," said Wendy. "It's going to get a whole lot worse from now on."

CHAPTER TWENTY

THE ABBOTS' HOUSE was packed with books, more than he'd seen in one place, even in Guz, where the libraries had been raided for flammable material to keep people warm in the first terrible days of the Long Autumn. There were novels by long-forgotten authors, encyclopaedias, guidebooks, recipe books, biographies, technical manuals for devices whose purpose seemed as remote and mysterious as that of Stonehenge. Hardbacks, paperbacks, books without covers and covers with all but a few pages missing. A whole lost world. He looked through them with the curiosity of someone researching an extinct tribe.

"They never stood a chance," Theresa told him one evening, sitting by the fire in the scullery. "All that technology and power and expertise, and The Sisters just took them by surprise."

"Life will do that," he said. "Every time."

"They thought it could happen," she said. "We've got a couple of novels here about it somewhere. Comets, asteroids, diseases, nuclear war. They weren't stupid; they just weren't ready. Or maybe they just stuck their heads in the sand."

Adam, who now had a better sense of what was going on in

the area, refrained from pointing out that Theresa and Paul and quite a few of the other farmers were currently sticking their heads in the sand. Sometimes it seemed to be the only rational choice.

"They had a thing they called 'nuclear winter'," she went on. "Do you know what nuclear weapons are?"

There had been nuclear weapons in Guz, in the early days, aboard one of the submarines caught in port by the disaster. When order, of a sort, had been restored, there had been much debate about what to do with them. Adam didn't know what conclusions the Committee had come to; there were conflicting stories. One said the warheads had been removed, taken out into the Atlantic south of Ireland, while they still had fuel for the destroyers, and dumped into the sea. Another said they were in storage somewhere, carefully maintained against the day when they might be needed again. He thought that was unlikely, but you never knew.

"It was really a catch-all term," she said. "A nuclear war, or a massive volcanic eruption, would send huge amounts of material into the sky and block out the sun for decades. Crops would fail, billions would starve. It happened before. Maybe a few times. Just a second." She got up and went over to the bookcase and took out a book, leafed through it and came back to sit down.

"About seventy-five thousand years ago there was a big volcanic eruption in Indonesia – that's way over on the other side of the world somewhere." She read a little. "Scientists before The Sisters thought it caused a nuclear winter that lasted at least ten years, and cooled the entire world for another thousand." She looked at him. "They thought things could have been so bad that the world's population went down to about ten thousand people. Imagine that." She closed the book and laid it in her lap. "They weren't sure; this was all a theory. But imagine that, the human race almost becoming extinct."

For Adam, everything before The Sisters was impossibly remote. He couldn't imagine living in the world portrayed in Theresa's books. It sounded ridiculously crowded and pretty. It might as well have been fictional.

"We were lucky," she said. "We didn't get a nuclear winter; we got a nuclear autumn. Eighty years of autumn. And that was bad enough."

He thought about his conversation with Betty, that night at Blandings.

"They thought a comet impact wiped out the dinosaurs," she said.

"The what?"

Theresa shook her head. "Doesn't matter; you can look them up, if you're interested. We were lucky. Lucky the comet didn't arrive all in one big piece, lucky it didn't cause a nuclear winter, lucky so many people died, because there wouldn't have been enough supplies for everyone if they hadn't. It's all luck."

He said, "I'm going to leave tomorrow."

She nodded. "I've been thinking you've been getting ready to do that."

"I can't thank you enough for what you've done for me, but I have to go."

"Oh, I'm not bothered about that." She got up and put the book back on the shelf. "I'm bothered about you going out there. More people died last night. Paul says there was a firefight about a mile from here."

He'd heard the shooting. "I do this a lot," he said. "Running away from people. It's easier than you'd think."

She thought about it. "If you head south until you reach Lambourn, you should be okay. I'll get Paul to put some stuff together for you."

"You don't have to do that."

"Oh, shut up. I'm not letting you go out there without as much as a map and a sandwich. You should go early."

He nodded. "That would be the preferred option."

"Right," she said. "Well, we'd better all get some sleep, then."

"Theresa?"

"Yes?"

"Why did you take me in? With all this going on? It would have been easier just to leave me."

She shook her head. "That was never going to happen."

BUT HE DIDN'T sleep. He lay staring up at the ceiling, turning the decision over and over in his head. He wasn't worried about slipping away from the madhouse this little corner of Berkshire had become; getting out of Thanet had, in the end, been perfectly straightforward, and he'd had the whole of Frank's army looking for him. No one even knew he was here. He could be in Goring in four days or so, back at Blandings early next week, and then he could ask what the fuck people were playing at. He was a month overdue; someone should have come to find him by now.

He heard quiet voices outside in the yard, below his window. He got up, lifted the curtain, saw three figures in the moonlight walking across the compound towards the wall. They were all armed, but that was a given, and they didn't seem alarmed or in a hurry, but something about their body language made him go and put his boots on, come back and open the window a fraction.

Now he could hear a voice calling, outside the compound. The three figures – one of them was Paul – reached the gate and climbed the steps up to the parapet. One of them called back.

There was shouting, but he couldn't hear the words. Looking down, he saw Theresa step out into the yard, a big coat wrapped round her.

He turned from the window, pulled on a jumper and his coat, and went downstairs and out the open front door. The shouting, from the people on the parapet and whoever was outside, was louder out here, but he still couldn't make out what they were shouting about.

"What is it?" he said, drawing up beside Theresa.

She was shivering, hugging her arms about herself. "I don't know."

More shouting from outside – much more shouting, it sounded as if there were dozens of people out there – and there was an almighty thud and the gate shook. Adam turned to Theresa. "Go back in the house and lock all the doors."

The people on the parapet started shooting down at whoever was outside; there were answering shots and one of the figures on the wall staggered back, caught their heel on the footboard, and cartwheeled down into the yard. Theresa screamed and started to run towards them as the gate shook again, and again. Adam heard splintering noises, more shouting, more shots. The Abbots' hands were running in all directions, completely lost to panic. Adam grabbed one by the arm as she went past. "Get out of here," he told her. "Get over the wall and make a run for it." But she just pulled away from him.

He went round the compound, trying to get the hands to flee instead of standing stupidly in front of the gate. One of them gave him a spare shotgun, but he had no intention of waiting around to use it. Everyone who stayed in the compound was going to die; from the noise outside the wall it sounded as if they were outnumbered at least two to one. He looked for Theresa but couldn't see her. The gate rocked again, and a long splinter of wood split off it and whined off into the darkness. People were still up on the wall, firing down on their attackers and then ducking down to hide, but it didn't seem to be making any difference.

Adam ran back across the yard, around the house, and up the steps on the wall at the back of the compound, saw the tops of two ladders poking up from the other side. Popped up, fired a shot, ducked down, pumped the shotgun, popped up, fired again. Looked over the wall. Two figures were sprawled on the ground outside.

There was a crash at the front of the compound. Looking around the house, he saw the gate come away from its hinges and fall into the yard, followed by a tide of people, all of them shooting. He hesitated for long moments, then put his leg over the wall and slid down one of the ladders.

At the bottom, he searched the two bodies for weapons and ammunition, came up with a crossbow and another shotgun and a couple of satchels.

As he turned and slipped away towards the trees a few hundred yards away, he smelled burning.

CHAPTER TWENTY-ONE

THE ATTACKERS LEFT after a few hours, and when the sun came up, he cautiously made an approach and went back up the ladder and over the wall.

Everyone was dead. Smoke was breathing from the broken windows of the house, farm equipment and furniture and clothes and personal possessions were scattered all over the yard. He found Theresa lying face down near one of the sheds; Paul was by the gate, half-trodden into the mud, his chest crushed and a crossbow bolt in his throat.

Adam did a slow circuit of the farm, hoping to find someone alive but knowing he wouldn't. Stood in the middle of the yard looking about him, at the bodies, the smouldering house.

The attackers, whoever they had been, had used a big tree trunk mounted on a cart to break down the gate. It sat just inside the yard, abandoned. He walked round it, touching the ropes that bound the trunk, his mind perfectly blank.

The attempt to torch the house had been hurried and amateur, burning for burning's sake, vandalism more than anything else. They'd managed to do little more than char some furniture. He found food and clothes and equipment, a sawn-off twelve-bore and cartridges, and an ancient revolver that looked as if it had been military issue long before The Sisters. Going round the yard and searching the bodies, he found dozens of shells for the pump-shotgun.

He should have left, but he couldn't. He hid out in the woods for a few days, keeping a watch on the farm. In time, some locals turned up and poked around and left. Then they came back and buried the bodies. Then some more came and stripped the farm of anything useful. Except the books. They left the books.

Peace, of a sort, settled over the community for a little while, as if the massacre had shocked everyone back to their senses. Adam didn't hear shooting, anyway. He would probably never know why the Abbots had come under attack; someone offended by their refusal to take sides, or someone trying to scare the other nonaligned farms into taking part in the war, it didn't matter.

He cautiously scouted out the area around the farm, working further and further out until he found an old overgrown road with a rusting signpost toppled crazily in a nest of brambles. The sign said *Lambourn*. He looked at it for a long time. Somewhere in the distance, echoing in the damp air, he heard a gunshot. Then another.

He turned away from the road and went back the way he had come.

No one talked about what had happened at the Abbot farm. It was as if, by not speaking of it, it had never happened. It was not like the other massacres; the Abbots had been well-liked, and had been trying to stay neutral amid the madness which had overtaken the Parish. It was a shaming thing, and with the exception of a few scavengers, the people of the embattled little farms and homesteads avoided the wreckage.

In the aftermath, some of the families who had tried to stay out of the escalating war rethought their position and decided they were probably safer under the protection of either the Taylors or the Lyalls. Ronnie and Sue Chapman's family were among them, and they found themselves walking patrols around the Lyall property.

It was actually quite fun. Ronnie was fourteen, Sue a year older, a solemn, quiet girl with auburn hair and freckles. They'd both grown tired of being cooped up in the family compound, and it was exciting to be given crossbows and responsibilities, although Ronnie kept being embarrassing by taking potshots at rabbits and then having to go and find the crossbow bolt.

Eventually, even that began to pall. They grew tired of trudging through the mud and undergrowth for hours in the drizzle. The crossbows were heavy and they made their arms hurt. It would have been nice to go home and get warm and have a biscuit and a glass of milk, but they were afraid of what Mr Lyall might do to them if they abandoned their duty.

"Boring," said Ronnie, who had taken to holding his unloaded bow by the stirrup at the front end and dragging it behind him.

"Don't you dare break that, Ronnie Chapman," Sue told him. "You'll get a slapping from Mr Lyall if you do."

The boy unwillingly gathered the bow into his arms. It was almost as big as he was. "Stupid," he muttered.

Sue glanced at her brother, dressed in a rain poncho two sizes too big for him, hugging the crossbow to him. She sighed.

"What's that?" Ronnie said.

Sue was suddenly alert, scanning the area around them. "Where?"

"There." Ronnie pointed and dropped his bow. "Bollocks."

Sue looked around, saw nothing. "*Where?*"

"*There,*" he said, waving a hand in a general way as he bent down to pick the bow up.

Embarrassing. Sue took a couple of steps forward, her own bow raised to her shoulder, and saw a flash of red between two trees a hundred yards or so away. She took a couple of cautious steps to one side and sighted through the bow's scope. The optics were old and not very good. She could make out what seemed to be a tall figure wearing a red coat and a red balaclava standing against a tree. She watched for a minute or so but the figure didn't move.

"What is it?" Ronnie said. "Let me see."

She shook his hand off her arm. "Be *quiet*." She took another few steps forward and looked through the scope again. The figure still hadn't moved. It suddenly occurred to her that her heart was beating hard in her chest. They'd been told not to engage anyone they saw, to come and find an adult and raise the alarm, but there wasn't any harm in making sure first. "Follow me," she said. "And be bloody quiet."

Together, they worked their way cautiously through the undergrowth, Ronnie crashing along and muttering and at one point dropping his bow again. When they had a clear line of sight again, Sue stopped and dropped to one knee and looked down the scope. The figure wasn't tall, as she'd thought at first, and it wasn't wearing a red coat. It was standing against the tree with both its arms raised above its head, and it seemed to be wearing a red shirt under its opened coat.

"Someone's got them standing at gunpoint," she reported quietly.

"Can you see who?"

"Not from here. Let's try to work our way around to the side."

This time, Ronnie seemed to get the idea, moving behind her with exaggerated care until they were level with the tree. Sue examined the scene, could see no one else. She shifted position, looked again, saw nobody.

She stayed where she was, thinking. Ronnie fidgeted beside her and she hissed for him to be quiet. She looked through the scope again, and saw a fox emerge from the bushes, walk right up to the standing figure, sniff its feet unhurriedly, and then walk away.

That was what decided her. "Stay here," she said, standing up.

"Fuck that," said Ronnie.

"Do as I tell you," she said. "And don't swear; you know dad doesn't like it."

She stepped forward slowly, alert for any movement at all, anything out of the ordinary, but there was nothing. She heard Ronnie following a few yards behind, and she sighed.

The figure was a man, and he was standing with his arms over his head because someone had crossed his wrists and nailed them to the tree. He wasn't wearing a red shirt and balaclava, either.

The two children had seen dead people before, but this was something different, and they stared at the body for some time before Ronnie noticed a piece of board lying on the ground near the base of the tree. There were letters scratched on it, but neither of them could read.

"Who is it?" Harry asked.

"We don't know," Wendy said. "Someone cut his face off, there was nothing on him that we can identify. He could even be one of the Taylors' men."

"Let's hope not," he said. "I'd hate to think any of us would do that." The Abbot massacre hung, noted but unmentioned, between them for a moment. "Are we missing anyone?"

"I'm asking around, but everyone's missing *somebody*, Harry."

He sighed. "How are the kids who found him?"

"They're fine. Down in the kitchen having a bowl of soup."

Children... "Whose bright idea was it to give kids bows and send them out on patrol, Wendy?"

"I don't know." She looked uncomfortable. "The Taylors..."

"I don't give a flying fuck what the Taylors are doing." He sat back and ran his hands through his hair. "Jesus fucking Christ, Wendy. This thing is bad enough without us using children. No one under seventeen's to go out on patrol. Starting now."

"Harry..."

"No one under seventeen, Wendy. I'm not having children killing each other."

"But it's okay if *we* do it?" she asked deadpan.

He gave her a long, level look.

"Just wanted to know if it's all right to shoot first if one of their fifteen-year-olds points a shotgun at me."

"Fuck off, Wendy." He looked at the board lying on his desk, reached out and picked it up. It was spattered with blood, but the word on it was clear.

"Maybe it was his name," Wendy suggested.

"Do we know anyone called Wayland round here?" he asked, tipping the board to the lamplight and examining the name carved deeply into it.

"There's Wayland's Smithy," she said.

He looked at her over the top of the board, then put it back on the desk. "No more kids with guns, Wendy. All right?"

"Yes, Harry." She turned and went to leave the study.

She'd reached the door when Harry said, "Saddle up a horse for me."

Wendy turned, her hand on the door handle. "Harry?"

"Saddle me a horse."

"You're not going out there on your own," she said.

"That was what I was thinking, yes."

"I'll come with you."

"You don't even know where I'm going yet."

"Doesn't matter; I'm not letting you go out alone."

"You're happy enough to let kids go round shooting each other," he pointed out.

She glared at him.

"I've been riding around here since you were three years old," he said. "On my own, quite a lot."

"You're being an arse, Harry."

"Yes," he agreed. "But it's my arse. Now are you going to get a horse ready for me or am I going to have to do it myself?"

"I should let you do it yourself," she told him. "Bloody fool of a Lyall."

IT WAS EASIER – although much more risky – to travel alone these days. A large group of armed people was obviously safer, but they also attracted a lot of attention and were more likely to come under fire. Harry kept to lesser-used paths and tracks, threading his way through woods and along the edges of old fields, took his time. He crossed his own property, made a meandering dogleg along the edge of the neighbouring homestead, and the next, and made his way, little by little, around Taylor territory.

Finally, he came to the Ridge Way. The old track looked deserted today; he'd heard that farmers and travellers from further east and west were cutting far to the south to avoid this part of the Chilterns.

Not to the north, though. He took his binoculars from his saddlebag and looked out across the Vale. Parts of Abingdon seemed to be burning; on its outskirts, he saw what he thought was a very large group of people marching down an old main road. It looked like things were no better down there than they were up here.

He turned the horse off the Way, walked parallel to it for a few miles until he came to an old overgrown glade filled with bushes and saplings. In the middle, almost hidden by weeds and overgrowth, was an old long barrow, a chambered stone tomb from the Stone Age. There had been legends about this place for centuries, how Wayland, the blacksmith of Norse legend, haunted the place and you could sometimes hear the sound of hammer ringing against anvil as he forged swords for the gods. There was a story that if you left a horse tethered here overnight, with a silver coin for payment, you could come back the next morning and find that Wayland had shod it for you.

"Shall we give that one a try, old son?" he asked, patting the horse's neck gently.

He got down, tied the reins to an overhanging branch, and looked around the glade. It was only a few miles from home, but he couldn't remember the last time he'd been here. He flipped back the hood of his coat, took his shotgun from the sheath attached to the horse's saddle.

There was no outward sign, at first glance, that anyone had been here in a very long time, but Harry was in no hurry. He walked around the tomb, keeping his eyes on the ground, noting where stalks of grass had been bruised underfoot and then sprang back, broken twigs on overhanging bushes, some of them too high off the ground to have been broken by wolves or foxes.

At the entrance to the tomb, the undergrowth seemed to have been pulled aside and then carefully put back.

"Hello?" Harry called. "Anyone home?" No answer. "I'm not looking for trouble." No answer again.

He pushed his way through the grass and bracken and brambles, down a corridor of waist-high stones, to a large rectangular hole. He called again, again got no answer, and ducked inside.

There was a little ring of stones on the earth floor, just inside the tomb, with a pile of ashes in the middle. Harry stirred a finger in the ashes, but they were cold.

Back outside, he did a circuit of the Smithy, then another a little further out, then a third. The fourth time round, he found a place where the undergrowth had been disturbed by a large creature of some kind but then rearranged to hide the fact that they'd passed through. He almost missed it. Following the path, he came on a place where a latrine pit had been dug and then carefully covered up with twigs and leaf litter. The fact that it had been covered at all should have been enough, but he poked around in it with a stick long enough to find human turds.

Back at the Smithy, he paused and looked about again. He was on the far western edge of the Parish here, a long way from any trouble. People mostly avoided the place, a vague superstition about Wayland keeping them away without being conscious they were doing it. That alone suggested that whoever had been living here was a stranger. He thought about the piece of board with the name carved into it, the corpse nailed faceless to a tree. There were few enough people round here who could read and write, and the thought that any of them could have done this made him shiver. He really hadn't known his neighbours, though. And that was the scariest thought of all.

CHAPTER TWENTY-TWO

MAX'S BREATHING IMPROVED, his temperature fell – although not by much and he still wouldn't wake up properly. Nell watched her mother moving as if in a dream, sitting red-eyed and tousle-haired beside the bed. It had been days since she had washed or changed her clothes and she seemed constantly on the verge of toppling over. No one could remember, exactly, when Rose had last left the house. The place seemed haunted by her.

It was left to Nell to take care of the day-to-day running of the house, making sure the kids were washed and dressed, making sure they got ready for bed in the evenings, reading stories to them, sitting up with them when gunfire woke them in the night. She saw less and less of Patrick, and braced herself for the day when she would never see him again.

When he did make a rare appearance at the house, slumped silently at the kitchen table, eating cold roast chicken with his hands or simply fast asleep, his clothes were torn and awry and his face was smeared with dirt. He didn't want to talk, which was fine by Nell because she didn't want to have a conversation with him.

One morning, though, she went down into the kitchen and found him standing there, shotgun in hand. He looked as wild-eyed and haunted as his mother. "You've got to come and see this, Nell," he said.

"I'm not going anywhere with you," she told him. "I've got breakfast to get ready."

He stepped forward and took her arm and started to urge her towards the door. "You've got to see this."

She shook herself free. "What's wrong with you? Look at the state of you."

"Nell," he said urgently. "Come *on*."

She sighed and grabbed a coat from the hook behind the door and followed him out into the yard.

If there was one thing the war had brought to the Taylor homestead, it was order. The place had always been amiably disordered but still capable, like her father, but now it was obsessively neat. Everything was squared away, tools in sheds and animals in their pens and outhouses. Everywhere, people were moving with a purpose, repairing equipment, cleaning weapons. Over in the forge, Alan Curtis the blacksmith was making crossbow bolts from old lengths of rebar. It was not, Nell realised with a sinking heart, her home any longer.

To one side of the compound, a small, heavily-barred door in the wall led through into a brick-walled herb garden where four hands were standing guard. Beyond that was another door. Patrick opened it and stepped aside to let her through.

"Oh!" She put her hands to her mouth.

Years ago, Max's father had dredged out and extended the little pond that lay adjacent to the property and stocked it with carp he'd traded for. Carp basically cruised the bottom of ponds eating rubbish and turning it into protein; Nell had never liked the muddy taste of the fish or the thousands of fiddly little bones, but the pond and its self-sustaining food source had been her grandfather's pride and joy, and after him it had been her father's.

Now the pond was still in the morning light, its surface carpeted with motionless glistening bodies, some of them of a considerable size.

Patrick walked up and stood beside her and together they looked at the vista of dead fish. Dotted here and there were the corpses of ducks.

"Jesus," she murmured.

He held out an ancient cardboard box with words she didn't recognise printed on the side. The top was open, and she could see the torn ends of clear sachets.

"Weedkiller," he said. "There's hundreds of these things over there." He nodded along the side of the pond, where she could see a considerable pile of boxes. "Someone did it last night. Must have taken them hours. Poured this stuff into the pond right under our noses and watched our fish die."

She couldn't process what he was saying. "Weedkiller...?"

"There's an old B&Q over to Wantage," he said. "There's not much left, it's been stripped of everything useful. I was over there a couple of months ago with dad to see if we could find something. There's tons of this stuff." He shook the box. "It's no use to anybody so it's just sitting there." He bent down and picked something up off the ground, a length of board with the word WAYLAND carved into it. "This mean anything to you?"

The carving looked fresh. She shook her head.

He threw the board away. "If this stuff seeps into the well, it'll make people sick," he said. "We'll have to find a new source of water. Fucking Lyalls."

She shook her head again. Ambushing people, shooting them, that was something she could understand. This was different. It felt... wrong. "I don't think the Lyalls did this," she said. She looked at the board lying in the grass.

"It's exactly what I'd do," he said. "Force us to leave the compound at regular intervals, slow-moving carts loaded with barrels. Sitting ducks."

She looked round, saw the guards from the herb garden had followed them out and were standing watchfully behind them. For a moment, she felt a wave of dizziness, of not knowing where she was.

"How's dad?" Patrick asked, and his voice seemed to come from a great distance. "Nell?"

She rubbed her face, took a breath, came back to herself. Was this how Ma felt all the time? "I don't know," she said. "He's stopped getting worse."

"You've been giving him the antibiotics?"

"Of course I've been giving him the antibiotics. Jesus." She turned to him. "If you came back now and again, you'd see how he is for yourself."

He looked out over the pond.

"How do you think Ma's going to feel when you get yourself killed?" she asked more gently.

Patrick looked at the box in his hand. He pitched it into the water and turned back towards the herb garden.

FROM COVER ABOUT four hundred yards away, he watched through the binoculars he'd taken from Paul Abbot's study as the boy went back into the compound. The girl stood where she was by the pond, looking out across the carpet of dead fish. The dynamic between them was interesting; they were both angry, but their body language suggested they were angry about different things.

The wall around the compound was impassable, old shipping containers, no way to cut or break through them. They were interesting; he hadn't seen anything else like that round here, and he wondered where the containers had come from and how they'd been brought here.

He'd spent two days familiarising himself with the Parish, finding boltholes and bivvies in places that seemed out of the way and overlooked. The farms and holdings were locked down and guarded, the countryside full of armed patrols. He moved among them like a ghost, silent and unseen, watched them take occasional potshots at each other. None of them seemed to know what they were doing; they were making up with frantic enthusiasm what they lacked in experience. According to the Abbots, bandits sometimes wandered into the area, looking for easy pickings – fewer these days than in the past, but still – and the farmers got together and either drove them off or killed them. But that was different. This was a form of warfare, and the farmers had no idea what they were doing. The only people who seemed remotely competent were the Taylors. The boy had a natural talent for leadership, and that made him dangerous. He thought back to long dull lectures on insurgency, a lifetime ago in a place impossibly distant. Back then he was being taught how to counter insurgent tactics, but the lessons applied just as much to him now.

THAT NIGHT, HE descended once more into the Vale. The weather had picked up and there was a moon, and he moved carefully down an overgrown road to the outskirts of Wantage and the old store where he had found the weedkiller. There was other stuff here he wanted, stuff that had been overlooked when the store was looted because no one could see any use for it at the time.

The town had been abandoned, but not all that long ago. Someone had been living here; many of the streets had been cleared of cars and rubbish, some of the larger supermarkets had been fortified. There was no way to tell for sure when whoever had been living here had moved out, maybe a couple of years, maybe longer, and there were no signs of why they might have gone. Maybe, like the family Betty had told him about, they had simply exhausted the resources here and moved on to pastures new.

Hearing a noise, he moved quietly off the road and into the

weeds and vegetation to one side, found himself in what had once been someone's lovingly-tended front garden but was now a dense tangle of brambles and overgrown shrubs.

Someone, or something, was coming up the road in his direction. As they drew closer, he heard the sound of boots on the crumbled tarmac, the swish of scythes cutting back the decades of overgrowth. Interesting that they were doing this at night, when the countryside was full of packs of feral dogs and most sensible people travelled as quietly as they could.

The noise drew alongside his position, and he moved slightly to get a view of the road, saw figures passing in the distance, completely silent save for their boots and the sound of their scythes. In the moonlight, he counted more than thirty of them, dressed in all-weather gear, their hoods up despite the fact that it wasn't raining. They didn't seem to be paying any attention to their surroundings other than concentrating on their work, and in a few minutes they were past him and gone. He waited a few minutes to make sure they weren't coming back and there was nobody bringing up the rear, then he retraced his path to the road.

The broken surface of the road was strewn with chopped-up vegetation, crushed by dozens of feet. It was rather impressive; a cart could have driven along here with not so much trouble. The road led up onto the escarpment of the Berkshire Downs, where it crossed the Ridge Way. He thought about that for quite some time. A lot of people could travel en masse along this road now, if they had a mind to.

NELL COULD STILL remember when the farm was an adventure, a place full of discovery and happiness. She remembered playing hide-and-seek with Patrick among the outbuildings in the compound. It only seemed like last week. Now all that was gone, and Patrick was out playing another kind of hide-and-seek. That, of all things, was what she could never forgive them for. Destroying her memories of childhood.

She looked into the bedroom. Her father was still feverish, his skin grey and hot, but she thought the antibiotics were having some effect. She'd had an armchair brought up from the parlour, so her mother could sit by the bed, and Rose was dozing, lost in some awful half-awake state where she would jerk into full consciousness at the slightest noise from Max.

The room was littered with the paraphernalia of Max's sickness. Bowls of water, damp cloths, piles of clean bedding. It took four of them to wash Max and change the bed, two of them just to turn him. Every day, they managed to get half a bowl of broth into him, spoonful by agonised spoonful, Max sitting up and only barely conscious. At the beginning, he had thrown them back up, but for the past few days he'd been managing to keep his food down. Still, the room smelled of sick, and Nell wondered if that smell would ever go away.

Downstairs, everything was quiet. To counteract the chaos upstairs, she tried to keep everything down here tidy. It was one of the few things she had any control over. A pair of old six-gallon plastic kegs, their blue surfaces scuffed and dented, sat over by the door. Mr Race had made a deal with one of the neighbouring farms which had a well to let them have fresh water, and Patrick had come back from a trip into Wantage with a wagon full of empty barrels, which sat outside collecting rain. It wasn't nearly enough, but it would have to do. There had been some discussion about what to do about the poisoned pond. Patrick wanted ditches dug, to drain it out into the neighbouring fields. Mr Race had pointed out that that would only spread the poison more widely. Patrick said it could be years before they could trust the water from their well any more. Mr Race said the damage was already done. In the end, nothing happened. Everyone was too busy going through the countryside killing Lyalls or anyone who associated with them. And the Lyalls were killing Taylors and their friends. Every death sparked another. It would not stop until they were all gone.

Thing was, if you talked to people individually, none of them wanted this. They expressed shock and horror at what was going on, said they hoped someone would find a way of stopping it. Get them in a group, though, and the mood changed. Everyone had lost someone, they wanted revenge. It was as if they reinforced each other.

Nell checked the water level in the kegs, stood at the kitchen window looking out at the darkness, remembering when it had all seemed safe and secure. That felt like a lifetime ago.

She took her coat from the hook on the back of the door and went outside. The rain had stopped, and the night air was cold enough to make her nose itch. She nodded hello to a couple of people crossing the compound to one of the other buildings, and made her way over to the wall.

Her mother had told her the story of how her grandfather and his friends had built the wall, back in the early days of the Long Autumn. The Taylor farm – it had been the Lakin farm, back then – had been here before The Sisters but the old farmyard had not been defensible against the bands of marauding refugees from London and other parts of the country, so her great-grandfather Lakin had gone out and looked for a quick solution. There had still been petrol and diesel back then, and engines that could run them. They'd found big, strong vehicles – 'heavy plant', Rose called them – and they'd raided a railway freight yard, got the container handling machinery working and loaded the containers, one by one, onto lorries.

Nell had sometimes tried to imagine what it had been like, those huge lorries – it was hard to picture what they must have been like, but she imagined enormous hulking machines with smoke coming out of them – making their way through the rain and the hail towards the Parish, the men fighting off looters as they went.

It had been a colossal enterprise. The roads were still in good condition back then, but they were choked with people and other vehicles trying to get to who knew where, and even when they got to the Parish they still had to get the containers off the lorries and into position. You could still see, if you looked carefully and knew what you were seeing, the marks in the ground, almost a century old, where the containers had been dragged into place around the farm. Then their doors had been opened and earth piled inside.

The 'heavy plant' had been driven some distance away on their last drops of fuel and then abandoned. Max had taken her to see them once, when she was little, but she couldn't make head nor tail of the great rusted masses of metal half-reclaimed by weeds and undergrowth. They looked as if they had been put there by careless gods.

Her great-grandfather had built another wall on top of the containers, a thick, shoulder-high wall of brick scavenged from a housing estate a few miles to the south, to protect people patrolling along the parapet. Later, a hole had been cut through the sides of one of the containers, and strong wooden doors fitted to make access to the walled kitchen garden.

All her life these high metal walls had kept out bad people and wild animals. Now, she thought, the bad people and the wild animals had been inside all along.

She walked across the yard to where a set of brick steps had been built alongside one of the old containers. She walked up until she could step out on top of the wall and look out across the darkened countryside.

Directly ahead, the track leading to the front gate of the compound ran straight through a little wood. Her great-grandfather and his friends had cut the track to bring the containers of the wall here, and they'd kept it clear ever since. The wood curved around half of the compound, about a hundred yards away, and between them was an area bare of undergrowth and vegetation, so no one could sneak up on them. There was still some hot-headed debate about how Doctor Ogden's murderer had managed to get so close to the gate without anyone seeing them, and even more about how they had managed to get away again. The general consensus was that the people on guard that day had been more than usually rubbish, and they deserved to be thrown out.

To one side, if Nell stretched up on her toes, she could look over the brick wall and see down into part of the walled garden beyond. And beyond *that*, lost in the darkness but making its presence known by the smell of rotting fish, was the pond. Patrick had told her not to bring any of the food from the walled garden into the house. He said it was probably contaminated as well.

At the back, the wall looked out over a vista of little fields and hedges, dotted with outhouses and animal pens. Nell wrapped her coat more tightly about herself against the chill and walked on.

Back at the gate, she started to turn and head back down the steps, but something in the corner of her eye made her stop and go back to the brick wall and look out into the wood.

For a moment, she thought she'd imagined it, but then she saw it again, a tiny spark of orange light moving between the trees. Someone coming to attack? No, surely not. Not carrying a lantern. Someone in need of help?

A couple of the guards on the wall had seen it too, and joined her to watch as the light bobbed along through the wood, almost as if it was floating along on its own. The light seemed to be rising and falling, dipping down to the ground and then lifting into the air again as it moved forward.

"Will O' The Wisp," said one of the guards. "Fairy folk. My ma told me about them."

"Oh do fuck off," said the other, momentarily forgetting that his boss's daughter was standing with them.

Nell barely heard them. She was watching as tiny flickers of light appeared on the ground along the edge of the clearing. They grew larger and brighter, and then with an astonishing *whoosh* that made everyone on the parapet take a step back, one of them leapt up the trunk of one of the trees. Then another. Then another.

It was impossible to understand what she was seeing, a wall of flame bursting out of the ground, illuminating the entire front of the farm. She could almost feel the heat, hear the roaring of the trees burning from the base of their trunks to their canopies. It was as if the whole wood was on fire, burning up, consuming her life.

THE NEXT MORNING, some of the trees were still smouldering fitfully, their trunks charred and their scorched branches bare of leaves.

"Well," said Mr Race, standing beside her and looking at the scene. "I don't know what would make a wet tree burn like that."

The air was full of the smell of burning wood and leaves, but under it was another smell, sharper, almost unnatural. Nell went over to one of the trees and ran a finger along its charred bark. There was some sticky residue there. When she sniffed her finger, she smelled that unnatural smell again. She went to wipe the finger on her coat, thought better of it.

"Where's Patrick?" she said.

Mr Race shrugged, and that told her all she needed to know. Off somewhere, killing Lyalls. She couldn't remember when she'd seen him last. Yesterday morning? The day before?

"I honestly don't know," Mr Race said again, looking at the trees. "If I didn't know better, I'd say it was lightning."

"It wasn't lightning," she told him. "Someone was out here last night and they set fire to the trees. I watched them do it." That bobbing, supernatural flame moving along through the wood...

"Lyalls wouldn't do this," said Mr Race. "I don't think anyone round here would know how. I certainly don't."

First the pond, now this. It was as if there were two wars going on: the one she understood and the one she didn't. The war she understood was just people wandering through the woods and shooting each other, attacking each other's farms. The one she didn't understand, *this* one, was different. It was being fought on completely different terms, she sensed.

She turned from the screen of charred trees and started to walk back to the gate. Mr Race looked at the trees for another few moments, then followed her.

"I want you to bring some people in from patrol, Mr Race," she said. "Set them to patrolling around the compound." If Patrick wasn't here to do this, she was going to have to do it herself. "I don't want them going into the woods or the fields, only around the wall."

Mr Race thought about that. "Yes'm," he said – he couldn't quite bring himself to say 'miz' – that was her mother.

"If they see anything out of the ordinary, anything at all, they're to raise the alarm. Nothing else, just to raise the alarm. I want you to make that very clear to them. I want people inside the compound ready to go out at all times."

"Yes'm."

She looked at the wall as they approached the gate, the great metal containers her great-grandfather and his friends had brought here so long ago to protect his family. *Her* family. No one had been hurt last night, but all of a sudden the wall didn't seem so strong any longer.

As she reached the gate, she looked along the wall and saw something half-hidden in the grass, leaning up against the streaked metal of one of the containers. She walked over to it and saw an old board – something from a fence maybe, or a bit of floorboard from one of the abandoned houses that littered the Parish. She bent down and picked it up, knowing before she even touched it that there would be a single word carved into the wood.

"Mr Race," she called.

He was standing at the gate, waiting to be let in. "Yes'm?"

She went over to him, the board in her hands, and showed him the carving. Mr Race couldn't read, so she said, "Have you heard of someone called Wayland?"

He frowned at the board. "There's Wayland's Smithy, away down on the west side."

She remembered her mother telling her the story, now. Wayland the demon smith, with his forge. Her father said it was just an old tomb, from thousands of years ago, all overgrown now. It wasn't really all that far away, but she'd never been there.

"Is there a family called Wayland?"

He shook his head. "Not round here, at any rate."

"You're sure? Nobody with an old grudge against us?"

He shook his head again. "Nobody's got a grudge against you."

She tipped her head to one side.

"Not an old one, at any rate," he added. "Is that what it says? 'Wayland'?"

She turned the board over in her hands, looked at the back. Both ends were jagged, freshly-broken. "Could you ask around, please? See if anyone else knows the name? Perhaps it's someone from over Goring way. Maybe dad got in a fight with them."

"Your dad never got into a fight with anyone," he told her. "Not since he was a boy, anyway."

"Maybe it's this Wayland who attacked him and killed Rob Lyall and those other two boys," she said.

He looked at her, and she knew she was grasping at straws. Even if someone from outside the Parish had started all this – even if she could somehow convince Harry Lyall of it – the people here weren't going to stop. Too many had died already. Nobody was going to back down now.

"Just ask," she told him. "Please."

CHAPTER TWENTY-THREE

MORTY MOVED THROUGH the increasingly-fraught landscape of the war he had helped to start as if it was not there at all. He felt quite at home in the chaos, a lone figure slipping unseen across a drenched patchwork of fields and woods and dense vegetation. It was as if he was invisible, invulnerable.

He no longer resembled the Morty Roberts who had left his home for the last time all those days ago. His clothes were filthy and torn, his hair matted, his skin covered in dirt. The only thing that remained was the Morty Face, looking trustingly out on the world, always ready to help, always ready to take whatever abuse the world and those in it presented to him and shrug it off.

He'd long ago stopped trying to keep count of those he killed. He was well into double figures now, he thought, and still the howling anger behind the Morty Face wasn't satisfied. It wouldn't be satisfied until everyone in the Parish was dead, everyone who had mocked him and patronised him and pitied him and abandoned him.

But he wasn't alone. He'd become aware, in recent days, of

something else at large in the Parish, another predator who moved through the countryside in much the same way as he did. He'd seen its handiwork nailed to a tree near the Lyalls', and it had pleased him.

He took to keeping an eye open, as he ventured out on sorties, gunning people down – Lyall, Taylor, whoever, it didn't matter – from a distance or close up with bursts from the machine gun. They were always unprepared, surprised, like little children playing at soldiers and finding a real soldier in their midst. The people of the Parish were acting on old angers and grudges, stored up over many years. Everywhere he went he saw signs of the predator – the *other* predator. The Taylors and the Lyalls and the others missed the signs because all they saw was another dead body, but Morty knew. It was like being able to identify an animal from the bite-marks it left on its prey. Like recognises like.

One night, heading back to what he was increasingly thinking of as his stronghold, Morty experienced a presentiment so profound that it made him halt in his tracks, standing absolutely still. He stayed that way for so long that he thought perhaps he was having a stroke or something, but then he heard something moving through the undergrowth a few yards away.

He didn't move, not even his eyes. He didn't see what it was, just heard a soft, confident tread in the leaf and twig litter on the ground, an almost-inaudible rustle of bushes being moved aside as something passed by. Morty himself was standing in a dense patch of undergrowth almost as tall as he was, invisible, barely breathing. He let whatever it was pass by, waited a minute or so, then set off silently in pursuit.

The quiet sounds from ahead of him led to a clearing close to a farm compound. In the middle of the clearing sat a brick outhouse. Morty saw a big, bulky shape pass along the wall of the outhouse, and at first he thought it was some fantastical creature, a thing out of legend. Then he realised it was just a man with a large rucksack strapped to his back.

The figure moved round to the door of the outhouse and stooped, doing something Morty couldn't make out. The door opened, and the shape went inside. A few moments later, it emerged and it was a different shape, slimmer, more agile, the rucksack gone.

It started to move towards him, and Morty froze, just barely fighting the urge to flee, but it passed by, just a few yards away and disappeared into the woods.

Morty had just begun to breathe again when the figure returned, this time dragging something heavy. There was no haste in its movements, just a careful plodding walk. Morty couldn't see what it was dragging, but it was large and it made a lot of noise as it passed through the undergrowth, but the black shape didn't seem to care. It was, like him, entirely outside time, invulnerable, intangible.

It dragged whatever it was dragging into the outhouse, and then went back into the woods, came back a few minutes later dragging another large object. It did this a number of times, and then there was a pause when it didn't emerge.

Morty was just about to move around to get a better view of the doorway of the outhouse when the figure reappeared. It was moving more quickly now. It dropped something to the ground. And then it started to run flat-out back into the woods the way it had come. Morty spent a couple of seconds processing this development, then he too turned and ran, off at a tangent, as fast as he was able.

He'd got quite a distance from the outhouse when there was a huge flat concussion behind him and the woods all around lit up. A huge, soft, hot hand pushed him off his feet and pitched him face down into a patch of brambles as hundreds of small heavy objects hurtled overhead and thumped into trees, dropping to the ground all around him.

He lay there for a few moments. The flash had ruined his night vision; everything was just a huge damp blackness that smelled of freshly-disturbed earth and broken vegetation and scorched meat and a sharper, more acrid and unnatural smell that he couldn't indentify. He closed his eyes, opened them again. Did it again, and this time he could make out enough detail in the darkness to stand and make his way uncertainly from the farm, while behind him shouts rang out through the woods.

"WELL," SAID HARRY.

"It happened last night," said Gracie Farr. "I was out in the yard and I saw this huge flash and heard a bang."

"Yes," Harry said. He'd heard the bang, too, thought it was thunder but it had sounded too flat, had echoed all wrong across the sleeping countryside. "Accident?"

She snorted. "We haven't run a brew since this fucking stupidity started; the fires were out."

They were standing in a clearing a few hundred yards from the Farr compound. As well as farming, the Farrs operated a distillery that made a particularly potent form of potato vodka. Gracie's grandfather had found all the copper vessels and piping in a microbrewery in Lambourn years and years ago, had built himself a little brick house to put them all in.

The little building was gone now, almost from the ground up. There were bricks scattered all over the area, for hundreds of yards – one had gone through the Farrs' roof. Branches and foliage had been shredded off the trees around the clearing, their bark scorched and chewed and some smaller saplings snapped entirely, and in the middle sat a broken, blackened square of concrete outlined by a jagged line of broken brickwork not much more than shin-high. Harry looked up and saw a copper pressure vessel sitting in the branches of a tree. There were bits of broken, twisted piping everywhere.

He walked across to where the distillery had stood, considered the ruined concrete square of the floor, looked around the clearing. He walked over to the other side and squatted down on his haunches, looking at something half-buried in the disturbed leaf and twig litter. He found a small branch and poked around experimentally.

Gracie came over and stood beside him. "Is that someone's foot?" she said.

In the end, they found four feet, but three of them were left feet. They also found, in the woods beyond the brewhouse, five arms, a leg minus a foot, and one ripped and bloody female torso impaled on a branch halfway up a tree.

"*This* is a hell of a thing," said Wendy.

"Mm," said Harry, looking at the body parts arranged on the ground beside the devastated distillery. "Have we found any heads yet?"

"Still looking." Wendy shook her head. "How fucked up do you have to be to lock people up in a building and then blow it up?"

Harry gazed around the clearing, ringed by armed guards in case the Taylors or some of their allies turned up. He had a sense that it was impossible to stop this now; even if he and the Taylors made peace tomorrow, there was enough enmity between the other holdings to last another hundred years.

"No glass," he said.

"What?"

"Gracie and Tim kept a stock of empty jugs and bottles in the distillery, but there's no glass anywhere."

She stared at him. "Harry. Really?"

"Yeah. I know. Not the worst thing." He stuck his hands in his pockets.

"If the Taylors have got their hands on explosives, we're in trouble."

On the other hand, if the Taylors had got their hands on

explosives, why not use them on the Lyall compound instead of... this...? He saw one of the hands on the other side of the clearing reach down and lift what looked like a piece of wood out of the leaf litter, look at it, and drop it again.

"See if you can work out who's missing," he said, starting to walk unhurriedly across the clearing. "Ask around and see if anyone's got an idea where the explosives came from."

"Well, *that's* an easy one," she said, following him.

He shook his head. "Betty wouldn't let them do this."

"Coghlans and Taylors go back years," she said. "You know the story."

"Yes, I do, and I know Betty well enough to know she's far too sensible to be arming the Taylors. Let's not drag Blandings into this, Wendy; we're in enough trouble as it is."

"What if you're wrong?"

He stopped and looked down and poked at the rubbish on the ground with the toe of his boot. "Bury what's left of these poor people at the farm. Whoever they are."

"Okay."

After Wendy had gone, Harry looked down again at the bit of wood lying on the ground. It was scorched and shattered, but it was still possible to see the letters *ay* carved into it.

THE WEATHER BROKE. Squalls of rain and sleet battered the Chilterns, rushing away up the Vale of the White Horse, harbingers of the monsoon storms which still lay a month or so in the future. Everywhere, farmers and homesteaders battened down for the approaching autumn. Everywhere but one small corner of the Hills.

More or less entirely cut off now, either by the efforts of its own people or by locals who shunned it, the Parish seemed to have dropped out of the world, become a hermetic pocket of violence. Word of what was going on there had spread as far as

Goring and Lambourn, and no one in the outside world wanted any part of it, as if there was a sickness there and they were afraid of it spreading.

Within the ad hoc boundaries, firefights and assaults went on daily, in rain and wind and hail. As resources dwindled, livestock and crops were plundered by both sides. Farmsteads were besieged and broken, their families executed.

And through all this moved Wayland, a dark faceless fear. Wayland could come into your compound in the middle of the day, into your house, and slit your throat without anyone ever seeing him. He could poison your animals just by looking at them. He worked for the Taylors, he worked for the Lyalls; he existed, he did not.

He'd been lucky with the explosive; some of the ingredients, scrounged from abandoned farm supply stores and the old do-it-yourself supermarket, were over a century old, and he was working from the memory of a long-ago field weapons course during which the instructor had said casually, "Of course, you'd have to be crazy to actually *try* any of this, sir, but you might as well know it, just in case." It was a miracle he hadn't blown himself to bits.

It was actually pathetically easy to move about the area, at night or during the day. The farmers were so busy killing each other that they didn't notice a lone figure moving through the undergrowth; if they'd actually put aside their differences and started to pay attention to finding him, he'd have been dead days ago.

He drifted through the embattled landscape, scrounging food and gear from abandoned farms. Sometimes there was ammunition, left behind in a hurry and overlooked by later visitors, but not so often. He had a sense that the war was reaching a tipping point. He never stayed in one place more than a few hours, snatching sleep where he could.

Strangely, he felt good. He'd reached a sense of clarity where all other priorities had been rescinded, where the time before he had ridden into the middle of this mess seemed distant and dreamlike. He was a point of concentration, dimensionless. Sometimes it was an effort to remember his name.

He went back to the Abbot farm, from time to time. The locals had seemed to shun the place after looting it of anything useful, whether from shame or superstition he didn't know. It was a safe place to lay up for a night, anyway. Someone – someone decent in the midst of the madness which had overtaken the Parish – had taken the time to bury the bodies of the Abbots and their people, and he stood by the graves without a thought in his head. No one knew he was here; if the people who had attacked him on that first day remembered him at all, if they'd somehow survived the war this long – if he hadn't killed them himself, along the way – they'd assume he was dead. He was a ghost, an avenging spirit.

HE FOUND THE two men sheltering from a rainstorm in the lee of an old brick outhouse, part of an abandoned farmstead which had been absorbed by the larger, neighbouring one. They went for their weapons when he appeared in front of them, but he subdued them with blows from the butt of his shotgun, gagged them, bound their elbows behind their backs and their knees with short lengths of rope, looped more rope around their necks, and urged them through the undergrowth to the site of his latest demonstration. They didn't make any trouble. Perhaps they thought a chance for escape would present itself. The older one tried to talk to him, in an exhausted voice, but he didn't respond beyond urging them on with pokes in the back from the muzzle of the shotgun.

It was only when they got to their destination – it wasn't far, he wondered how it hadn't been discovered yet – that they saw what he was building, and they panicked. The younger one managed to pull the rope out of his hand and tried to make a hobbling, shuffling run for it, but he shot him in the back. The older one just stood there and watched with sad eyes. He didn't try to resist, even when the rope round his neck was thrown over a branch and he was hauled up into the tree.

Everything had started to seem like a dream. Patrick couldn't remember the last time he had slept properly, or had a decent meal. He spent days out in the countryside with a group of hands, hunting down Lyall supporters, sleeping rough. He and his men moved across the drenched landscape like ancient warriors called back from a long absence to do battle against a modern evil. It was hard, now, to recall how many he had killed, how many of his family had died. It just went on, day after day.

Heading back towards the farm, one of the scouts came running through the undergrowth shouting, "Guv! Guv!" and for a moment he thought they were calling Max, that his father would step up and take over and make everything right again. But that didn't happen. They were calling him.

The scout led them along a track between two fields, an old farm lane that had slowly and patiently been reclaimed by vegetation. Sometime shortly after The Sisters, a sapling had started to grow here, at an intersection with another track, in defiance of the Long Autumn. Now it was almost fifty feet tall, a great gaunt monster of a tree. Patrick and his men walked up to it and stood there in horrified wonder.

Seven bodies were hanging from the branches of the tree, all of them bound and gagged. They swung gently to and fro in the wind and the rain. Patrick's mind refused to process what he was seeing. The Lyalls – or their allies, anyway – were prone to hang their captives, but not en masse like this, adorning a tree like some sick form of Christmas decoration.

"They're not all ours," said one of his men, looking up at the bodies. He pointed. "That's Neil Latham; he's with the Lyalls. And there's Connor Lyall..." His voice trailed away as one of the bodies turned slowly on its rope and they found themselves looking up into the darkened, suffused face of John Race. Patrick felt the world stagger a little, as if it had stubbed its toe and lost its footing momentarily.

When everything steadied, he was still standing there. John was still hanging above him.

"Guv?" said one of the hands, looking at him from the other side of the tree. Patrick walked around to him and together they looked at the single word freshly-carved into the trunk. Deeply and calmly carved, as if whoever had done this had all the time in the world.

"Cut them down," he said. "Bury them in the field there. And then I want someone to get word to the Lyalls."

WHEN EVERYONE HAD gone, Morty emerged from hiding. He walked over to the tree and stood looking up into the branches for a long time. He ran his fingers over the word cut deeply into the bark. This was marvellous work; the other, the predator, was an artist. Morty realised all of a sudden that all he had been doing was blindly killing, when he should have been doing something like this, sending a real message to the people who had abused him all these years.

He went over to the field where the bodies had been buried, considered the graves. It really was the most wonderful work.

CHAPTER TWENTY-FOUR

BACK BEFORE THE Sisters, there had been a village here. Not a big village – half a dozen houses and a little local shop, arranged around a village green with a duck pond. The houses had been abandoned for years, as everyone in the area withdrew into fortified compounds. The pond had flooded, over and over again, during the Long Autumn, and had overwhelmed the green. Now the deserted and ruined houses, at the confluence of four small roads, rose from the fringes of a large shallow lake.

There was a pub at the edge of the village, looted and burned by refugees from London in the early days of the disaster, a blackened shell almost submerged in bushes and small trees. It was, they had decided, the closest thing to neutral territory they could find.

Patrick arrived first, and spent some time scouting the village before ordering his men to pull back onto one of the old roads. Harry and about a dozen of his men turned up a few minutes later, and they too stopped just short of the pub. The two groups watched each other for a while, and then Harry stepped forward alone and Patrick went to meet him.

They reached the ruined pub and stood in what had once been the car park, in plain sight of both armed groups. Patrick had some kind of automatic rifle slung over his shoulder, something Harry didn't recognise.

"Harry," said Patrick.

"Patrick," said Harry, a little taken aback by the changes in the boy. He seemed almost feral. "You wanted to talk."

Patrick held out an old piece of board, the one he'd found by the pond the morning after all the fish had been poisoned. Harry looked at the word carved on it and nodded.

"So you know about this?" Patrick said.

"I've seen the name."

"Who is it?"

"I don't know. It's not us."

"Who the fuck is it, then?"

Harry shrugged.

Patrick walked to the edge of the car park and stood looking out across the lake.

"You didn't think it was us," Harry said. "Otherwise you wouldn't be here."

Patrick turned and said, "I –" and then he fell down into the bushes around his feet and for a moment, everything was perfectly calm and silent save for the crack of a single gunshot echoing flatly into the distance.

"Oh, fuck," said Harry. Then everyone was shooting.

Harry threw himself to the ground and elbow-crawled around behind a pile of tumbled brickwork. People were shouting, firing at each other, running from cover to cover. Someone jumped over the pile of bricks and landed right in front of him. They looked at each other for a dazed moment, then Harry lunged up, grabbed the barrel of the man's rifle, and punched him hard in the stomach. The man – Harry had no idea who he was – folded up, and Harry grabbed a brick off the ground and belted him round the head with it and kept hitting him long after he'd fallen and stopped moving. Harry searched his pockets hurriedly for spare ammo, then moved quickly away through the weeds and bushes around the pub. Popping his head over a broken wall, he saw two people standing thigh-deep in water at either end of the lake, shooting repeatedly at each other without success. A crossbow bolt banged into the wall near his face and whined off into the bushes, and he ducked down and duck-walked quickly through the weeds away from the ruins.

He made it to a screen of bushes and crashed through them into a dense stand of trees, turned, and lifted the rifle to his shoulder, but it all seemed to be over. There were bodies everywhere. The two people in the lake were both floating face down in the water. There was sudden movement out in the open, right in front of him, and someone he didn't know was running directly towards him waving a huge and very antique revolver. Harry shot him in the chest.

He emerged cautiously from cover, rifle at the ready. In the distance, two figures were running up the road away from the village as fast as humanly possible, and Harry couldn't blame them. The whole thing couldn't have lasted more than two minutes.

Patrick lay where he had fallen, a bloody hole in the breast of his coat and a surprised look on his face. Harry looked at the houses on the other side of the lake, then back down at Patrick. He looked like a little boy again, the way Rob had. All of a sudden, Harry didn't know what to do. It was out of the question to do the right thing, which would have been to take Patrick back to his family. Burying him was also impossible; someone would be coming soon, drawn by the gunfire or by those two people who had escaped. He dithered for long moments in the drizzle, remembering getting drunk with Max on the night Patrick was born. He remembered seeing Max the next morning, massively hungover and sheepish; Rose had given him hell. But he was still the happiest man in the world.

From far back in a bedroom of one of the houses overlooking the lake, he watched through the scope as the lone figure turned and walked back into the woods.

That had actually been quite gratifying. He'd taken the hunting rifle from the body of someone he had shot a few days previously, and the scope had been cannibalised from a crossbow. It was by no means the finest scope he had ever used, and he'd had to lash it to the rifle with string, but the shot hadn't been difficult. He hadn't been prepared for both sides to start blazing away at each other, though. That was a bonus.

He slung the rifle over his shoulder, picked up a shotgun, and made his way downstairs. Halfway down, he stopped and listened. He turned and went back into the bedroom and cautiously looked out through the broken window.

A horse was standing by the lake, its rider sitting comfortably and without fear, looking around at the scene of carnage. The rider was wearing a long hooded coat, and there was a long gun cradled in its arms. Its body language was quite unlike anything he had seen since he had arrived here. Utterly relaxed and without fear.

He reached into the satchel hanging round his neck and took out the pair of binoculars he had taken from Paul Abbot's study, uncapped the lenses, and raised them to his eyes. At the same moment, the rider turned to the houses across the lake and lifted its head, and he found himself looking, from a distance of maybe a hundred and fifty yards, directly into the eyes of Albie Dodd.

CHAPTER TWENTY-FIVE

IT STARTED TO rain hard as Harry got back to the farm. The hands, used now to his frankly suicidal wanderings around the surrounding countryside, opened the gate just far enough for him to slip through, then closed it again behind him. Wendy was waiting in the yard.

"We need to get ready," he told her. "It was a catastrophe. Patrick Taylor's dead. Everyone's dead."

"Oh, for fuck's sake, Harry," she said.

"They'll be coming," he said. "All of them."

She didn't know what scared her more, the news Harry had brought or the fact that he seemed completely lost, bewildered. She took hold of his upper arms and said, "Harry. Harry, listen to me. It will take them time to get organised. We have time."

He stared at her, and someone called, "Gaffer!" from the wall. They both looked round at the voice, and the hand shouted, "Someone's coming! Riders!"

They looked at each other. "It's too soon, Harry," she said.

He turned from her and ran up the steps to the parapet, heard her running after him through the rain. At the top, he looked over the wall and saw ten or twelve riders making their way unhurriedly down the track towards the compound. They were all dressed in long hooded coats and they were all armed with rifles and shotguns, and they moved as if they owned the ground their horses walked on.

"Who the fuck are *they*?" Wendy said.

For Harry, the day had long since stopped making any sense at all. If an army of elves had come down the track riding badgers, it would have seemed perfectly reasonable. He watched the riders reach the wall and stop. They all looked up at him.

"Who are you?" he said in a voice which didn't seem remotely strong enough. "What do you want?"

"We want Adam Hardy," called one of the riders, the one at the front of the group.

"*What*?"

"Adam Hardy. We know he's here."

"I don't know anyone called Adam Hardy."

The rider shook his head sadly and pulled back the hood of his coat. He was a bulky, shaven-headed man with a round face and the eyes of a murderer. "We know he's here," he said. "They told us at the ferry."

Harry turned to Wendy, who shrugged helplessly.

We're busy; we have things to do. "There's nobody called Hardy here," he called down. "Adam or otherwise."

The rider thought about that. "You see," he said, "I don't believe you."

"I don't give a flying fuck what you believe," Harry said, and it occurred to him that his voice sounded ever so slightly hysterical. "Who *are* you?"

The rider thought about that, too. "Friends of Adam's," he said. "Come to take him home."

"Are you *serious*?" Wendy said.

"Yes," said the rider. "Actually, yes."

"There's no one here called Hardy," she said. "Or Adam, come to that."

"No strangers?" the rider asked. "People passing through?"

Harry suddenly thought of Wayland and tipped his head to one side. "No," he said.

The rider smiled. "And I don't believe you again."

"People pass through here all the time," Wendy told him. "We've not heard of your Adam. He's not here."

All the time, Harry was standing in wonder that the riders could just sit there in the pouring rain with a dozen guns pointed down at them and *not care*. As if things weren't already bad enough. *Don't have time for this.*

"You'll have to go now," Wendy said.

"No, we don't," the rider said casually. "We don't *have* to do *anything*." He seemed, if anything, faintly amused to be sitting there in the rain and having this conversation. Harry felt his heart pounding in his chest.

"Your friend isn't here," he said.

"You know, we've come a long way," the rider told him. "It'd be nice if you let us in so we could have a bit of a rest before we carry on looking for Adam."

"Not going to happen," said Wendy.

"Not very friendly, are you," he mused. "I noticed you were having some trouble. Maybe we can help."

Harry didn't doubt they could. He also didn't doubt that letting them into the compound would be one of the worst mistakes he could ever make. "Your friend isn't here," he said again. "We don't know him, we haven't seen him, we haven't heard about him. Sorry."

"Eh well," said the rider. He ran his hand over his smooth, bare scalp. "We'll be around for a while. If you do hear about him, come and let us know. Yes?"

"Sure. Okay." By this point, Harry was prepared to promise anything at all so long as these strange and scary men – and they were all men, he realised – went away.

"All right, then," said the rider with a smile. "Be seeing you."
He flipped up the hood of his coat, took up the reins, and urged
his horse to turn away from the farm and back up the track.
One by one, the others followed him, and in a minute or so –
they were in no hurry at all – they were gone.

"What in fuck was that all about?" Wendy said.

But Harry was still looking down the track, his mind
somewhere else entirely.

THEY DIDN'T TELL Rose, not then. Max's fever had broken in
the night, and so had she. Nell came into the bedroom in the
morning and found her mother slumped half in her chair and
half across the bed, and for a second there was a thunderstruck
feeling in her heart that they had both died, that it had just been
too much for both of them in the end. Then she saw Rose's
shoulders moving as she breathed and a moment later Max
turned his head slightly and opened his eyes. "Hallo, Nelly,"
he said, and then he closed his eyes and fell asleep and she ran
downstairs to find Patrick.

But Patrick, of course, was nowhere to be found, so she got
her mother to bed and tried to keep the routine of the day going,
making the children breakfast, tidying the kitchen. Through the
kitchen window, from time to time, she saw another kind of
routine going on. Hands patrolling the wall, making repairs
to buildings and weapons, people returning from the outside,
wounded or worse. She thought no one knew who they were
fighting any more, or why. It just went on, incident after
incident, action and reaction.

Drying her hands at the sink, she looked out of the window
and saw the gate slide open a fraction and two men come running
through. They looked exhausted, as if they'd run a very long way,
but they seemed frantically excited too, shouting and gesturing to

the other hands who came running to them. They recounted, in what looked like quite a chaotic fashion, some story or other, and as the story reached its climax everyone around them turned and looked at the house, and Nell felt her heart die.

There was some discussion among the men in the yard, then two of the hands left the group unwillingly and started to walk over to the house. Nell watched them and willed that short walk to last for ever, because until she heard them say it, Patrick was still alive. They moved out of view and a moment later there was an unenthusiastic knock on the door, as if hopeful that no one would hear it. She neatly folded the tea towel she had been drying her hands on, draped it over the back of one of the kitchen chairs, and went to answer it.

THEY TOOK TWO wagons, and nobody said a word as they drove over to the village where Patrick had arranged to meet the Lyalls.

There were bodies everywhere. They walked through the village, turning corpses over, looking at faces, trying to decide which were Taylors and which were Lyalls. It was harder than Nell expected. Not all the faces were familiar; some were from outlying farms and holdings, people who had come from distant parts of the Parish to join one side or the other, either out of a sense of loyalty or out of fear of being isolated and caught in the middle, like the Abbots. She was tempted to just load all the bodies up and take them home, but there wasn't room in the wagon, and her hands wouldn't have stood for burying Lyall dead after what had happened here.

She found Patrick lying on his back in the weeds beside a ruined old building. For a moment, she didn't know him; so much of what had made him Patrick had only been present while he was alive. This empty shell was like a badly-rendered model of him, recognisable only by his clothes and his earring and the fancy gun still slung over his shoulder. Stolen, she suspected, from some other poor soul. She stood looking down at him and remembered them playing together as kids, remembered him giving her a toy for her seventh birthday, a rather poorly-carved wooden dog that he'd made himself. Bingo, he'd called it, a word he'd seen in one of Ma's old books. Bingo was still sitting on the dressing table in her bedroom, one of his back legs broken off during a particularly vigorous playtime. Patrick had tried to glue it back, but somehow it never stuck properly. She wondered why she didn't feel more sad, and realised she had given Patrick up for dead days ago. It had already happened, in her head, and she was only going through the motions now.

Some of the hands were going from body to body collecting weapons and ammunition, and that *did* make her achingly sad, seeing them stripping the dead like that. She knew they were short of stuff, but it was disrespectful. She knew they were better than that, or had been once upon a time, at any rate.

She knelt down and took one of Patrick's hands in hers. His hand was cold and stiff, the fingers clenched into a fist, and his arm wouldn't move. It was as if he was carved from wood.

And then she started to feel angry. She felt angry with Rob Lyall and those two unknown boys, with Harry Lyall, with all the people of the Parish who had taken up arms and refused to bring this madness to a stop. She felt angry, in the end, with Patrick.

So they loaded their dead – those they could identify - onto the wagons, and they drove off, and in time Morty Roberts came walking down the road, although by now he was staggering a little, and he looked at the scene of the slaughter, trying to reconstruct what had happened and failing.

He searched the bodies, but everything useful had already been taken. He found a lump of cheese wrapped in paper in someone's pocket, overlooked by those who had come before him, and he gnawed on it as he walked towards the houses on the other side of the lake.

He went through these too, carefully and methodically. It was obvious they had been abandoned for far too long for there to be anything edible here, but people had left behind many things when they tried to flee the Long Autumn, and sometimes he could make use of them.

In an upstairs bedroom of one of the houses, there were signs that someone had been there recently. Some of the furniture had been moved; there were lighter patches in the dirt on the floor where they had been originally. He looked round patiently, and eventually a dull brass shine half-under a chest of drawers caught his eye. He knelt and reached down and retrieved a spent rifle cartridge, lifted it to his nose, and sniffed. Recently fired.

After that, it was just a matter of checking amongst the rubbish piled everywhere in the bedroom, and there it was, a piece of board with a single word carved on it. He didn't know what it said, but it was the same word that had been carved into the tree from which the predator had hanged his prey. It was his mark, and it was beautiful.

Morty went to the window and looked out over the lake. He could see some of the bodies from here, crumpled and contorted or spreadeagled in the undergrowth. He took the spent rifle cartridge from his pocket and looked at it.

Wonderful work.

THE LIGHT, SUCH as it was, had begun to fail as the wagons made their way back to the farm. They had not seen the Lyalls, neither on the way out nor on the way back. The countryside, for the first time in days, was silent and still, save for the steady hiss of the rain.

Nell sat in the front wagon beside Anthea Reese, her brother's fancy new gun across her lap and his body and those of seven other hands covered in tarpaulins in the loadbed behind her. She watched the track unwind before her, emerging from the rain and growing dusk like a dream, and for a moment, when she saw the two mounted figures blocking their path, she thought that they too were a dream.

Anthea brought the horses to a halt, and the other wagon stopped behind them. Then everyone just sat there. The riders were large and bulky and they wore hooded coats and carried rifles. They made no sign of being prepared to move.

One of them pulled the hood of his coat back, revealing a bald head and a face with a mean little mouth. "Hello there," he called.

Nell's fingers curled slowly around the shotgun. "We don't want any trouble," she said.

"Neither do we," he said. "We're just looking for our friend. Adam Hardy. Do you know him?"

"No."

"He might just have been passing through." Nell thought there was something in his eyes like a predator weighing up a prey animal, a cool emotionless assessment. "You might have seen him."

"He'd have to be fucking crazy to want to come through here," muttered Anthea.

"Sorry?" said the rider amiably. "Didn't quite catch that."

"We haven't seen any strangers for a long while," Nell said. "Who are you?"

"Friends of Adam's."

"Where are you from?"

The rider smiled, a slow, small, sly and utterly disgusting smile, and he and his companion moved to one side to let the wagons by. As they passed, he sketched a mocking little salute at Nell.

"Scary cunts," Anthea said when they were clear, but Nell was already forgetting about the newcomers.

At the farm, a large group of people – more people than Nell had ever seen in one place before – had gathered, inside and outside the compound. Hundreds of them. They were all armed and they were all angry.

Nell got Anthea to stop the wagon just outside the compound, and she sat looking at Patrick's army – *her* army.

"All right," she said, almost inaudibly. "All right."

MORTY, SKELETAL AND filthy and almost entirely feral, picked his way across the rubbish-littered yard of the abandoned farm. He didn't know who it had once belonged to, and he didn't care. It was a long time since he had eaten properly; the chunk of cheese he'd found at the predator's latest tableau had barely even taken the edge off his hunger. He was moving in a dream, the exterior world unreal and drifty. He shot everyone he encountered; sometimes he killed them, sometimes not, it didn't seem to matter any longer.

The farmhouse had been looted and burned out, but a couple of chickens remained in one of the henhouses, had probably returned here after whatever had happened was over. He caught them quickly, wrung their necks, tied their feet together and slung them over his shoulder.

In the house, he found a couple of jars of dried meat. He popped a couple of strips in his mouth and chewed them, put the jars in his satchel. He was searching for more food, or anything useful, when he heard voices out in the yard.

Unslinging the semi-automatic – conscious that he didn't have a lot of ammunition left for it now – he went to one of the soot-smudged windows and peered out. Two men were outside, wearing long, hooded coats and cradling shotguns in their arms. Behind them, near the gate, two horses were tied up to a smashed wagon.

They didn't seem to be searching for anything, just wandering about, poking at bits of broken furniture and equipment lying on the ground. One of them looked at the house, gestured to the other. Neither of them seemed in the least bit nervous or worried. Morty thought they looked rather amused, cocky. They started to move towards the house.

When they were almost there, Morty stepped out into the open doorway and shot them both dead. He quickly searched the bodies for ammunition, went over to the horses and looked through the saddlebags, finding wrapped bread rolls, cheese, apples. He hadn't seen an apple since he was a boy, and he bit into it hungrily, the juice running down his chin and through his beard while he looked at the two dead men lying in the mud. They didn't seem local; something about their clothes and their body language was different. He wondered who they were.

He took out his knife, stooped down, pulled back the hood of the first body, and began to cut.

CHAPTER TWENTY-SIX

HE AND CHRISSIE had been stupid. They'd forgotten all about Eleanor's field equipment, presumed stashed and lost somewhere in Thanet. Frank's people had obviously found her radio at least, and had heard Chrissie giving him map references as she navigated him towards Blandings. All Albie'd had to do was follow him, and he doubted Albie had come alone.

The thought that it was utterly ridiculous to send people halfway across the country just to retrieve a gun and the person who had stolen it never occurred to Adam, because it certainly had not occurred to Frank.

How they'd got to here from Blandings was something he was going to have to worry about later. He could leave the area, head south towards the coast, hitch a ride back to Devon with one of the trading boats; he might even get lucky and find a boat from Guz in harbour somewhere. He could stay here, hide out and let them give up looking for him and go away.

Adam went to the window and looked out into the compound of the Abbot farm. Hail and sleet were battering down, the yard slowly flooding now there was no one here to clear it. Lightning was blinking in the clouds, answered by long slow rumbles of thunder. As he watched, a bedraggled sheep wandered across the yard and out through the broken-down gate.

There was a door in the corner of the kitchen. He'd locked and bolted it, but he needn't have worried; the locals were treating the place like a sacred shrine. He unlocked it, found a lantern, lit it, and went down the steps on the other side.

The cellar ran the full length of the house, ankle-deep in water now, jars and bits of rubbish floating on the surface. There were racks along one wall where Paul had kept his tools, and most of those were empty, stripped by the Abbots' neighbours the morning after the slaughter. At the far end, Adam hung the lantern on a hook in the wall and moved a stack of wooden crates until he uncovered a wheelbarrow full of bottles. He checked the seals, then shook the little plastic box of homemade fuses. All the time he was going through the two options. Slip away, head south. Stay and hide until the enforcers left. He kept seeing Rhoda's battered face, kept seeing bodies hanging from the gallows at the Clock Tower, turning in the wind and spray.

THEY HAD A rough perimeter around their camp, patrolled in pairs. He sat in a tree and watched them through his binoculars. It was hard to tell just how many of them there were, but he estimated over forty, maybe as many as fifty, which in one way was rather flattering but in another was just a demonstration of how Frank accomplished everything. Has someone offended you? Make an example of them by sending a ridiculous number of people to bring him back. Because you can, and because it will dissuade others from doing the same. He wondered how they'd got here; if they'd tried to pass through the High Weald in numbers like that they'd have run up against the Nassingtons. Not that it mattered. They were here now.

The enforcers were a long way from being professional; they

relied on simple brutality to get things done. But compared to the locals – particularly at the moment when everything was in a state of utter chaos – they were like an invading army. Fifty well-armed and relatively organised men could take over the Parish with not a lot of effort, if that was what it took to find him and take him back to Margate.

He watched Albie moving among the tents pitched between the trees, stopping at a fire and tasting whatever was cooking in a pot suspended over it. What was going on under that shaved scalp? Far from home, was loyalty to Frank starting to wear thin? Had his journey across the country with his little army put ideas in his head? Was he, with his patient predator's eye, regarding the Parish as a place to start his own kingdom, far from the rot and struggle of the Kent coast? Was he actually thinking of staying here? Adam thought he might be, because that was how his own mind would be working, if their positions were reversed.

There was a commotion in the camp, and he watched as two men rode in, each leading a horse. Each of the horses had the body of an enforcer draped over the saddle. Albie and some of the others went over to the new arrivals. Adam watched as Albie lifted the heads of the dead men to get a look at their faces, then dropped them again. He turned to the waiting enforcers and said something, and then they were all in motion, breaking down the camp, getting ready to move out. Even at this distance through the binoculars, the look on Albie's face was one which Adam was familiar with, the look he got when someone had offended him and he was about to dish out a beating.

The enforcers weren't concerned with being neat and tidy. It only took them a few minutes to fold up their camp and move out. When they'd gone, Adam climbed down from his tree and went over to where it had been. Rubbish everywhere, fires not properly extinguished. The whole place stank of horse piss. He picked up a discarded boot, its upper completely separated from the sole at the toe, and thought about Betty Coghlan talking about bootmaking machines, and Paul Abbot telling him that the people before The Sisters had been too reliant on civilisation. The people of the Parish had relied on themselves for too long, shut themselves off behind their walls, looked not much further than the boundaries of their own little world. And now the monsters from outside had come, hothoused by Frank Pendennis.

Movement in the bushes made him turn, bringing up the rifle, thinking Albie had left someone behind to guard the camp, but the figure which stepped out was not an enforcer. Was only, really, vaguely recognisable as human. It was filthy, smeared with dirt and blood and ordure, its clothes in tatters, hair and beard matted. Its eyes were wild, and it raised hands which were covered in blood. Its face was twisted into a truly horrible smile.

"Don't shoot," it said, in a voice which sounded as if it hadn't been used in a very long time. "Please." Its face was twisted into what looked like a child's impression of innocence.

The figure didn't seemed to be armed, but it had a satchel slung over one shoulder. Adam kept the rifle trained on its chest. "What do you want?"

"I'm..." The ragged man's voice trailed off. He tried again. "I'm...." His face contorted in grief. "I've been killing them," it said.

Adam had thought the Parish had exhausted all its surprises, but obviously he'd been wrong. "What?"

"I want to help you," said the ragged man. "I'm like you."

Adam stared. "I'm a bit busy right now," he said.

"I've been doing your work," the ragged man said, hands still raised above its head. "I brought you a present. Can I show you?" He started to reach for the satchel.

"Oh no," Adam said. "You stop right there."

The ragged man lifted his hands in what looked a lot like supplication. "I brought it for you," he said, and he sounded on the verge of tears.

Adam thought of the enforcers, riding off who knew where, to do who knew what. "I haven't got time for this," he said.

The ragged man said, "It'll only take a moment," and he reached for the satchel again.

"Stop," Adam told him.

"I only want to show you your present." The words were almost a sob.

'Absurd' didn't even begin to cover it. Adam said, "Put it on the ground and step away."

The ragged man broke into a grin which was the most awful facial expression Adam had seen, and he nodded enthusiastically. "Of course. Of course. You'll want to look for yourself." And he slipped the strap from his shoulder and let the satchel fall to the ground.

"Now step away," Adam said. The ragged man took a step to one side. "Further. Further. Okay. That'll do. Keep your hands up."

Keeping one eye on the ragged man, he stepped forward and flipped open the satchel with the muzzle of his rifle. He poked inside to widen the mouth of the bag, glanced down.

Inside was a mass of blood and flesh and human hair.

"I did it for you," he heard the ragged man say.

Adam took a step back from the satchel, then another. He looked at the ragged man, and it was like looking in a mirror. He felt the full horror of what he had been doing for the past few days wash over him like a wing of darkness. He took another step back and raised the rifle, sighted on the ragged man's chest.

"Go," he said, voice almost a whisper. Then louder, "Go. Go before I shoot you."

"But..."

"Fuck off!" Adam shouted. "Go away!"

The ragged man was actually crying now, hands still over his head, tears cutting tracks through the filth on his cheeks. "I only wanted to help you," he said between choking sobs.

"Just go," Adam said, suddenly bone-weary of this madhouse and everyone in it. "No, leave that." The ragged man was moving towards the satchel. "No souvenirs. Go away. Go home."

"This is my home..."

"I don't care. Get out of here."

The simpering, inept impersonation of a smile disappeared, replaced by something appalling. "I thought you were different," said the ragged man, and his voice was level and emotionless.

Adam started to back away. One step, then another, then another, until he felt confident enough to turn and start to run.

Behind him, the ragged man shouted, "I thought you understood!"

WORN THIN BY lack of sleep, Harry walked out into the pouring rain and looked around the yard. The compound was full of people, all of them armed, all of them fidgety. They watched him as he passed, as if waiting for him to give orders, which he thought was sourly funny because he didn't have the first idea what to do. He should, it suddenly occurred to him, have got everyone in here right at the start. Just sat them down and told them to stay here until things cooled down and tempers calmed. The irony was, nobody would have listened to him back then. They were happy enough to want him to tell them what to do now, when it was too late. He had a sudden and very strong urge to tell them to all fuck off home and take their chances on their own.

Up on the wall, Wendy was standing looking over a revetment of sacks hurriedly filled with earth. She glanced at him as he climbed the steps and stood beside her.

"You look awful," he said.

"You can talk." She didn't look as if she'd slept much, either.

If at all. He stared down the track leading into the woods. "How the fuck did all this happen, Wendy?" he said.

He hadn't expected an answer, but she said, "Well, your Rob and his mates decided to have a go at Max, who killed them. Then young Walter decided to kill Faye Ogden. Then the Taylors decided to attack those farms down south, fuck knows why. Then the southsiders came up and attacked the Taylors. And then everything just got really fucking stupid, Harry. Just really fucking stupid."

Harry supposed it was as good a summary as he was going to get, even if none of it made any sense. He said, "They might not come."

Wendy looked at him. "We killed Patrick. Rose is going to come here and wipe us out."

"Rose is sick. John Race said."

"Well, then nobody's in charge over there now. This isn't going to stop until we're all dead."

"Their Nell will take over," he said. "She's got a level head."

"Nell's fifteen. And if you think *she's* going to let us get away with killing Patrick, you're in for a shock."

"We didn't kill Patrick." He'd been going over the events in the village again and again in his mind, and he was sure the shot that had killed the Taylor boy had come from behind him, behind his men. Maybe in one of the deserted houses. "It was Wayland."

Wendy snorted. "Wayland. Fucking hell, Harry, I wish you luck trying to talk Nell into believing *that*."

"He's been here all along, sniping at both sides, setting us against each other."

"Why? Why would anyone do that?"

"You saw what he did over at Gracie Farr's distillery. Is there anyone here who has explosives? Who even knows how to make them?"

"Betty Coghlan and that Andrew know how."

They'd had this conversation before, but now he thought

about it. Actually thought about it very carefully, because it was the only explanation that really made sense. He didn't know the Coghlans very well – had only met Betty a handful of times, and all those times she'd been perfectly civil to him – but they and the Taylors went way back.

"If they were involved, we'd be having this conversation at the bottom of a smoking hole in the ground," he said finally. "And why would they kill Patrick, anyway?"

"Did you find a sign? Something with Wayland's name on it? Not that that would prove anything."

He'd been too busy trying to save his own life to look for one. He rubbed his eyes.

"They're not going to care who did it, Harry," Wendy said with a heavy sigh.

"I should go over there and explain."

She stared at him. "Don't be so fucking soft, Harry. They'd kill you before you even got near the farm. It's a miracle they didn't kill you last time. Explain. Jesus Christ, they *wouldn't listen*. Seriously." She shook her head and looked down the track again. "You're a nice man, Harry, and you've been a good boss, but you do talk some bollocks sometimes."

For some reason, that made him smile, and he was still smiling when movement down the track caught his eye and a single rider came into view.

"Ah, shit," he said.

"I'll give her this, she's got guts," said Wendy. Raising her voice, she called, "Hold your fire! Anyone shoots, I'll have your fucking ears!"

All alone, Nell Taylor rode unhurriedly up the track towards the gate. She was wearing a rain poncho with the hood thrown back, and her soaking wet hair was plastered to her head. She seemed to be unarmed. She rode right up to the gate and stopped and looked up at Harry.

"Mr Lyall," she said.

"Good morning, Nell," said Harry.

"I'm sorry this had to happen," she said.

"Me too. It didn't have to."

"Dad's fever broke yesterday. He's going to be all right, I think."

"That's the first piece of good news I've heard in quite a while. Give him my regards, will you?"

She didn't answer, just sat there looking up at him. "I know a lot of this was down to Patrick," she said. "But he's dead now."

"I know. I'm sorry, Nell. That had nothing to do with us."

Nell smiled a sad little smile. "That doesn't really matter, does it?"

"No. No, I suppose not."

She sat up straighter in the saddle and her voice grew stronger. "You've been a good friend to us in the past, Mr Lyall, and I wanted to thank you for that."

"You're welcome, Nell," Harry said past the lump in his throat.

She looked at him a few moments more, then nodded. "Goodbye, Mr Lyall."

He sensed Wendy starting to move along the parapet. "Goodbye, Nell."

She turned the horse slowly and rode away, as unhurriedly as she had arrived. Harry watched her go, and as she vanished round the curve of the track, he sank down behind the revetment and a few moments later gunfire erupted from the cover on all sides of the compound.

FOR ALBIE DODD, life was a fairly simple equation. He got respect, and that made him happy. If he didn't get respect, that upset him, and he hurt someone until he got respect and he was happy again. Respect was the key. Everything else – food, clothes, a warm, dry place to sleep – was just a natural side effect.

He had received a marked lack of respect here. These *farmers* in their ridiculous little castles had refused to help him, had actually been pretty fucking rude about it, really. He'd been prepared to be magnanimous about that – they didn't know him, after all, and you had to make some allowances – although he had been planning to come back here at some point after returning Adam and Gussie to Margate, and teaching them some manners. Now they'd killed some of his people, though, and that changed everything.

Albie still had no clear idea what they had ridden into. The farmers were certainly angry about something, although quite who or what was not immediately obvious. Scouts had reported seeing firefights and lynchings and all sorts of chaos throughout the area – the mass gunfight he'd witnessed the day before was obviously not an isolated incident. But Albie didn't care about the sensitivities of these people. He had not been afforded respect, and his first instinct was to hurt somebody. He'd deal with everything else later.

The two biggest farms were far too well-fortified, but he'd seen smaller ones with nothing more than wooden walls and a couple of dozen people defending them. One of those would do. All he had to do was get their attention and make his point and then everything would be just fine.

So Albie and his little army rode through the rain towards a farm he'd seen yesterday. They rode silently and in formation, like the invaders they were. Somewhere off to their right, the sound of a lot of shooting echoed through the woods, but they'd been hearing a lot of shooting since they arrived here and it didn't worry Albie. One of the farmers might have been able to take two of his lads by surprise and bring them down, but they were a different prospect en masse. They could take care of themselves.

All of a sudden a figure stepped out onto the track twenty or so yards ahead of them. It was wearing a tattered old raincoat and there were twigs and leaves in its hair and beard, and as it pulled back the hood of its coat, Albie saw that it was Adam Hardy.

"Don't shoot!" Albie called out. "Frank wants him alive!" Actually, Frank wanted Adam dead, but he wanted to do it himself and only after he got Gussie back. He was already fucked-off enough with Albie for bringing Adam to Margate in the first place; the last thing Albie needed was someone shooting Adam and then having to go back without Frank's fucking gun.

If Adam was alarmed to see them, he didn't show it. He stood there quite relaxed in the middle of the track. He even seemed to be smiling a little, and that made Albie pause and wonder. As he watched, Adam turned his back on them, dropped his jeans and underwear, and slowly and deliberately bared his arse at the mass of enforcers.

"Oh, you cheeky cunt," Albie murmured, not without a small amount of admiration. He shouted, "Get him!" and the front ranks of the enforcers surged forward towards Adam, who was already pulling up his jeans and haring into the undergrowth beside the track. The horses turned and crashed through the bushes in pursuit, but the woodland was dense and there were no real paths through it and they could only manage a fast walk at best, while Albie watched the running figure of Adam disappearing into the distance. In a corner of his mind, he noted that they seemed to be moving towards the shooting he'd heard earlier, but the sight of his prey getting away blinded him to all other considerations. He'd come too far and gone through far too much to give up now.

They burst from the trees and into a wide, deep clearing full of chaos and running people. On the other side of the clearing was the corner of a high brick wall that ran off into the distance in both directions, broken on one side by what seemed to be a solid wooden gate, and people standing on a walkway on the other side of the wall were firing down at hundreds of other people who were firing back and trying to manoeuvre ladders into position. Dozens of bodies already lay in the churned-up mud near the wall. Albie reined in his horse, and for the first time in his life he felt a pang of doubt.

The defenders of the farm noticed the newcomers and started to fire on them. Some of the people with the ladders noticed, too, and also started shooting. The enforcer beside Albie took a round in the chest and fell sideways out of his saddle. Then everyone was firing at everyone else.

Something came flying through the air – it looked like a bottle, turning end over end and trailing sparks, Albie couldn't see where it came from – and hit the wall, and there was an almighty bang and a cloud of smoke, and when it cleared a number of people, and pieces of people, were lying at the base of the wall. Two more bottles looped across the clearing and struck the wall, and this time when the smoke cleared, there was a hole in the brickwork, and as Albie watched, a portion of the wall collapsed in on itself and farmers boiled out through the gap, firing at anything that moved.

Albie's people were fighting for their lives. Half of them were already dead, half the rest were off their horses and trying to fire from cover at the edge of the clearing. Panicked horses were running everywhere. Albie had no idea what to do. This was so far outside his experience that his mind could suggest no course of action at all.

Abruptly, there was a hissing sound, and Albie watched in astonishment as a line of smoke drew itself through the rain right in front of him and hit the gate to the compound, and there was a bang like the world ending, and when the echoes of that had died down, the gate was mostly just gone, reduced to splinters.

The shooting stopped, and there was a moment of shocked silence. Everyone just stood there, the rain pouring down on them, bewildered by the explosions.

There was another hissing sound, and another line of smoke.

This time it passed straight through the gate, across the compound, and through an upper-storey window of the house. There was a fraction of a second's pause, and then the entire top of the house belched smoke and flame and blew off in a concussion of brick and woodwork and roof tiles.

Then there were yet more people in the clearing, a line of them marching towards the farm, and the air was full of the racket of automatic weapon fire, something Albie had only ever heard once before but had never ever forgotten. The newcomers were not farmers, and they were not enforcers. They were all in uniform, and they looked like a picture of soldiers Albie had seen a long time ago in a book, and there seemed to be hundreds of them and they were shooting at everyone, and that was enough for him. Heart pounding, he turned the horse and rode back into the woods.

CALM, OF A sort, finally returned to the clearing around the farm. Hundreds of bodies lay in the mud, Taylors, Lyalls, enforcers. Smoke drifted in horizontal panes across the scene as the Marines strode through it all, shooting the wounded, disarming the dead. Adam watched it all from the branches of a tree some distance away. He'd seen Marines do this once before, to a community down in Cornwall which had put up a token resistance to Guz. Shock and awe, they called it. Carrot and stick, but with a very large stick and no carrot.

"Well, you took your own sweet time," he said to himself. Then he dropped to the ground and was gone.

CHAPTER TWENTY-SEVEN

EARLY THE NEXT morning, riders began to arrive at the Lyall farm. They came in threes and fours, pulled up outside the shattered gate. The soldiers camped outside the wall seemed to know them. The exhausted defenders of the farm watched them come. They were all dressed in black coveralls and festooned with weapons, some of which the Lyall hands couldn't even recognise. It never crossed their minds to offer up any resistance at all, not for a moment.

Someone went to get Harry, and he came out into the yard slowly, pulling on a coat, smelling the drifting smoke on the air. The compound was littered with covered bodies, people sitting around listlessly, too spent to move.

He walked out of the gate and stood looking at the riders. Two horses stood just in front of the silent ranks. On one sat a red-headed woman wearing a duster coat. On the other sat Betty Coghlan.

Harry drew himself up to his full height. "Hello," he said to the red-haired woman. "I'm Harry Lyall. Morning, Betty." Betty glared at him.

"I know who you are," said the redhead. "We're in charge now. If you try to resist, we will use force."

The idea of resisting was so absurd that he almost giggled. "Who are you?"

"We'll talk about that later. From now on, there is going to be order here. I want you and your people to put down your weapons."

"Have you told the Taylors that?"

"Just listen to yourself, Harry," Betty said heavily. "Don't be such a fucking embarrassment."

"We've spoken to the Taylors," said the red-haired woman. "They saw reason. We want you to see it too."

Harry looked at the two women, at the ranks of hard faces behind them. For a moment, the thought of going out in a blaze of gunfire seemed almost attractive. It would be a suitably ridiculous way to end this fiasco.

Instead, he stepped aside. "Come on in," he told the woman. "We haven't got much, but you're welcome to what we have. I don't think we even have any tea left."

"That's okay," said the woman, urging her horse forward. "We brought our own."

OVER THE NEXT few days, once it became obvious that the locals weren't going to cause very much trouble, the bulk of the Westerners packed up and departed for home. Twenty or thirty of them set up camp in the Abbot compound, whether by accident or design it was never quite clear, but nobody could mistake the message either way.

It didn't all go smoothly, of course, nothing ever does. A few locals were unable to accept that the war was over and they were now under martial law, and some hangings were necessary. Shock and awe. Guz was fair, but it was not, by and large, forgiving.

A week or so after the final firefight, a wild-eyed, disordered figure came walking down the track towards the Abbot farm. Its clothes were filthy and torn, its hair matted, but it didn't stop. It seemed to be unarmed, and the guards were somewhat confused about what to do until their commander, recognising the figure, told them to let him pass.

He went through the lines of tents pitched in the farmyard, looking inside each until he found the one he was looking for, then he marched right up to the desk inside and stopped.

The person sitting at the desk finished making some notes on a piece of paper before looking up at him. "Oh, hello," she said.

"I resign," he told her.

"Oh, don't be daft," Chrissie said. "Sit down. Do you want a brew?"

"No, I don't want a fucking brew," he said, before realising that, actually, he did. He sighed and sank down into a camp chair.

"Do you want to tell me what the hell's been going on in your head these past few weeks?" she asked.

"You sent me into this," he said.

"No, I didn't. I sent you to Blandings."

"'Go and deliver Betty's stuff for her, Adam. It'll be a nice trip, Adam. How can it hurt, Adam?'"

"I didn't authorise you to start a war," she said. "We had a conversation about that, I remember."

"That was in Thanet."

"Thanet, here, anywhere. No wars."

"It was already going on when I got here."

"Dim sod," she said.

"You knew what I was walking into."

Chrissie sat back and rubbed her face and looked at him. "I didn't, actually. Betty Coghlan probably did. And don't you dare go making trouble for her. She did it with the best intentions."

"Struggling, here, with that 'best intentions' thing."

"I told her what you do for us. Contacting communities, negotiating with them. She thought you'd be able to put a stop to the fighting before it went too far." Chrissie looked at him. "Judging by what we found when we got here, I may have oversold your abilities."

"Oh, for fuck's sake, Chrissie."

"There's no law here," she said. "Nobody in authority. That's one of the reasons everything broke down so completely so quickly. All those petty little grievances seething away for years and years and years, and one day people have an excuse to settle scores and there's nobody to stop them. Betty thought you could reason with them, as the representative of a greater power, and then we'd turn up a few days later to underline the message."

"Well, as stupid fucking plans go..." An aide arrived with a tray on which sat two metal mugs. He handed one to Adam, one to Chrissie, and left the tent again. "And speaking of which, what took you so long?"

She shrugged. "Ran into a little trouble in Wiltshire. Father John's people."

"Oh, that's just wonderful."

"He wasn't there, but they said he's still alive. Went up north somewhere. Anyway, we had to sort them out."

"Shock and awe?"

She thought about it. "Just shock, really. We didn't leave anyone behind to benefit from the awe."

Good old Guz, slashing and burning its way across the countryside, imposing Order. They'd been cooped up down there in Devon for too long, he thought; now they wanted to flex their muscles.

"Anyway, by the time we got to Blandings Pendennis's people had been and gone. Betty just told them to fuck off. She's got a couple of Gatling guns, did you know that? That boy of hers built them; I'm going to have to arrange a visit to Guz for him."

Adam shook his head. "What a fucking mess," he murmured.

"The best we can guess is that they asked around and someone on the ferry remembered you coming this way and they thought it was safer to take a look for you round here than annoying Betty. They're a bit *amateur*, really, aren't they?"

"It's all relative," he said, thinking of the starving, frightened people of Margate. Someone had told him that the inhabitants had trapped and eaten so many seagulls down the years that the birds avoided the town entirely now.

"You should have got out of here when you could, gone back to Blandings."

He gave her a hard stare.

"But you just couldn't leave it alone, could you?" She sighed. "Like those farmers in Wales. You had to get involved."

"According to you, that's what you and Betty Coghlan wanted me to do."

"Not like this." She waved a hand towards the entrance of the tent, the ruined farmyard beyond, the wreckage of the Parish. "I had a long chat with Harry Lyall. He says there was someone else here during the fighting. Not a local, he doesn't think. Someone killing his people and the Taylors' people and really anyone they could get their hands on. Called themselves 'Wayland'. That ring a bell with you?"

He thought of the ragged man, the satchel full of scalps. "It wasn't just me."

"Lyall's foreman thinks it was someone from Blandings, and so do a lot of other people, from what I hear, so that's going to poison relations between Betty and this place for a very long time, so thank you for that."

Right now the status of Betty Coghlan's friendships was quite a long way down his list of priorities.

"There's going to be a hell of a lot of rebuilding needed here," she said. "And not just of physical stuff. And we need it fixed, we really do."

"Can we go home now, please?"

Chrissie sat perfectly still, and he knew she was about to deliver bad news.

"We've known about this community for a long time," she told him. "Mainly through our contact with the Coghlans. But until now there was never any point in making a direct intervention; they're so far from our own territory, it makes no sense."

He sipped his tea, looked down into his mug, sipped some more. That was the Navy for you; always ready with a tot of rum.

"Betty got in touch a while ago and told us about some rumours of something going on in the Vale of the White Horse, maybe further north too, in Oxford and the Cotswolds," she went on. "She sent people up there to have a look, but they never came back."

"You could have told me," he said.

"You were coming back from Thanet anyway. I thought you could have a look around, get the lie of the land, help us make a decision about whether or not to set up shop here. Not," she added, "to start killing people."

"And what did you decide?" he asked.

She let the sarcasm pass. "We took some of Pendennis's people alive and we've had a little chat with them and decided they're not a threat for the moment. They can sit and stew over there in Thanet and we'll deal with them when we're good and ready."

He looked blankly at her.

"I know you don't like them. *I* don't like them. But we're not in the business of imposing peace."

He bugged his eyes and looked around the tent.

"Not in *general*," she said. "This thing up north is of greater concern to us. We need a foothold in the Chilterns to keep an eye on it. We're planning to garrison this place, open supply lines from Southampton up round Winchester and across the Downs."

"They're not going to like that," he said, wondering in passing just how long this decision had been before the Committee. They never acted in haste, always weighed up the options. He was, he realised, always going to come here, one way or another, as the point man for Guz's takeover. He thought about what he'd seen, that night in Wantage, the silent figures clearing the road in preparation for the movement of a lot of people and their wagons. Was someone preparing for an invasion?

Of course, Betty had known all this. She was playing a long game; that was why she'd sent him to the Parish in the first place, to provoke some sort of response from Guz, bring the Chilterns under the control of someone who could protect them from whatever was going on further north. It was no wonder she and Guz got along so well. They had a lot in common. Always planning, always plotting, always preparing. Not bothering to tell anyone what was going on in their heads, no matter how many people got hurt.

"Well, they're not going to have any choice," she told him. "Not that they could do much about it at the moment, even if they wanted to. Completely disorganised. It's a miracle they didn't wipe each other out years ago." She looked at the note she had been writing to herself. "We do need someone to have a wander up there and have a shufti, of course," she said vaguely. "How'd you feel about doing that? A few days' rest here, we can have a chat about Thanet, then you can go when you're ready. No rush. Hm?"

She looked up from the desk, expecting Adam to stand up and storm out of the tent, but he had fallen asleep in the chair.

Two DAYS AFTER the firefight, Albie emerged from hiding and saddled his horse. Peace had settled over the Parish, a silence broken only by the hissing of the rain and some occasional hail. He'd managed to avoid the soldiers and some black-clad people who looked even worse than the soldiers, had somehow slipped through their cordon in the chaos and found shelter in some little brick sheds behind a wall deep in the undergrowth. It looked as if someone else had been living there until quite recently. The sheds stank of piss and shit and human grease, and there were bits of abandoned clothing and gnawed rabbit bones everywhere. He'd spent the first night there too terrified to sleep, in case the soldiers or whoever had been using the sheds came and found him, but when it became obvious that he was secure, he fell into a fitful period of nightmares, from which he woke feeling even worse than before.

He let the horse walk slowly through the woods, senses at breaking point, listening for approaching danger. But nothing came. He found a track leading north, and shortly afterward he came upon a sign indicating that he was on the Ridge Way, and he turned towards his distant home. After a couple of hours, he began to relax.

Sudden movement right at his side, and he glanced round just in time to see what looked like a scarecrow rushing straight at the horse. He tried to bring his shotgun up, but the scarecrow made a remarkable leap and tumbled him out of the saddle, hitting the ground face down heavily enough to drive the breath from his lungs and break one of his arms. Something big landed on his back and a filthy hand like a bundle of bones clamped itself over his mouth and nose, and he smelled a terrible foul odour and heard a high, wordless sobbing, and the last thing Albie Dodd ever felt was something cold and razor-sharp sawing back and forth across his neck.

CHAPTER TWENTY-EIGHT

It was a long time before Max was well enough to drive the wagon. Rose didn't want him to go, but one morning he got stiffly out of bed and washed and dressed and went out and hitched up the horses. He looked around the compound and noted the marks of the war and he shook his head.

Outside, on the road, the marks were even more obvious. He drove slowly past the scorched trees and burned-out buildings. He'd been expecting it to be worse than Rose had told him, but he hadn't expected it to be this much worse. The road took him past the Tomlinson compound, and through the trees he could see that it was just gone. The gate stood open and the buildings inside were smoke-blackened ruins already being reclaimed by weeds.

It seemed that the area had been hit by an invading army. More than one, actually. At breakfast this morning, Sophie had leaned over to him and informed him, in a grave six-year-old's voice, that Wayland was a devil who had come "to stop us all being cunts," and Rose had lost it completely, cuffed her round the ear and shrieked at her about swearing and then stormed into the bedroom and locked the door. She still hadn't emerged when he left.

No one could tell him with any great certainty what had happened. Nell sat in her room, refusing to speak to anybody. John Race was gone – when Max had asked after him, the hands had just shrugged and muttered, "Wayland," and refused to look him in the eye. Patrick was dead. "Lyalls," the hands said, and again refused to look him in the eye. While he lay in his bed, the whole world had changed.

At the Lyall farm, some of Harry's labourers were working to repair the gate and the hole in the wall. Some of them looked up as Max approached, but most of them seemed shell-shocked.

Max pulled up just outside the ruined gateway and nodded down to one of the workers. "Morning, Reg," he said.

"Max," Reg said dully. Max saw a couple of people with guns among the group, but they kept them slung over their shoulders.

"Harry about?"

Reg gestured towards the main house.

"Mind if I go on in and have a word?" Max asked.

Reg shrugged and looked over at one of the guards, who also shrugged, so Max shook the reins and the horses walked on through the gateway and into the compound.

Inside, if anything, it was worse. The whole top floor of the Lyall house, the house Alice Lyall had been so proud of, was shattered and burned out. The compound was littered with rubbish and wreckage. People were working to clear stuff up, but more were just sitting around hollow-eyed, exhausted. Max took a brief, empty pride in thinking that at least his own people were in better shape.

He tied the horses up to a piece of farm machinery lying on its side near the house, got down, and walked over to the house. The front door was open and he rapped on the frame and called, "Lyalls?"

Charlie, the youngest of the Lyall kids, stepped into view

down the hallway. "The old man in, son?" Max asked in what he hoped was a kindly voice. "Just want a word." The little boy just stared at him. After a moment, he brought his fist up to his mouth and started to gnaw his knuckles.

Harry came out of one of the rooms behind Charlie. He looked at Max for a moment, then put his hand on his son's shoulder and said gently, "It's all right, Charles, it's only Mr Taylor come to see us." His voice sounded as if it was coming from some awful distance. "Say hello to Mr Taylor, there's a good lad."

Charlie muttered an almost-inaudible "'lo," and then bolted down the hall towards the kitchen.

And then it was just Max and Harry, standing staring at each other.

THEY WALKED. NOT because Harry didn't want to rub the wreckage of his home in Max's face, particularly, but because the house was all but uninhabitable. They were quiet for quite some time, neither of them willing to start the conversation. Eventually, they came to the brow of the hill and looked out over the flooded Vale, two middle-aged men standing side by side, hands in pockets, contemplating unimaginable loss.

"How's Rose?" Harry said in the end.

"Poorly. But getting better."

They stood there in silence for a few more minutes. Harry asked, "What happened?"

"They were waiting for me on the road," Max said. "Rob and two other lads, I don't know who they were."

"Brannings," said Harry. "From up Risborough way."

Max nodded. "They wanted my stuff, although fuck knows why. I shot Rob, he shot me, I killed the two Branning lads. I'm sorry it happened that way, but that's what happened."

Harry scratched his unshaven chin, put his hand back in his

pocket. Max thought he looked shrunken, diminished. His clothes seemed too large for him. They stood in silence again. Birds sang, the sun continued its battle to break through the clouds. Max thought that if the sun ever did come out properly, people would fall to their knees and worship it.

"Brannings legged it," Harry said eventually. "I sent their boys' bodies back but the place was empty. Last anyone saw of them, they were heading west. Dunno what they thought they had to be afraid of. We buried the boys at their house." He shrugged.

"I never knew them," said Max.

"She was all right," Harry said. "Antoinette. The husband was a twat. Boys took after him, I expect."

Max sighed at the thought that all this had been caused by three cocky lads. If they'd killed him on the road that day, none of it would ever have happened. He'd just have disappeared quietly, no one would have been able to prove anything. Maybe Rob and the Brannings would have done it again and again until someone finally stopped them. Maybe not. He started to say something, then wondered what on earth he could say that would do any good.

"People keep talking about Wayland," he said instead.

Harry nodded. "Don't know what that was all about. It wasn't us. I went over to the Smithy and someone had been living there." He shrugged. "Hard to work out what was him and what was us, really. Your Patrick..." His voice trailed off.

"What about our Patrick?"

Harry shook his head. "Doesn't matter. We were all to blame. Maybe there never was a Wayland. Maybe it *was* us all the time." He looked at Max. "I want to apologise for what my boy did." It sounded as if he was saying it from the depths of his soul.

There was still a dead place in Max's heart where Patrick had been. He didn't think it would ever go away. "We're never going to be able to apologise enough to each other," he said. "Best we can do is stop all this and try to sort ourselves out."

Harry bunched his fists in his pockets, and Max saw there was something else, another weight to add to the already huge burden he was going to have to carry for the rest of his life. "It was James shot Faye Ogden," he said finally.

Max groaned and closed his eyes. "Oh, fucking hell, Harry."

Harry didn't look at him. "He told me a couple of days ago. Said he wanted to get back at your family for Rob, and for killing our chickens."

Max snorted a laugh. Couldn't help himself. "Chickens."

"Someone broke into one of our hen runs and killed all the chickens, not long after you were hurt. Sort of thing an angry kid would do."

Max felt a falling in his heart. "Patrick."

"I don't know. Doesn't matter now."

"What are you going to do? With James?"

"Sent him down to Newbury." He sounded as if he was fighting back tears by an effort of will. "Faye's people will want him dead if they ever find out, and I can't..."

Max reached out to put his hand on Harry's shoulder, thought better of it, put his hand back in his pocket. They were silent for some time, looking out over the Vale. Max thought he could see smoke rising from distant buildings, here and there.

"So," he said finally. "What are we going to do now?"

"You and me?"

"No. We'll sort things out. There's been too much killing. No, I meant everything else."

Harry thought about it. He said, "The others, they were from Kent, as best we can work out. Some of them got away. If they ever make it back there and talk about what happened here, whoever sent them's going to be pissed off with us. That's on top of whatever they were already pissed off with us about."

"Someone said they were looking for a traveller."

Harry nodded and fought to remember the name. "Harvey.

Hardy?" He shrugged. "I wasn't exactly paying a lot of attention. Maybe I should have."

"Poor fucker probably wasn't even here."

"Not if he had any sense."

Max said, "If these people in Kent *are* pissed off with us, we'll need to be ready for them. Just in case."

"I was thinking of sending someone over there to talk to them, find out what the fuck's going on."

"You think that's a good idea?"

Harry shrugged. "That's what Betty Coghlan said, but she's caused enough trouble round here."

"None of this had anything to do with Betty. From what I hear, she's the one who stopped it, bringing those soldiers with her."

Harry hawked and spat. "Plymouth," he said. "Call themselves *Guz. Sailors.*"

"Soldiers, sailors. Whatever."

"I talked with Betty and the woman from Plymouth."

"Hm." Max had missed them; he was going to have to go over to Blandings at some point and have a quiet word with Betty himself.

"They say there's something bad going on in the Cotswolds."

Max thought back to the last conversation he'd had with Betty, the conversation which had, in its way, started all this. "*I* told her that," he said. "Sort of."

"She says someone's going up there to take a look, report back. Then she and the Plymouth people are going to work out what to do."

Max had driven past the Abbot farm on his way to the Lyalls', had seen the Marines camped there. They'd started to make repairs, cleared out the compound. "They look like they're settling in for the long term."

"I think that's the plan. Nobody knows what to do about it yet."

Max made a rude noise.

"They're quite scary actually," Harry allowed. "But they're on our side."

"*They* say."

"The woman who was here, she seemed to know what she was doing. I wouldn't mind going down there one day and seeing what they've made of the place."

"I might come with you."

Harry nodded. "I'm not going yet, anyway. The monsoons will be here soon, then it'll be winter. Spring'll be soon enough."

"There's too much to do here, anyway."

"That'll be right."

"And there's always Wayland," said Max, and he saw Harry wince. "I was thinking," he went on, "that maybe we should go and knock that fucking tomb down."

"No." Harry seemed to gather himself a little. "No. We leave it. To remind us."

ON THE WAY back to the farm, Max saw a figure some distance ahead of him, marching along the track in a determined manner. It took him a few minutes to catch up. The figure was wearing a long hooded coat, a big rucksack on his back, and a battered nylon case slung over its shoulder. Max pulled the wagon alongside, but the figure made no sign of paying any attention.

"Afternoon," said Max amiably. "Give you a lift?"

"No," said a voice from within the hood. It sounded angry.

"Just passing through, are we?"

"Trying to get out of this fucking madhouse as quickly as humanly possible."

Max couldn't fault him there. "Where are you off to?"

"Oxford."

"I've heard some bad things about Oxford."

"Yes. Me too."

They made their way, side by side, down the track for a little while, until they came to the turnoff leading to the Taylor farm.

"Well, this is me," Max said.

No reply.

"You take care," said Max. This time, there was a quiet grunt from the figure marching along beside him. He drew the horses to a stop and sat watching for a few minutes as the figure stomped off into the distance, then he flicked the reins and clucked his tongue and turned the horses towards home.

A MINUTE OR so later, what had once been Morty Roberts stepped out onto the track. Muttering to himself under his breath, he looked in the direction the wagon had gone, then in the direction the determined figure had taken. Where to? To stay? Or to go? Whole vistas of possibility opened up in his mind. He shouldered his rifle and picked up the sack containing Albie Dodd's head, and set off for Oxford.